Offer of Proof

OFFER OF PROOF

Robert Heilbrun

The LARGE PRINT
BOOK COMPANY

SANBORNVILLE, NEW HAMPSHIRE

Library of Congress Cataloging-in-Publication Data

Heilbrun, Robert, 1957-
  Offer of proof / Robert Heilbrun.
     p.   cm.
  ISBN 1-59688-020-1 (alk. paper)
  1. Businesswomen—Crimes against—Fiction. 2. African
American youth—Fiction. 3. Attorney and client—Fiction.
4. Trials (Murder)—Fiction. 5. New York (N.Y.)—Fiction. 6.
Large type books. I. Title.

PS3608.E37O36 2004
813'.6—dc22   2004025780

Published in Large Print by arrangement with
William Morrow, an imprint of HarperCollns Publishers.

Published by The Large Print Book Company.
PO Box 970 Sanbornville, NH 03872-0970
ISBN 1-59688-020-1

Typeset in 16 pt Times New Roman type.
Printed on acid-free paper and bound in the
United States of America.

For Laura

ACKNOWLEDGMENTS

First thanks go to my agent, Amy Rennert. Luck has a lot to do with any first novel, and I got lucky with you. I will always be grateful for your hard work, your great judgment, and your good humor.

Carolyn Marino is a wonderful editor, who never stopped using her vast skills and experience to make this book better. Thanks also to her assistant, Jennifer Civiletto.

Thanks to John Cohlan and David Sand, my dearest friends and most patient readers, for support from day one.

I wish to express my gratitude to the following readers: Neil Altman, Linda Biagi, Nina Bjornsson, Dena Fischer, Emily Heilbrun, Jim Heilbrun, Margaret Heilbrun, Pat Holt, Jimmy Nicholson, Tony Rudel, Julia Serebrinsky, and, most of all, my wife, Laura Buonomo.

Finally, the biggest thank-you is to my mother, Carolyn Heilbrun, who always told me don't chase the dime, do what you care about, and whose many wonderful Amanda Cross mysteries made me think, just maybe, I could do this too.

CHAPTER 1

SAY YOUR LIFE BREAKS DOWN, or your luck goes bad, and you get arrested, busted, taken into custody for some damn thing here in Manhattan. You'll drop out of sight, just disappear. You'll be going through the system, from the precinct where they print you and take what they call your "pedigree" information—which sounds like you were bred in captivity and are up for sale, but which actually just refers to your name, address, and date of birth—then on to central booking, where they fax your prints to Albany to see if you have a criminal record, and, finally, to court.

When you do pop up in a jail behind the arraignment court after a day or two of waiting around in filthy grimy cells with tiled walls like old bathrooms, sharing a few square feet with a lot of other desperate-looking people, you might be pleased to find that your court-appointed attorney is me, Arch Gold, working the night shift. You won't ask yourself why a young man who could have worked at a big corporate firm, making in a month what he makes in a year as a public defender, does this dirty work. You won't ask yourself, doesn't he have anything better to do on a Saturday night? You'll just be very happy to see me, because my friendly face, and my apparent desire to help you, whatever your alleged sins, will make you feel better, will give you hope.

I grabbed the top file off the pile of cases the court clerk had just thrown into the wire basket bolted to defense counsel's table. When I first started as a public defender, I used to look through the files and select the ones that appealed to me, secretly hoping my shift might run out before I got to a particularly nasty case that I'd left at the bottom of the basket. Not anymore. After ten years of this work, I just take the cases in the order they appear. Picking and choosing isn't part of my job description.

I looked at the name on the first file—"Kathy Dupont."

When you get arrested, your lawyer is given three pieces of paper with which to defend you in front of the judge at your arraignment: the criminal complaint, which purports to set forth exactly what laws you've broken and exactly how, all in stilted legalese; your rap sheet, based on your fingerprints, which lets everyone know if you've got a criminal record, no matter what name you happen to claim for yourself this time around; and, last, a joke—the CJA sheet. This is a form filled out by a career pencil pusher from something called the Criminal Justice Agency, who interviews you, and to whom you're expected to give a home address, your supposed occupation or lack thereof, and your supposed contact person, so the court can decide if you have sufficient "community ties" to maybe risk releasing you or setting a bail you could make.

I checked out Kathy Dupont's rap sheet. Twenty-eight years old. Second arrest. She had an open case for assault, just like this new one. The complaint here said she'd stabbed a fellow by the name of James Johnson, on Fifty-second Street and Ninth Avenue, at 4:45 in the morning. The CJA sheet said she was a dancer. Probably not with the New York City Ballet.

Kathy Dupont's file was a little curious, since the contact person listed on the CJA sheet was the very same James Johnson whom the complaint said she'd stabbed in the ass. Sounded like a complex relationship.

I walked back to the pens, to the women's interview cage, and called out her name. Through the steel bars in the door at the back I could see into the women's pen. You've probably never been in jail even for a day or two, locked up behind a courtroom in a twenty-foot-square cell. Right now approximately twenty-five women were packed into the pen, some sitting on benches, some passed out on the floor or curled up in the fetal position, all waiting to see the judge. The women were mostly hookers, shoplifters, and crackheads. These were mixed in with the occasional woman arrested for assault, usually in self-defense against some man who wanted something he couldn't have. The threat of violence didn't hang in the air here, as it did in the men's pen.

"Kathy Dupont," I yelled out. One of the sleeping figures on the floor came to life. She was wearing a short skirt over a tight, low-cut black leotard, stockings, and purple knitted leggings. Her boots were next to her on the floor. She tiptoed around various sleeping bodies on her perfect little stocking feet and slid into the interview booth.

She was a knockout—big, dark, hurt-looking eyes, high cheekbones, long brown hair, and a body that appeared to have everything just where it was supposed to be.

"Cigarette?"

"Aren't you sweet."

She had a real Southern drawl. I passed her a cigarette through the bars. I don't smoke, but I've found that a cigarette often eases the difficult discussions that are inevitably central to my job. For some reason, people who get arrested tend to smoke way more than the general population. There were probably a million reasons why, none of them good. She put the cigarette between her lips and leaned forward, her big eyes checking me out as I lit it for her through the bars.

"You my lawyer, cutie?"

She leaned back and took a long drag.

"Yes, I'm your lawyer. My name's Arch Gold. Who's James Johnson?"

"An asshole that used to be my boyfriend."

"Has he been bothering you?"

"You might say. He's obsessed with me. He won't let me go. He comes to my shows, he follows me everywhere. This time he was bothering me after the show."

"Where did you stab him?"

"In the ass."

"Why the ass, Ms. Dupont?" I asked with a straight face. She flashed a little anger.

"Because if I hadn't stabbed him there, I would've killed him. That's why. We were on the street. He grabbed my arm, twisted it really rough, and spat in my face. All because I told him to leave me alone. Then he walked away like I could never hurt him. He's lucky I just poked him, that little asshole. He probably didn't even need stitches."

"How'd you get arrested?"

"I guess he went to the precinct and pressed charges. The cops were kind of apologetic, but they took me in."

"Funny, you're charged with a felony here."

"Big deal. He'll drop it. He doesn't want me in jail. He wants me out where he can . . ." The sentence trailed off.

She exhaled, a long sigh, and shook her head. She was a little too resigned to the whole thing.

"What's this other case?" I was flipping through her rap sheet. "It looks like there's a warrant for your arrest on this one, because you didn't come back to court. Now, that could be a problem for you tonight. The judge might not let you out without some bail. Let me guess. Mr. James Johnson is the complainant in this one, too, and you thought he'd dropped the charges, and didn't think you needed to come back. How's that sound?"

"Honey, just get me outa here tonight. I don't belong in here."

"What do you do?"

"I'm a dancer at a club. Not a stripper, a dancer. But I make good money. That's the only reason I do it. I don't do drugs. I don't turn tricks."

"How much do you make a week, Ms. Dupont?"

"What's the difference?"

"You may not qualify for a public defender. You probably make more a year than I do."

She rolled her eyes.

"I don't need a private attorney. You'll do fine."

I didn't argue. If the case went anywhere, which I doubted it would, some judge down the road would order her to get a private attorney.

"Where you from?"

"South Carolina. Small-town girl wins beauty contest, comes north to big city, seeking fortune and fame."

She pronounced fame as if it were spelled "fime."

I got lawyerly for a minute. I could have sat and talked to her all night. But there was work to be done, and most of the folks in the jail had problems a whole lot worse than hers.

"Ms. Dupont, I think the judge should release you without bail, but I can't guarantee it, because you didn't come back on your last case. So, if the judge sets minimal bail, can you make it? Like five hundred dollars? Otherwise, you could be in for a little while. After six days, if your ex-boyfriend, the asshole, hasn't come in to testify against you in the grand jury, they'll have to release you."

"Honey, just get me outa here and you'll be my new best friend."

I left the pens quickly, trying not to think about what it

might mean to be Kathy Dupont's new best friend.

Back in the courtroom, I grabbed the next file. Joe, one of the court officers I'd known for years, one of the guys who stood around all day in court in a pressed shirt with a fake black tie and, of course, a gun strapped on, making sure nothing got out of hand, started talking to me.

"Hey, you must of picked up the kid who shot the lady in Chelsea. I saw it on the news at six. Kid's in deep shit. It's gonna be big. Didja see that chick's picture on TV? Wall Street executive. What a shame. Just for a few bucks. The kid's going down big time. Pressure's gonna be on Leventhal on this one. Wonder if the governor will take over, to fry this kid."

Joe knew what everyone in the building knew, that Leventhal, the grand old man still head of the district attorney's office, age eighty-one, had never sought the death penalty in a case, and never would. Still, the wily old DA maintained the fiction that each new homicide was evaluated on its merits, and that the right case could still come along. This was to mollify the governor, who had already removed the Bronx district attorney from a high profile murder of a cop, because that DA had announced that he would never, under any circumstances, seek the death penalty. Here in Manhattan, anyone who had ever seen the old man off camera quietly explaining that he did not believe the state should be in the revenge business knew that, for him, the appropriate case would never come along. Yet all the senior assistant DAs who handled homicides pretended, right up until the statutory deadline, 120 days after felony arraignment, that there was some possibility that Leventhal would seek the death penalty. Their loyalty was touching. So far, the governor hadn't wanted to tangle with him.

Joe nodded over toward the half-dozen reporters sitting in

the first row. I knew their faces and names, but only because I'd watched them in action, chatted with them occasionally, and read what they wrote. I had never been asked a question on the record by any of them. That was about to change. I looked down at the next file. It was the kid.

CHAPTER 2

"THE PEOPLE OF THE STATE OF NEW YORK against Damon Tucker."

That's what the complaint said, the official piece of pink paper sitting in my file, opened on the steel desk, in the steel cage behind the courtroom, where I was interviewing Damon. The People had always been against Damon, as far as I could tell. According to the CJA sheet, he lived with his mother uptown, on 132nd Street and Lenox Avenue. Ms. Tucker was a nurse's aide at Harlem Hospital. Damon worked at a video store on the West Side and attended City College. His rap sheet said he'd pled guilty to assault in the second degree, a Class D felony, when he was fourteen years old. He'd received "youthful offender" treatment, so technically he didn't have a criminal record, but his life was not off to a great start. He'd been arrested four times since the assault case, twice for jumping the turnstyle to get on the subway and twice for petit larceny.

He'd never done real time, but the "People of the State of New York" had been having a lot of problems with Damon. Now they said he'd robbed and killed a woman named Charlotte King in Chelsea.

"How you feeling, Damon, all right?"

Damon's eyes gave away how scared he was, behind his

valiant attempt at impassive coolness. He was a black kid, huge, well built, and handsome. He needed a doctor. He was cut and bruised over his left eye.

"What they got me in here for? I didn't rob no lady."

I've been around too long to attach much importance to my clients' protestations of innocence. I flicked a cockroach off the steel desk.

"Tell me how you got arrested."

Damon looked at me through the grating, terrified, trying to decide whose side I was on. For the first time in his life, it was going to matter just exactly what kind of lawyer he had, and he knew it.

"Did my mother hire you?"

"No, I'm a public defender. I haven't spoken with your mother. Do you think she's out there?"

"Na. She's working."

It didn't really matter. Damon was going to be remanded without bail, no matter who showed up for him.

"Mister, we got to get something straight right now. I did not do this crime. I did not rob no white bitch, and I certainly didn't shoot her. I ain't coppin' to nothing. Ever. I was just running down the street, going from work to the subway, with my Walkman on, like I always do, when these two cops pulled me over for no fucking reason at all. They beat me. They threw my Walkman in the gutter. Police reports say anything 'bout that?"

"Damon, I don't have the police reports yet."

"How come? What kind of lawyer don't have the police reports. You ain't trying to defend me. Fuck it."

I didn't respond. It was pointless to get into this kind of argument with him. Most of my clients couldn't believe that in New York state defense counsel didn't get the police reports about a case until the day of trial, couldn't believe that it was a big game of hide the potato between the DA's office and counsel. Only if a defendant decided to push the case to the limit did he really find out its merits, often long after he'd turned down whatever offer the People were inclined to make early on, usually less in the interest of justice than in the interest of doing less work and moving things along as quickly as possible.

Fewer than 3 percent of all felonies in New York City go to trial. The system is geared toward guilty pleas, which is understandable, since most defendants are in fact guilty. Still, if every defendant exercised his constitutional right to a trial by jury, the whole thing would freeze up like pipes in winter, in a house with no heat.

"After these cops stopped you and threw your Walkman in the gutter, what happened?"

"They put me in the squad car and drove me over to where this white woman was lying on a stretcher on the sidewalk."

"How far away was that?"

"Maybe two blocks."

"Were you cuffed when she looked at you?"

"Fuck, yes. An' too tight. I still got the burns." He lifted up his hands and showed me the wounds on his wrists, wounds any cop could claim came from an attempt to escape or a failure to follow directions during transit.

"And did she identify you?"

"Whatchyumean, identify me? Fuck, no. Bitch started shaking every which way, and then I think she died. I never seen her before in my life!"

His face twisted bitterly.

"Yeah, this lady, after she got robbed, described someone to the cops. And they picked me up. And I bet you I know what that description was."

I broke in. "Black male. Black coat."

"Mister, just cuz I'm a black kid with a black North

Face down coat, like every other fucking nigger in this city, does it mean I did this crime? Fuck, no."

He spat out the last words like bullets.

"Do you think I'd be stupid enough to rob some woman two blocks from where I work?"

I didn't answer. I knew from years of experience that when presented with the question "Do you really think my client could be so stupid as to . . ." jurors usually answered with a resounding "Yes," whatever the level of stupidity displayed. The "too stupid" defense didn't work. But I kept these thoughts to myself.

"Tell me more. When you were arrested, what did you have on you?"

Damon sneered with disgust.

"Don't go there, man. Yeah, I had one hundred eighty dollars in my jeans pants pocket, and another thirteen big bucks in my wallet. That one eighty was separate. I was on my way to buy my moms a present, a DVD player, straight up. And I'd counted out that money because I knew exactly how much that DVD player cost at Circuit City, where I was going when they busted me."

"What brand were you buying?"

"What is this, a pop quiz? A Sony, that's what."

"And the thirteen was what you had left over after you took the one eighty out of the wallet?"

"Man, you ain't *trying* to help me, are you?" He paused, fighting to get control of himself.

"I got paid yesterday. I cashed my check at the video store where I work at. My paycheck is one eighty each week, and you can check that shit *out*."

The kid sure had an answer for everything. But I got no sense of bluster, which I often did from the first far-fetched story I'd hear from those clients, quite numerous, who felt obliged to lie to their attorneys.

I try never to leap to conclusions. Some of my clients' stories are predictable, and the truth, usually a confession. Some are the truth, yet utterly improbable, and some are perfectly possible, but lies. At least nothing Damon had said so far fell into the most common category—the ridiculous explanation. I'd have to check it all out. But the bottom line in the case, based on what I knew so far, was the quality of the ID by the dying woman. This was not a "how'd it happen"; this was a "who done it." This was what defense lawyers called a "one-witness ID case," except in this case, the identifying witness was dead. And the only remaining witnesses to the identification were the police officers involved. They'd be testifying in the grand jury in a matter of hours. Damon wasn't going anywhere soon.

He looked at me through the steel grating.

"What's with this girl, anyway? Maybe somebody wanted her killed. Maybe she stepped out on her boyfriend. Maybe it was drugs. Maybe it wasn't no mugging. You guys ever think of that? You all just assume it had to be a young black kid. Well, it didn't have to. Why don't you check this broad out? Or the state don't pay for that kinda investigation? State just assumes if it wasn't me, it was some other wild-ass young nigger, so what's the difference."

"Damon, to be honest, it seems like a long shot. The thing looks like a street crime, nothing more, nothing less. It looks like a mugging gone bad. That's probably what it is."

"You legal aides are all alike. I hope my moms can afford a *real* lawyer."

I ignored this comment. On a case like this, even the cheapest private attorney would want at least a ten grand retainer. I doubted Damon's mom had that, if she worked as a nurse's aide.

"Damon, did the cops take the coat?"

"Watchyuthink, that makes me guilty?"

"Listen to me, Damon. I do not give a rat's ass whether or not you committed this crime. Right now, I'm not sure I even want you to tell me what happened. There's only one thing I care about. That's how much evidence they have against you. Do you understand?"

"Yeah, I speak English. I understand. But that canned bullshit ain't good enough for me. That rap may work on criminals and crackheads, but I ain't neither. Sure, I got a little record, but if you check it out, it's all bullshit, including that assault charge. I go to college Monday through Friday, and I work weekends and evenings in a video store. And like I already said, you can check that shit out."

Damon was very angry. It didn't mean much. A lot of my clients were angry because they'd been caught, not because they were innocent. Damon was obviously a smart kid. Smart enough to be angry with himself for messing life up so badly.

A certain percentage of my guilty clients believe the best approach with their free lawyer is to bitterly protest innocence right up until the inevitable guilty plea. On the other hand, a small handful are actually wrongly accused. With Damon, it was impossible to tell yet.

Although I might come to my own conclusions, the truth is, it really doesn't matter to me. I really don't care whether my clients are guilty or innocent. Layden, my boss at the public defender's office, who trained me years ago, and is the only lawyer from whom I'd ever wanted to learn anything, always said: "If you have a moral problem defending guilty people, then you're in the wrong job." Obviously, a small number of my clients have done truly horrible things. But most of them haven't. I am still moved more by my clients' obvious misfortune than by their misdeeds. I know I am their last line of defense, and I like stepping into that small space between their fate and the forces arrayed against them: the People of the State of New York, whoever they are, other than the police, the prosecutors, and the judges, the ones who have the power to point and say "You did this, you did that, and now we're going to lock you up for a chunk of your life." Well, they couldn't just point. First they had to deal with Arch Gold.

Damon was on the verge of tears, but I knew he'd rather die than let me see him cry.

"Mister, I know I ain't gettin' outa here tonight. But listen up. I need a good lawyer, or else they're gonna make this shit stick. You a good lawyer? You *look* good. That counts for something. You know what you're doing?"

I smiled. "Yes, I do. Damon, tonight is just the beginning of a long fight. I'll see you in front of the judge in a few minutes."

I folded my slim file, left the pens, and went back out into the courtroom.

CHAPTER 3

AMERICANS LIKE THEIR COURTROOMS OPEN—it's right there in the Constitution—"a speedy and public trial." Tonight, 210 years after the Founding Fathers used that phrase, there seemed to be a lot of German tourists on hand, sitting in the back rows, trying to size things up in the huge courtroom, staring at the prisoners coming and going through a big dirty steel door in the back. The German tourists were tying to figure out what the prosecutor was saying, trying to guess which prisoners would walk out the front of the courtroom, and which would go back through the steel door. Some German guidebook to New York must have put in a paragraph about night court. Lately the usual collection of mothers, lovers, and friends waiting for a particular case to be called found themselves sitting side by side with these groups of wide-eyed young tourists on holiday.

Americans go to Europe to sit in the back of beautiful old churches. Maybe this decrepit old courtroom was the best we could offer in return. This was no church, but the rows of thickly constructed carved wooden benches did look like pews, and the high ceiling, the grand space, the judge sitting at his altarlike desk high above it all, with the words "In God We Trust" carved above him, did lend a kind of religious gravity to the event. Outside it was freezing, and the wind howled against the windows high up on the sides of the courtroom. They weren't stained glass, but the ice made a sublimely intricate pattern on them.

There was a feeling of shelter about the place, as if it were the last warm open public place of refuge in the whole city. What happened to the thousands of shackled people passing through—twenty-four hours a day, 365 days a year—a steady stream of arrests, for crimes heinous and petty, what happened to them wasn't always just, and was frequently very sad. Though the sense of shelter was an illusion, it was still powerful.

I looked out into the audience. Several dozen black and Hispanic faces stared back at me expectantly from the first few rows. Farther back, the German tourists took it all in.

"Anyone here for Damon Tucker?" I asked, standing at

the low wooden partition, the "rail" that separated audience from participants. "Anyone here for Damon Tucker?"

I always try to speak to family or friends before my client sees the judge. Sometimes, the presence in the audience of a mother, or an employer, can help secure a client's release. On a homicide, there was no chance of that, but if Damon's mom was in the audience, she would need some emotional support, and no doubt she'd be full of questions.

There was no answer. I walked over to the defense counsel area, just a little table with a few chairs around it where I could read, joke, stare off into space, or actually watch the whole damn process. I picked up the phone that the court had finally agreed to provide a few years ago and dialed Damon's mother. No answer. Damon was striking out tonight.

Meanwhile, they'd brought Kathy Dupont out from the pens. Very few good-looking women came through the system, and she was turning some heads. Tom, the court officer calling the cases from the "bridge"—the area between the table at which the accused stood and the high bench where the judge sat—grinned at me as he announced the case in a voice loud enough to quiet the buzz of the large courtroom.

"Docket 98N124876. People of the State of New York against Kathy Dupont. Step up, hands out of your pockets, face the front."

So Kathy Dupont, the 124,876th person arrested in Manhattan as the year drew to a close, sashayed up to face the judge with me standing beside her. She was now wearing her black cowboy boots with silver tips over her purple leggings, black leotard, and short skirt.

"Waive the readings but not the rights thereunder?" intoned Tom.

"So waived," I said.

That was how every arraignment began, with this meaningless litany, a reminder to everyone who might have forgotten that the law was still an arcane world unto itself, with vestigial phrases and procedures that meant nothing and served no purpose other than to intimidate the uninitiated.

"The defendant is charged with assault in the second degree, based on the sworn complaint of Officer Paul Scarponi. People, bail?"

The prosecutor, a conservatively dressed but friendly looking young man just out of some mediocre local law school who had been unable to find a high-paying job in the private sector, and, like many of his peers, figured locking folks up was the next best thing to making piles of money, read the information from the file in front of him. For the first time, the judge looked up.

"Sorry," he said, "where are we?"

It was Judge Everett, perpetually unfocused, good-natured, but dense, a man forever stuck in the bottom rungs of the criminal justice system, whose occasional attempts at innovation or originality left nothing but confusion in their wake. He might lock up a first-arrest shoplifter one night, contrary to the most settled past practice, and do so with a smile, commenting on what he perceived to be the recent turn for the worse in the attire the youth of America were stealing for themselves. Five minutes later, he would release a pathetic burglar, caught red-handed for the thirteenth time in some Upper East Side home and certainly facing many years in prison, for reasons he couldn't ever hope to articulate but that were probably rooted in some unconscious identification with the futility of the poor old bum's life. Most judges eventually moved upstairs to Supreme Court, where they heard exclusively felonies. Only the especially dull judges remained mired in misdemeanor court. And only during arraignments did misdemeanor judges have any contact at all with serious crime. So it was here, in arraignments, that Judge Everett's muddled legal instincts, for better or worse, had their greatest effect.

For the first time, Judge Everett took note of Kathy Dupont. As his gaze fell on her, he began to blush uncontrollably. Did he know her? Had he gotten hot watching her dance at some club? Or was he that awkward kind of man who still blushed like a kid at his first high school dance when he was near a very sexy girl?

"Just a moment. Let me take a look here," he said, shifting his attention from Kathy Dupont to the court papers now in front of him.

"There appears to be a warrant. That's a serious problem."

I decided it was time to jump in, even though I am supposed to stand mute while the prosecutor makes the first arguments.

"Judge," I said, in a tone that I hoped spoke volumes, a tone that was meant to convey a deep understanding between myself and His Honor that this was a nothing case, a mere disagreement between a beautiful woman and her old boyfriend who didn't understand that no means no.

"Judge, as you can see, this earlier case involved the same complainant, a Mr. James Johnson, who at one time had a relationship with my client. As you can also see, that case, which is over a year old, never went anywhere. The People never managed to obtain a corroborating affidavit from Mr. Johnson. In fact, my client thought the case was over. She absolutely understands the importance of making all her court dates."

"Mr. Gold, your client stabbed this man in the ass, are

you aware of that?"

I had no idea what significance the judge attached to this particular fact. Did he think it ruled out self-defense? Or indicated some kinky sexual encounter? The trouble with Judge Everett, tonight as always, was that the smoothest, most direct bail application, where the defense strategy would be clear to the most incompetent counsel, could suddenly veer into uncharted territory. And the lovely Ms. Dupont wasn't taking any of this well. She was beginning to pout. She'd crossed her arms over her ample breasts and begun swinging her hips back and forth, in the kind of slow dance children sometimes do when an authority figure is causing irritation.

"Hands at your side, stand still, and face the front," ordered Tom, although he was in fact deeply pained to have to bring to an end her slow-motion tantrum.

"God," exclaimed Kathy Dupont, stamping her boot in disgust. "Could we just get this over with? That schmuck is never going to prosecute me. He's in love with me."

"That's enough, Ms. Dupont," said the judge. "Bail is set in the amount of one thousand dollars. This young woman has to learn a little respect for the judicial system. And for the sanctity of a man's rear end. Oh, and I'm issuing an order of protection. Young lady, you're to stay away from this man. Any contact with him, and I'll give you thirty days."

The prosecutor hadn't even opened his mouth, and my first case of the night was a disaster. Kathy turned toward me and whispered, "Honey, how could you fuck this up so bad?"

I said nothing as they led her into the back. Tom intoned, in his usual loud mournful voice: "One going in. You have the right to communicate with your lawyer free of charge."

The court officers didn't refer to prisoners other than as numerical units. It was always "one coming out" or "two going in." There were no men or women in the pens, there were only "bodies," as if the city were running some kind of large-scale scientific experiment. On a very busy night, the chief clerk might come out and say "We got three hundred bodies in the system, it's gonna be busy." Only when someone got out could they regain their status as a living entity.

The court officer by the men's pen started off the next case.

"One coming out."

The bridgeman echoed the cry.

"One coming out."

Into the huge courtroom walked Damon Tucker, looking scared, trying to find a familiar face, and seeing only yours truly, Arch Gold.

CHAPTER 4

WHEN DAMON CAME OUT to stand before Judge Everett, the hum of the courtroom died down. Murder gets everyone's attention, even in the arraignment part. Two or three people are murdered every day in New York City. Most of the victims are black or Hispanic, as are most of the accused. But even the most routine killing, say, a knife fight between two drunks, or a gang shooting—the kind of violence that to most New Yorkers is in the end just a statistic—even these acts of violence change the rhythm of the court. Everyone wants to look. Everyone wants to hear. Everyone wants to know what this particular killer looks like. How does he walk and talk? How did he actually do it? How did he snuff out the other life? Is he admitting, or denying? How much evidence is there against him anyway? Even the court officers, who've seen thousands of cases come through, to whom crime is just the reason they come to work every day, even they crane their necks and cup a hand around an ear.

I have defended thirteen homicides in my career—more than most lawyers anywhere. Each one of them was different, but they all had one thing in common—my client had done it. In most the question was not identification, but choreography. I've won a few of those. And I've lost my share, mostly cases with no real defense, where my only choice was to claim mistaken identity—the last refuge of the cold-blooded contract killer. But as I stood next to Damon in front of Judge Everett, I realized that in every case, my client had in fact killed someone, even if the act was legally or morally justified. And in every case where the defense was mistaken identity, the evidence had been overwhelming, and my client had been convicted. This one would probably not turn out any differently.

Judge Everett did things by the book. The earnest young prosecutor had stepped aside, supplanted by Paul McSwayne, one of the old pros of the DA's office, a career prosecutor, smarter than most and, most irritating to me, a nice man, who pulled no punches, and in the eight years I had known him, as far as I could tell, had told no lies. I resented McSwayne precisely because I couldn't find a reason to dislike him.

He was speaking in even tones.

"People serving Section 250 notice. We'll be seeking either the death penalty or life without parole. As Your Honor knows, under the death penalty statute, we have 120 days from Supreme Court arraignment to decide between these two alternatives. Based on the seriousness of the charge, and the strength of the case, the People are asking that this defendant be remanded without bail. The defendant was arrested two blocks from the scene, as he was fleeing on foot. He had 180 dollars loose in his front left pants pocket, and 13 dollars in his own wallet when he was arrested. A show-up was conducted moments later, and shortly before the victim died, she identified this man as the shooter. The wallet was recovered in the street under a parked car several yards from the victim, with no cash inside, next to a .9 millimeter automatic. The defendant has five prior arrests, and this is a strong case. Based on these facts, the People feel that remand is justified."

There had been no doubt that Damon would be held without bail, no matter who the judge, or, for that matter, who the prosecutor making the presentation. But McSwayne had just painted a tough picture for Damon, a little preview of the difficulties facing the accused and counsel at trial.

Judge Everett shifted his gaze to me.

"Anything?"

"Judge . . ."

Before I could say another word, Judge Everett had begun to address Damon directly.

"Young man, I don't know if you're guilty or innocent, only the judicial process will determine that, but I just wanted you to know it really doesn't matter what your lawyer says right now; there's no way I'm going to do anything but lock you up with no bail. So don't blame Mr. Gold here. He's a very fine lawyer."

The judge banged his gavel. "The defendant is remanded. The case is adjourned to next Thursday, December 10, in Part F, for grand jury action. I hope you have a good week, Mr. Tucker."

As they led Damon back into the pens, the courtroom was quiet, except for the squeak of chalk. Cameras were still forbidden in New York State courtrooms, and for high-profile events, the big papers and TV networks still hired artists to sketch the proceedings, a curious nineteenth-century tradition that survived the fast traffic of the electronic highway. The sketches usually showed the defendant and his lawyer standing together in front of a judge, with the defendant scowling and the lawyer frozen in some desperate gesture.

Later, outside in the darkness on the curb, with the huge Criminal Court Building looming behind me, the biggest building in the world devoted solely to "criminal justice," I found the TV networks waiting for me, mikes all jammed together into a little stand, a little pulpit from which I was supposed to say something helpful to my client when it was still possible, early in the case before some judge issued the inevitable gag order.

"Well," I said, half smiling, "they're prosecuting the wrong kid. Damon Tucker had nothing to do with this horrible crime. The police made a quick arrest. Much too quick. Thank you very much."

That was it. There wasn't much else to say at this point. Walking away from the media, heading around the corner, where the taxis sometimes pull up, I saw Kathy Dupont, waving down a cab. A small bearded man was running toward the same cab. He got to its door just as it pulled away. He looked after it with deep desperation, his pointy little bearded face contorted in agony. I stood next to him, waiting for another cab.

"I just bailed that whore out, and she snuck into that cab without even so much as a hello."

"You must be Johnson," I said, sounding too much like a colonial explorer. "I represent Ms. Dupont. As I understand it, you're the reason she was in jail in the first place, am I right?"

"What is this, cross-examination or what? Who the fuck are you, anyway, scumbag?"

I was in the process of opening my mouth when the left hook hit me.

I never saw it coming.

Looking back, I see the punch as the beginning of a new phase of my life, a phase of violence I could have never imagined back in law school when I didn't know the difference between a tort and a tortoise. But compared with what was to follow, it was a love tap. It didn't knock me out, it just knocked me down. I hadn't been hit since college, when I'd been punched by a heroin addict in Amsterdam from whom I'd decided not to buy some unimpressive-looking hash.

By the time I pulled myself up, Johnson was gone. The street was quiet. The local networks, who had focused on me so intently moments ago, had already moved on to their next story.

CHAPTER 5

DEATH CAME to Charlotte King on the sidewalk in front of a commercial printing plant on Twentieth Street off of Twelfth Avenue. Early Monday morning, before going into the office, flashlight in my coat, I walked up the West Side to the spot where she died.

This part of town was physically unchanged since the turn of the century. Lofts, warehouses, and commercial buildings of all sizes and shapes hulked over narrow streets. A few pedestrians were heading to work, and a few prostitutes, male and female, mostly in short skirts, halter tops, and spiked heels, were wobbling up and down the sidewalks looking for business. Once in a while a car, usually from New Jersey, stopped, and things like price and service to be provided were negotiated. Supply and demand. Twenty-four hours a day in this city, someone was selling, and someone was buying.

The last few years had created an alternative world for some of the gloomy old buildings. Art dealers, squeezed out of Soho by rising rents and unable to compete with the designer clothing stores and fancy restaurants, had discovered this part of town and moved their galleries here. This was where Charlotte King had come on her last day on earth, looking for art.

The spot where she had been shot was no longer taped off. There was no sign of Friday's mayhem. New York wasn't an efficient place in many ways, but how quickly it could process violence, clean up a little mess on the street, and carry on. Over the weekend the city warmed up, the dirty air stirred, the rain came, and the quart or two of Charlotte King's blood that had stained the old slate sidewalk of Twentieth Street was washed away into the gutter.

Gutter. I wanted to check out the gutters over on Twenty-second and Twelfth. According to McSwayne, that's where the two Street Crime Unit cops had stopped Damon, before bringing him back to Twentieth Street, where Charlotte King lay dying, for the "show-up."

When I got to Twenty-second Street, I walked over to one of the four ancient iron sewer grates that were set into the street, one on each corner, and that led to the dark gutter beneath. I squatted down and shined my flashlight into the blackness. I saw nothing unusual in the first three.

But shining the beam through the fourth grating, I could see a Walkman, its wires leading to the earphones, all caught on something, dangling from the sewer grate, not yet fallen into the darkness below. So far, Damon's story was checking out.

Now I had a complicated situation on my hands. It's always tricky when the defense finds potentially exculpatory physical evidence in a sensitive location. I wanted that Walkman tested for prints. I was sure it had Damon's prints all over it, and also one of those two cops' prints—whichever one threw it into the gutter, failed to note it on the paperwork, failed to preserve it as evidence, and generally fucked up every conceivable police procedure. Most jurors would agree with me that you might not choose to flee a crime scene wearing your Walkman. Wouldn't a juror or two want to know why these cops were so unreliable about preserving evidence that might help the defense? What did that say about their ID testimony?

I pulled out my cell phone and dialed McSwayne's number. I had no choice but to let the DA's office handle it while I watched. I'd lose the element of surprise, but otherwise, I could never prove it up at trial. McSwayne was skeptical but told me he'd be right down, with forensic and video, to do the whole thing right. That was what I liked about the Manhattan DA's office. They were pros. They didn't hide evidence, they didn't sit on stuff, and if it cut your way, they lived with it. The "system" I fought wasn't the DA's office itself, it was all the lying cops, and the sentencing laws, passed by disingenuous politicians looking for easy votes. But even though I trusted McSwayne, after I got off the phone with him, I called the local papers and TV stations. I told them who I was and that I thought I'd discovered some important

evidence in the case that the police had deliberately
overlooked. I told them I thought they should haul ass
over to Twenty-second Street to watch what went down.
As I clicked my cell phone shut, I could hear the wail of a
siren approaching. It was McSwayne. He jumped out of a
black Chrysler, came up to me, and shook my hand.

I pointed down to the iron grating, and the darkness
below it.

"Think I got something here, Jim. According to my
client, the cops ripped off his Walkman and threw it in
the gutter. Funny, I see a Walkman dangling right in that
gutter there. Bet you my next paycheck it has Damon's
fingerprints on it, along with the prints of one of those
idiot SCU cops, who likes to lie and get rid of evidence
just for the fuck of it. Wanna have your forensic team pull
it out?"

"Looks like we will, Arch. Here they come now."

A black van was pulling up to the curb. Out hopped a
swat team of DA forensic techies, ready to retrieve and
record.

I got in McSwayne's face.

"This whole case turns on some cops' testimony about
the totally improper ID of my client by a woman who
is now dead, and therefore unavailable to testify at trial.
Now, turns out these same cops hide evidence. Sounds
like a problem for you, Jim."

"Let's wait for the prints before getting overly agitated,
okay?"

McSwayne scratched his head.

"We're gonna be under some serious pressure to make
this the first big one."

Now it was my turn to laugh out loud.

"Your loyalty to the boss is touching. Come on, Jim,
this is an eighteen-year-old kid. Leventhal's not gonna

suddenly decide he's the first to fry. It's not happening."

"An eighteen-year-old kid who's six four, two thirty, and shoots rich, white lady executives shopping for art in Chelsea. Not exactly kiddy-type behavior. Gold, this kid had 180 bucks in a wad of bills in his jeans pocket when he was running from the scene, and 13 dollars separate cash in his wallet. He matches the description that went over central, which I've already listened to a couple times on tape, a dub of which I am sending over to your office, literally as we speak. And my cops say this lady ID'd him before she died right there on the sidewalk. Not to mention whatever fingerprint evidence is gonna come back tomorrow."

"That's not how it went down, Jim. Those cops are trying to make a bad arrest stick. That poor lady's description was shit. It described every fourth black kid in New York City She didn't ID my guy. She just went into a spasm and died as he was standing in front of her, illegally cuffed during a show-up. Talk to those cops a little more."

"We'll see," said McSwayne evenly. "You and I both know there's politics way over my head that says I don't make this kid an offer. So let's not pretend that there's anything on the table. If your kid doesn't want to plead to life, we'll go to trial."

"Thanks for that wisdom, Jim."

"No problem, Arch. I'm just a friendly civil servant with no secrets. And your kid is fucked. It's all routine. I'll fax you the reports. How's that? Have I actually interviewed the cops about the details of the ID? No. But when I do, which will be real soon, I'll let you know what they say. Tomorrow, we'll see whose prints turn up where. And despite your hard-on about getting this ID tossed, trust me, it ain't happening. You may be the best trial lawyer in your office, but that'll only get you so far, handsome."

The whole thing was videotaped, not just by the DA's guys, but also by the local networks. Forensic pulled out the Walkman and bagged it just like they were supposed to. And for the second time in two days, I found myself standing in front of a bank of microphones, giving everyone my sweetest look and answering questions about how this helped my case: Did I think the police deliberately withheld evidence? What did I think the fingerprint analysis would show? Were these the same cops who would testify about the identification? Was the DA's office going to ask for the death penalty? Did I think my client could get a fair trial?

Finally, when the last question had been asked and answered, I got on the number one train and headed downtown to the office.

CHAPTER 6

THE NEW YORK COUNTY Public Defender's Office is a big old outfit. We have offices on four floors of a run-down office building several blocks from the courthouse. We exist because in 1963 the U.S. Supreme Court declared, in *Gideon v. Wainwright*, that every indigent person accused of a crime has a right to a free attorney. Since less than 5 percent of the folks arrested in New York City can actually afford private lawyers, *Gideon* seems only sporting.

The right to counsel, of course, doesn't include the right to counsel with a nice office. I sat at my brown Formica desk, leaning back in my government-issue plastic chair, which balanced perfectly in the cracks of the faded linoleum floor, as I dialed into my voice mail.

"You have three messages," the off-key computer voice sang into my ear. At first, I'd hated the advent of voice mail in my office, the further dehumanization of so-called human contact. But my feelings had changed. I'd grown to savor the intimacy of the messages, which were far more revealing than a pink slip with a name and phone number scrawled illegibly. Of course, I hadn't appreciated the disgruntled client who told me, in no uncertain terms, "Gold, if I ever see you again, it's two in the head." That dude was doing twenty-five to life. Hopefully, he'd forget about me after a decade or two. He was less irritating than my ex-wife. Right now, she was carrying on about my new status with the local media. She'd left me as soon as she figured out I wasn't going to be making partner and hundreds of thousands of dollars a year in some big firm. But now, if I could get on the six o'clock news, well, that was worth at least a phone call.

"Archibald, I can't believe that was you! You look great. Maybe this'll set you up in private practice, even if that kid is guilty as hell. Bye."

Typical. The only upside was monetary. The downside was the work itself.

We'd met as first-year associates at Davis White & Wardell, a huge Wall Street money machine of a law firm, back when her long lean body, her fascination with corporate law, and her ambition to make a zillion bucks seemed to fulfill all my needs, day and night, back when neither of us understood that I couldn't take orders from older attorney assholes in large corporate settings, and that it mattered to her, and didn't to me. We'd married after a year, and it was over within a year and a half. I quit my job with Davis White, where they thought they owned you for a hundred thousand bucks a year, and she quit me. Now she was pulling down five times that a year as a partner somewhere else, merging large corporations, and then breaking them apart, and then putting them back together, still single like me. That was about all we had in common.

Then there was a message from Kathy Dupont.

"Hi, Mr. Gold, I just wanted to tell you I made bail, and to talk about the case, and stuff. I don't think Jimmy's gonna go forward with it. Do I still have to come to court next week? Call me. Or come see my show. Bye, cutie."

The last message was from Damon. The voice was sad and hurt.

"Yo man, I saw you on TV. When you gonna come out here and talk to *me*? You the big TV star now. I'm still locked up in a goddamn cell."

"I'm coming, Damon, I'm coming," I said, to no one in particular, as my phone rang. It was Kimberly, the receptionist at the front desk. She was a young black woman with attitude, an essential asset in her job, which involved dealing with some awfully upset people from time to time.

"Mr. Gold, there's a Hyman Rose sitting here who says he wants to see you. He's been waiting all morning."

"Never heard of him. What's he look like?"

"Old white guy. Not our type."

"What the hell, send him up."

Hyman Rose was ancient. At least eighty. He was a tough old piece of gristle. He was wrinkled, and he moved stiffly as he sat himself down, but he wasn't particularly fragile. Still had a nice head of white hair. I tried to place him, tried to figure out what he was doing in my office, but I couldn't.

"You look just the same, Archie. The last thirty years been kinder to you than me. Your father would be happy about that. I know it."

"Sir, I don't believe we've met. Do I represent you?"

I wasn't supposed to take in new cases off the street. The PD's office had a special "intake" unit for people with a criminal problem who hadn't yet been arrested. This old man wasn't exactly who they had in mind.

"I worked with Noah."

That took me right back to Clinton Street. I don't go back often, not even anymore in my dreams. They've been dead twenty years. Now, this Hyman Rose put me right back behind the counter of my father's electrical supply store, running around and around the floor-to-ceiling metal shelves all full of fuses, circuit boxes, switches, wires, cables, the best hidden playground on the Lower East Side, and me too small to be seen by the customers, the general contractors, and electricians on the other side of the counter. When you came into Noah's store, you had to know what you wanted. Nothing was displayed. It was all in the back. You could stand in the little service area between the front door and the short counter with the circuitry diagrams and standards on it, but if you didn't know what you wanted, nothing and nobody was going to tell you. Maybe you needed a circuit breaker box, or maybe you wanted to place a bet on the Knicks or the fifth race at Belmont.

I can't remember how old I was when I first figured out that my father ran more than one business at a time. Neither one seemed more or less legitimate. I can remember hearing my mother, Isabelle, crying late at night, hearing her through the thin walls of the apartment, talking in a desperately low voice, hoping I wouldn't hear, begging Noah to give up the book, to forget about the "vig" and just sell the goods. And Noah laughing, and going through her closet, and fingering all the nice dresses, and saying did she think fuses and switches could put a kid through a good college, and law or med school, and shouldn't Archie go to a good college, he's got the grades.

"What kind of work did you do with Noah?" I asked Hyman Rose, pulling myself back into the present, back to my drab office on Lafayette Street, in lower Manhattan. Would my parents have understood why I worked in this dumpy office, for the dregs of society? I liked to think so. I would never know.

"Your father was a business partner of mine, many years ago, and I'm not talking electrical supplies, y'understand?"

Rose looked intently at me, pursing his thin lips, sucking in a little around his dentures.

"I was bigger than he was, ya see? I helped set him up, and I could keep him in business. He could always lay off a bet with Rose. I kept him liquid if he needed. I was bigger, but his heart was twice the size of mine. If he loved you, like he did you and your mother, and me, you could feel it, you felt part of something. His word was always good. He did what he said he'd do, even if it cost him. If you got half his heart and balls, you're gonna be okay."

He waved his hand around at the office, a valiant gesture, considering how drab it was.

"But I'm wandering. Last few years, harder to stay on track. Yunno what I mean, sonny? I'm talking, suddenly I'm on a goddamn new subject, and I don't know how I got there."

He sucked his lips again.

"Old ain't fun. Not for me."

I nodded.

"What the DA's doing to me, that ain't no goddamn fun either. Freezing my bank account. Forfeiture proceeding. I'm an old man. A grandfather. I ain't in business no more.

Where was the government back when they coulda made a real case against me?"

Better they waited, I thought.

"Tell me about it."

"I don't work no more. Saved enough, don't need the stress, don't give a damn anymore. Worked hard in a scummy game so my son could make it legit, like you. He has, and he hasn't. The DA's crawling into his *tochas*, and taking an awful good look around. He owns a couple Big Burger franchises. Looks like there's some hanky-panky when it comes time to renovate the joints, know what I mean. Big Burger pays for the renovations, see. My son picks the contractor and gets a little cash back. I call it a rebate. A discount. They call it a kickback. What do I know? So the DA taps his phone, and the rest, and what do they find out? They find out that once in a while, I take a bet for my son and his friends. I'm not in the business. I'm just like a cash box. I take the dough, I pass it on to the guy with the book, and I pay out later in the week. It's all peanuts. Every few weeks I even it up with the bookman, and that's it. It's nothing. I make nothing. Not a dime. You could call it volunteer work. I'm just a branch outlet. Like an ATM. But I don't even charge a buck fifty. 'Course the DA don't see it like that. I'm on tape, talking bets and amounts, and next thing I know, they fucking froze my IRAs, and mutual funds, all dough I've had for years, though from where, I wouldn't wanna hafta say."

Forfeiture laws stink. They can take your money without notice, without a hearing, and with only the vaguest connection ever established to illegal activity. I explained it all to Rose, told him we'd move for a hearing, we'd fight it tooth and nail, but that he might have to settle in the low six figures. I didn't tell him that I wasn't supposed to even handle civil forfeiture cases like this, that this was a big favor, for Noah.

I watched Rose glide out the door the way well-preserved old men do, old men moving slowly, but with a strong will to stay in this world, old men trying to hide the stiffness in their bones.

I walked down to the big corner office with the two windows and the slightly better-looking furniture, where the attorney-in-charge sat. I wanted to talk about Damon Tucker.

CHAPTER 7

KEVIN LAYDEN was leaning back in his huge chair, feet up on his desk, exposing the holes in his soles to my view as I walked in.

"You need tips and heels, maybe half soles, Kev. Looking a little ragged for a guy at your level."

"When did you become the keeper of men's soles, Arch?"

Kevin sat up and threw the *Post* at me.

"Nasty fucking crime," he said. Now he was scowling. The cover had a photo of Damon Tucker, in cuffs, as they hauled him out of the Thirteenth Precinct and down to central booking. Great pretrial publicity. Just what Damon needed.

Kevin knew about nasty crime. He'd seen a lot of it in thirty years at the PD's office. He presided over a huge operation. He had a budget of 120 million per annum, paying four hundred lawyers and three hundred support staff, and handling 80 percent of the city's criminal defendants. Not surprisingly, he hadn't started out his legal career planning to become the CEO of a large organization. He joined the PD's office right out of law school, when it was in its infancy, in the 1960s. Within a few years, he was the best trial lawyer in the place. He knew every corner of the law, no mean feat. But he also had a style, a look, that was perfectly suited for juries. He wasn't leading-man handsome, he was character-actor handsome. He was very tall, 6'5", thin, but surprisingly graceful. He had short dark hair and a closely trimmed salt-and-pepper beard. Full beards make you focus on the eyes. You can't read a face full of hair. So it was with Kevin. His deep-set green eyes were never quiet.

Outside the courtroom, his expression was generally pained. Even those who'd known him for years, like me, never knew if it was empathy or irritation. A decade ago, before his promotion, he'd trained me—taught me how to try a case. Now we were friends.

The only tension between us was recent. Several months back, he tried to make me assistant attorney-in-charge, number two behind him. I refused. I like trying cases. That's what I am good at, not fighting for a budget with the mayor's office, and hiring and firing lawyers. I was still hoping he hadn't taken it personally.

"How's it look for this kid, Arch?"

"Too soon to say. Of course, he's denying. The ID's not real solid. I mean, she was dying when she saw him. He says she died right after looking at him. And, of course, the cops threw his Walkman in the gutter, instead of vouchering it."

"No shit!"

I told him the story of my early-morning discovery. He seemed amused.

"Cops can fuck up any case, can't they? It never fails to amaze me."

"I don't think this woman ID'd him at all," I said.

"Shit, she was probably in shock, seeing triple. We'll get an expert to say that, no problem. Any physical evidence?"

"Not yet. We should hear about prints today."

"Did you see who the victim worked for?"

I shook my head.

"Yates Associates."

I looked blank.

"Come on, Arch, you gotta keep up on this stuff. It's a big world out there. And Yates probably knows more about it than any private individual alive. He's a private investigator. Runs the biggest PI firm on earth. Takes in millions. Has a file on everyone."

I shrugged. Layden understood.

"Guess it doesn't mean much for your kid, does it? A street crime's a street crime. Doesn't matter who the victim works for. You're going to have to go ID. Let's face it, you're not going to produce the 'real' shooter. If it wasn't this guy, it was some other black kid who you'll never find. So get an expert to look at her injuries, to testify about the speed with which she must've died, to say she was totally gone, unable to see or think clearly long before Damon was illegally paraded in front of her.

"How's Tucker?" he asked me. "Can you work with him?"

"He's a smart kid, very angry, with a big mouth. Maybe he's angry because he's innocent."

Layden gave me a look and laughed for a second. I resented it.

"You're such a goddamn cynic, Layden. I guess you've seen one too many homicides come through this place."

The laugh went away. He sighed. His expression became drawn. He got up and closed the door. He spoke to me in a tone I didn't know.

"Arch, Lisa's kicking me out. She told me to leave. She says it's over."

There were tears in his eyes.

"You know how much I love my kids. I don't know how I'm going to deal with this. I don't."

"No," was all I could manage to say. I felt a wave of affection for him, for his heroic effort to talk to *me*, about *my* problems, about *my* case, when his world had just blown up on him. He was a trooper.

He'd always seemed the perfect family man. His cute preppy wife, Lisa, who was ever perky and appropriate, had lots of dough. They lived in an elegant nineteenth-century town house on the Upper West Side with their three beautiful smart bambinos. Kevin lived for those kids. He didn't have much of a social life, as far as I could tell. When he wasn't working to keep the indigent well represented, he was hanging out with his kids. I didn't quite see how he could get along without seeing them.

"What happened?" I asked.

"I don't know. I'm in shock. I knew things weren't perfect, but . . ."

His voice was breaking. Neither of us knew what to say next. We weren't used to talking about painful personal things. We had a close, professional relationship. No emotional displays. I'd never seen him like this.

"I rented a place nearby. I'll see the kids most weekends, and vacations. Oh, God. How did this happen?"

He put his head in his hands. I walked around his big desk and patted him on the back.

"I'm sorry, Kevin. I really am."

He sat back up, trying to pull himself together.

I'd worked with him for years, played with his kids, eaten dinner at his house from time to time, admired his wife—all from a certain distance. It had seemed close to picture perfect. Had it all been a facade? I had no idea.

"You can't help, Arch. These are just very tough days for me."

I was worried about him.

I walked back to my office. The phone was ringing. Reception again.

"Mr. Gold, we have a Ms. Tucker here to see you. Says you represent her son."

"I sure do. Tell her to come up."

Evelyn Tucker was still dressed in the white uniform of a hospital worker, probably just off a long shift. She was a chunky woman, with a handsome broad face and a determined look. I motioned to one of the plastic chairs. She sat on the edge.

"How are you, Ms. Tucker?"

"Not too good, Mr. Gold. You have kids? You never imagine your kid is going to be locked up and charged with murder."

"I'm very sorry, Ms. Tucker."

"Sorry isn't going to do it, Mr. Gold. He needs a good lawyer. I guarantee you, he didn't do this crime. My son's a little wild. He has a fast mouth. But he doesn't hurt people. He doesn't fight. He doesn't rob. He'd never go near a gun. Shit."

She started to cry. Everybody was trying to cry on me this morning.

The fact was, I hated making speeches to the relatives. I'm way too direct. If they ever isolate the "sugarcoating" gene, they won't find it in my DNA. That's why I couldn't make it in private practice. I'd tried it again after a few years at the PD's office, working for one year at a boutique white-collar criminal defense firm that paid me six figures as a senior associate, and wouldn't let me do anything but write memos to the file, much less try a case to a jury, one of the real thrills of my job at the PD's office. The biggest problem for me, though, was watching the two partners for whom I'd worked go out and get business. It was more than enough to turn me off for good. The dog and pony show in front of the prospective client, usually incarcerated, who was looking to get something for nothing—which was the reason he probably ended up in jail in the first place. The puffing about the possible results. The haggling over money. I wasn't made for it. I have problems with the first premise of private practice—that your clients should pay you money to represent them. I considered the fact that I was, inevitably, trying to make money off my client's difficulties to present an insurmountable conflict between myself and my client.

Out there in the white-collar world, I was supposed to be charming, to make nice talk with the right people, and to get rich. I'd always been an excellent student, gotten great grades, and gone to all the right schools—Yale College and Harvard Law School. Looking back, it all seemed almost accidental. I'd supposedly made all the right connections, wired myself in, solidified all those old school ties that were rumored to pay off down the road. Well, I was down the road, and although it didn't bother me, nothing much seemed to be paying off. Truth is, I'd spent the last ten years sliding away from the well-pressed shirt-and-tie crowd that my parents had wanted so badly for me.

So I'm back at the public defender's office, where I get to try cases and don't have to fight anyone over money. I much prefer the gritty purity of the work. My meager salary comes in, week after week, and I defend folks that everyone I know considers the scum of the earth.

"Where do you work, Ms. Tucker?" I asked.

"I work at Harlem Hospital. I'm a nurse's aide. I check up on patients, see if they need a new bedpan, or water, or a new bandage, or if they're plugged into the right equipment, if their leads are tangled. It's not the most complicated stuff, but it's stressful, and it's the work that makes every hospital run. I work hard. I learned that from my parents. They came from Barbados in the early sixties with me when I was a little girl. They're both dead now. My papa worked in a dry-cleaning plant; my momma was a home attendant, keeping one rich old white lady after another alive. They both taught me how to live right. I taught Damon, too. That's why I can't believe this is happening to my son."

I told Ms. Tucker what I knew about the case. I told her to call me anytime. I promised to call her right away if there was any news. I told her I'd fight like hell for Damon. What else can you tell a mother whose son is locked up for murder?

I went out to Rikers Island to visit Damon.

CHAPTER 8

RIKERS ISLAND is New York City's local jail and also, by the way, the largest penal colony in the world, housing over twenty thousand inmates on the sixty-five-acre island sitting in the dirty water between Manhattan, the Bronx, and Queens.

Leaving Manhattan, going over the Triborough Bridge, and through Queens, I saw the New York skyline glowing like gold in the crisp blue sunny air. From a distance, it looked like beautiful science fiction, created on a scale no one could believe. This was real talent. You could almost forget that there was no design to it at all, that up close, it was a big mess. But the illusion never lasted more than a few minutes anyway. Then the endless gravestones in the cemeteries along the highway told the story again of the human anonymity that was the price of the glittering city.

It is almost as hard for an attorney to get into Rikers Island as it is for a defendant to get out. There is only one bridge, and to call it a bottleneck would seriously understate the situation. Clearance takes forever. The city is so busy transporting thousands of inmates to court in Manhattan, the Bronx, Brooklyn, and Queens that it barely has time to process the lawyers who, ever so rarely, decide to actually visit their clients in jail. From the last checkpoint on the bridge, which arched over the East River, I could see the whole island, the acres and acres of fenced-in land, more like some kind of third world plantation than an American prison. I surrendered my car, got my security clearance, and waited for the "attorney" bus.

The various building complexes on Rikers were connected by a network of small highways, used only by Corrections vehicles. One was approaching now. It was a converted school bus. All of the windows had been covered with thick steel grating, and the familiar yellow color was gone, replaced by a deep blue. Still, the thing looked like a school bus, and when you saw it, you still wanted to think of small-town America and innocent kids hopping on and off in front of cute houses on tree-lined streets. You wanted to, but you couldn't. The city bought the buses used, from the Board of Education, and even though they carried some innocent passengers now and then, the scene was several dark twists away from the false brightness of the mythical American child on the way to school.

The attorney bus circled the island's roads every half hour or so, often riding empty. Few lawyers found it a profitable use of their time to visit a client all the way out here. Riding over to the Men's House of Detention, where Damon was housed, I was alone on the bus, except for the angry-looking driver, a middle-aged white man who looked like he drank his lunch and was at war with the world on and off the Rock, as everyone called Rikers Island. He wanted to talk.

"Know how many fucking niggers and spics they got on this island? Twenty thousand. Big waste of time."

I said nothing. I wished my face didn't attract conversation, didn't seem to send off a signal "Talk to me," but it did.

"Costs the city sixty thou' a year to house each one of 'em. I say fuck it. Give 'em the goddamn sixty thou'. Prison don't do shit for these kids. They go in with nothing, and they come out with less. Just give 'em the sixty thousand, each, and we'd all be better off."

My views on the situation hadn't evolved quite that far, but I wasn't in the mood to argue. The bus pulled up to the curb outside the Men's House of Detention, and I got off. Ten minutes later, I was sitting in the counsel visit room, waiting for the guards to bring in Damon. This was what penologists would call a contact visit. No wire grille, no glass, no Lucite, just the two of us sitting in a little room.

Damon walked in very slowly, dragging each foot as if it weighed two tons. He finally reached the beat-up chair, sat down, and put his head in his hands. He looked up after half a minute.

"Man, I ain't doin' too good."

I was quiet. I knew from long experience that silence

was better than some half-assed response when the talk turned to life in jail. Words just couldn't bridge that gap.

Damon looked up.

"What's this I hear 'bout the death penalty?"

"Not happening. Whatever you hear, it's not happening. But life without parole is no picnic. Not when you're eighteen years old."

"You think I'm guilty, don't you?"

"I do not, Damon."

"But you don't care, right? You do your best anyway, don't you? It's so touching!"

I said nothing. He had to vent.

"Man, what do you really think? Think I did it?"

"Your word is good enough for me."

"Mister, can I say something? I did not rob that woman, and I did not shoot that woman. Someone else robbed her and someone else shot her. Those four cops are lying motherfuckers. That woman started shaking, and died right in front of me. She didn't ID me. She just shook every which way and died. All those cops know it, too. For some fucking reason, they're framing me."

I nodded, only half in assent.

"They know she didn't really pick you out, but since you match the description they got, and since they caught you running away from the scene, and with the separate cash in a wad in your pocket, they're positive you did it, so they have no trouble reinterpreting that death scene."

"You can call it what you want, those cops are still framing me. Shit. Don't the truth matter? This ain't some fucking performance art. The whole goddamn city wants a conviction, don't they?"

" 'Fraid so, Damon."

Damon definitely wasn't just another gangsta kid proving he had heart. Those kids didn't know from "performance art."

He banged the metal desk with his huge fist. He was trying hard not to cry. His handsome face was contorted in pain. His lips trembled as he took several big breaths, trying to control himself.

"Man, I am the unluckiest nigger alive."

I told him about finding the Walkman. I told him about my conversations with McSwayne. I explained that we'd have a pretrial hearing to contest the legality of the victim's identification. I tried to sound upbeat. I told him it was early in the case. I told him there was a lot we didn't know yet. He took it all in. We sat in silence for a few moments, and then he spoke.

"As long as I live, I will never forget standing in front of that woman, in cuffs, watching her die. All those cops looked at each other, and then they put me in the car. I said to the cop in the backseat with me, 'What are you guys charging me with?' He laughed and said, 'As if you don't know, asshole. Murder one.' I knew my life was never gonna be the same again, no matter what happened."

He stared at me, to see if I was listening. I was.

"Bottom line, they're trying to lock me up for the rest of my life for this, and all they have is these lying cops to say this woman actually identified me."

"You got it right. As of now, they don't exactly have a rock crusher case against you. What we're looking at now, we can beat. Let's hope there's no bad fingerprint evidence coming at us."

"Mr. Gold, there is no way her prints can be on that money. No way."

"Good. I look forward to hearing it for sure, from the prosecutor."

"Seen my mom?"

"Yes. I filled her in on everything I know. Obviously,

she's really upset."

"She's way too religious," he said. "Guess she better start praying her ass off. We're gonna need all the help we can get."

"You don't buy that religious stuff?"

"My mom's a good lady. She works hard. She always gave me what I need. But the religious stuff just didn't rub off on me. Man, how could you believe in God when you're accused of a murder you didn't do? What kind of God does that to you?"

He had a point.

"You found out anything about this chick?" he asked.

"Haven't had time yet, but I will."

I was just appeasing him. The fact was, not for one second did I think this was anything other than a mugging gone bad, whether or not Damon was the mugger. The odds of catching the "real" mugger were slim—he'd have to get caught on an unrelated case and then confess to this one. It happened, but not often.

"So you still assuming if it wasn't me, it was some other dumb black kid?"

"What do you think?" I asked.

"I think you should check this broad out."

"Honestly, Damon, I think it's more likely to be a mugging gone bad by someone other than you, than some kind of hit. That's just the way it looks to me."

It was the wrong thing to say.

"How long you been doing this, mister? Ten years? Man, you've seen too many homeboys go upstate. It's messed up your thinking."

He was getting angry.

"Fuck it, then. My owns gonna hire a lawyer, spend every dime they got. You state-appointed lawyers all the same. Fuck you."

This kid had a short fuse. Was it just the stress, or was it possible that he was actually innocent? The thought crossed my mind as he got up and started to stomp down the tiled hall. I followed him, trying to keep up with his long strides. Our voices echoed off the hard surfaces.

"Damon. I will investigate Charlotte King. I just told you it seemed like a long shot. I didn't say I wouldn't do it. I'll do it. I already told you, we can win this case. And by the way, you don't know how good you got with me. Whatever kinda money your mom's got, it's not enough to buy her a good lawyer. You already got that in me. Except you don't have to pay me, and I'm not interested in taking your money. I'm interested in winning, okay?"

He turned and looked at me stone-faced. He still didn't trust me. I couldn't blame him. We've all been brought up to believe that nothing good comes for free. Why should a free lawyer be any different?

On the way back to the city, I called McSwayne. It wasn't good news. There were no prints on the gun, or on Charlotte's wallet, and sure, Damon's prints were on the Walkman, along with one of the two cops who collared him. Maybe that was a little awkward. Damon's prints were also on the money, the eighteen 10 dollar bills found in his jeans pockets, on each and every one of them. Oh, and Arch, I almost forgot, Charlotte King's fingerprints were on three of those bills as well. Just thought I'd give you a heads-up before we put out a press release.

Things weren't looking too good for Damon.

CHAPTER 9

THE SERGEANT WHO had supervised the crime scene on Twentieth Street was thorough for a cop. He'd bagged the gun, the wallet found in the street, Charlotte's purse, and its contents. McSwayne had put all the vouchered property out on a big table in his office, a large room that was dumpy, yet functional. Everything was in a sealed clear plastic envelope, the standard method for preserving crime scene evidence. The criminal justice system is obsessed with the "chain of custody" when it comes to such stuff. For me to actually look at the evidence in these thick plastic bags, a cop had to be present to cut them open, and then reseal them, and put them directly back in the property clerk's office. This was done so that no enterprising defense counsel could claim the authorities had lost track of the evidence. The O.J. trial had shown the whole country how jurors could buy into this kind of reasoning.

"Ya really want this all cut open, Arch? It's a pain in the ass. And try not to touch everything. We haven't printed it all, and we may want to. We don't really need defense counsel's prints popping up."

I looked the stuff over. The gun was in one envelope. The wallet in another. The contents of the wallet in a third, the purse in a fourth, and its contents in a fifth. McSwayne had given me a photocopy of each piece of paper in the purse and wallet. I could look at that later. I picked up the envelope holding the contents of Charlotte's purse. The biggest object was a video, an apparently new videocassette of *Fatal Attraction*.

"Look at this. She had a video in her purse. Did you print it?"

"Not yet. Don't see the need."

"Would you mind?" I asked.

"What for? You looking for more evidence against your client?"

"Yeah. For better or worse, I wanna know the deal. You mind?"

"We'll do it," said McSwayne, "just to nail your guy every which way."

I walked back to my office, two blocks away, trying to imagine how Damon could be innocent. I wasn't making much progress.

When I got out of the elevator at the PD's office, I found Kathy Dupont sitting in the waiting room. She was fuming.

"I had to wait all day for them to call my case, and you never even showed up. I thought you were my lawyer. Believe me, I have better things to do than sit around in a filthy courtroom with a bunch of court officers staring at my tits."

She was wearing a tight black turtleneck that left no doubt as to her topography.

"Finally, at ten to five, they call my case, and some smelly old lawyer I've never met stands up next to me and doesn't say a goddamn word. What kind of lawyer docsn't open his mouth?"

"Ms. Dupont. Calm down. Come into my office, and I'll explain what happened, okay?"

She stomped back into my office with me and flounced into one of the plastic chairs.

I looked at her patiently.

"Ms. Dupont," I began.

She cut me off.

"For Christ sake, call me Kathy, okay?"

Boy, she was cute. Maybe she was a stripper, but in my office, dressed in black, she was almost my type. Of course, the Lawyers' Code of Ethical Conduct forbids anything but strictly "professional" contact between us, at least while her case was still pending. The Disciplinary Committee came down hard on lawyers who got involved with their clients. I banished the thought from my mind.

"Okay, Kathy, here's how it works. I don't keep every case I pick up in arraignments. I only keep the serious ones, like a robbery, or a murder. Since your case isn't going anywhere, and will probably just be dismissed a few months from now, you don't need a lawyer with my experience."

"Don't I at least get a guy who shaves and washes?"

She had a point about Mathew Cleary. He was an embarrassment to the PD's office, an old guy who wore filthy suits, stained shirts, and thought about nothing but what he was going to have for lunch. He was kept around because he was willing to handle meaningless cases, to spend his workday, year in, year out, standing up in Part F next to a parade of clients on cases going nowhere, all of which were simply being adjourned to their dismissal dates. The Constitution requires a lawyer at every court appearance in a criminal case, but he might as well have been a potted plant.

"Look, I'm sorry. But it really doesn't matter who stands up next to you in court. If you're so upset, hire a private attorney. I'm sure you can afford it."

"I work hard for my money. You think I like taking off my clothes? I'm not spending a penny extra just because that asshole won't leave me alone."

She smiled. "Maybe I want *you* to be my private attorney."

"Kathy, you can't hire me. I'm only available for free."

"Boy, don't *we* ever have principles."

I laughed, walked her back out to the elevators, shook her hand, and told her to call me if she ever got into real trouble.

Back in my office, I sat back in my desk chair and took a breath. Damon's angry face popped into my head, yelling at me.

"You state-appointed lawyers all the same . . . State just assumes if it wasn't me, it was some other wild-ass young nigger, so what's the difference."

My computer monitor, on by default to the *New York Times*, already had a headline about the Walkman: "Defense Attorney Discovers Evidence Police Threw in Gutter." A nice break for us. Every prospective juror in New York City would know the cops screwed things up on Damon's case.

I clicked off the *New York Times* on the screen and picked up the old-fashioned paper version. There was a little feature on Charlotte King. Predictable details. Middle-class girl, grows up on Long Island. Father dead. Mother owns small store. Devoted. Devastated. Charlotte described as having "fashion model" looks, but also brains. Went to work for Yates Associates right out of Harvard Business School five years ago. Expert in "data retrieval and recovery," whatever that meant. A quote from Yates himself, saying "We are all devastated by this shocking crime."

CHAPTER 10

As the workday ended, I found myself at a hip-looking video store on Eleventh Avenue and Twenty-second Street, checking out Damon's story. Yes, he had worked there. I was speaking with John Taback, the manager, a pasty-faced man in his forties, a wannabe in the movie business, who had probably started out trying to write movies and had ended up running a store that rented them. He was too skinny, with a ponytail and an earring. He looked like he'd abused some choice substances, perhaps to console himself over his lifelong failures. Or perhaps the drugs had come first and caused the failure. You couldn't always tell where talent began or ended, or why.

"Damon has a mouth," he told me, "but he isn't a street kid. He's very bright. Very funny. He related to everybody, white, black, old, young, rich, poor. I liked him. He knew the inventory. He figured out how the computer worked pretty quickly. He was responsible. I can't believe he'd rob someone, or shoot them. Not in character. Goes against type, if you know what I mean. But nothing's predictable in this world."

I showed him the picture of Charlotte King in the morning paper.

"Recognize her? Know anything about her?"

"Me, no. But let's pass this around, and see if anyone else does."

He called over the four other younger employees, who between them had a pound of metal poking through various holes in their ears, noses, tongues, and eyebrows. To me, it didn't appeal, but who's to judge style.

"I remember her. She came in a couple days ago. I helped her out. She was hot-looking. Kind of a Sharon Stone type. Bought a video of *Fatal Attraction*. Looked like she could've starred in the sequel."

A girl named Debbie Ringle was speaking, the type for whom punk had been invented. Her hair was purple and looked like a rabid dog had just finished chewing on it. She was wearing cut-up black jeans, a white T-shirt, and huge boots. She looked terrifying. Her small pleasant voice was a surprise.

"Do you remember if Damon was working at the time?" I asked her.

"Sure he was. I think he was doing the register and getting the films. He said something like 'Be careful out there, sister' to this woman. She rolled her eyes. Not too pleasant."

"You've got a pretty good memory, Ms. Ringle," I said.

"This girl looked like a movie star. That's why I remember her."

"You could be a witness in this case. Would you mind?"

"I tell it like it is, lawyer. Damon's a cool dude. He's big, but he's a gentle guy. And real smart."

"Were you friends?"

"Only because we worked together. Nothing more. I don't date men, you know."

I turned to the manager. "How much does Damon make a week?"

"He takes home about one eighty per week, I believe. Technically he's not full-time. I think he makes nine bucks an hour, no benefits, no withholding, works twenty hours, so yeah, one eighty per week. He's paid on the books. I usually cash his paycheck for him. Want me to look it up?"

That night I tossed and turned. I dreamed that Damon came into the shop on Clinton Street to place a bet with Noah.

CHAPTER 11

IN THE OFFICE the next morning, I started looking through the photocopied contents of Charlotte King's purse and wallet. Some people prepare for death, even unexpected death. They make wills, they try to keep their financial affairs in order. These are people with an overdeveloped sense of responsibility, most often those with young children, or big piles of money. Single types just as often have no will, and their financial affairs are a mess, usually consisting of a bunch of credit card debt, and a car loan. They say you can't take it with you, but if you die in debt you sure can.

Few of us think about having the contents of our purses, wallets, or lives, for that matter, laid bare after we die unexpectedly. I felt a little like a Peeping Tom, going through Ms. King's personal effects. I didn't often get this kind of opportunity. Not every prosecutor gave me this stuff so early, and without a fight. McSwayne obviously didn't believe he had anything to hide. He had already concluded, without the slightest doubt, that this was a street crime and nothing more.

Charlotte King's wallet was part filing cabinet, part wastebasket, full of useless receipts, ATM records, business cards, and of course, the usual assortment of credit cards. I counted two Visas, a MasterCard, an American Express, a Bloomingdales, a Bergdorfs, and a Saks Fifth Avenue. Upscale taste. Her driver's license photo showed a very attractive woman, with a wide clean jawline, a delicate nose, deep-set eyes, and a high forehead. Even with the poor quality of the photo, her looks jumped out.

In addition to the credit cards and driver's license, there were three business cards in her wallet. Two were stockbrokers' cards, one from Smith Barney, and one from Schwab. In addition, there was one doctor's card, a Dr. Hans Stern, psychoanalyst, with an office on the Upper East Side. Very interesting. I took a look at the photocopy of her calendar, which she'd carried in her purse. Thumbing through the last month, I found very few entries, just occasional lunch and dinner dates, and written in small letters, "Dr. Stern," every Tuesday at 5:00 P.M. Her therapist. What did this guy know about Charlotte King? Whatever he knew, I was probably the last person on earth he'd discuss it with. I leafed through her address book. Under "M" I found Mom's phone number.

Layden poked his head in.

"Anything new, Arch?"

I looked up. "Tucker's screaming and yelling at me to check out Charlotte King, as if this was something other than a goddamn mugging gone bad."

Layden nodded, a little grimly. "You just gotta tell him, someone gets robbed and shot, doesn't mean you get to poke around in their lives, without some offer of proof, that's the law, and that's how most judges see it. So there's not much we can do."

"Kevin, why does it never occur to us that maybe, if you wanted to do a hit, the best way is to disguise it as a robbery gone bad, play to the racism, the expectation of this kind of thing, that we all live with? Damon's right. The one thing we never really do is investigate the victim in a case like this. We just assume that if it isn't this particular black kid, then it's another. It leaves kind of a big opening for real murder."

He looked irritated. "Focus on the possible, kid. You can win with the possible here. You don't have to resort to the improbable. Do you really think this was a hit, that someone wanted this woman dead? Why? Does that mean they framed your guy? Or was it just an accident that he got arrested? Come on, Gold. This is a winnable one-witness ID case, but it's not a TV show. Get real."

He left. His divorce wasn't adding to his general charm, that was clear.

The receptionist buzzed me.

"It's Tom Twersky, again, Mr. Gold. Should I tell him you're in court?"

I didn't like to lie to Tom. Besides, he might hang around outside and spot me heading out later. You never knew with Tom Twersky.

"Send him in."

Tom Twersky was a professional stickup man. He did one to three stickups a week depending on the yield. He wore a black mask and used a real unloaded gun, working all over the city. He'd been caught a number of times, of course, and he was well acquainted with the amenities upstate. In fact, he'd earned his BA at Plattsburgh State College while doing four to eight at Danemora, the first member of his family to get a college degree in the fifty years since his grandfather came over from Poland.

When you win a trial for a guilty man, you have a friend for life. I was high on the list of good things in Tom Twersky's world, since I had gone to trial with him on a one-witness ID case last year, a case in which the best he could plead to, given his record, was twenty to life. He'd get at least that after trial. We went for it and won. I saved the dude twenty years. Since then he came to see me every few weeks, usually to complain that he couldn't find a job, and to ask me if I knew of any legitimate work for him, since he didn't want to go back to his usual schemes.

Ironically, a trial win, while saving a guy time in the short run, can cost him big in the long run. I can remember more than one career criminal who decided, after pulling out a squeaker in front of a fluky jury, that his lawyer was a miracle worker and threw all caution to the wind, quickly getting busted again on a dead case, then insisting on taking it to trial, and doing several decades more time than if he'd just lost his first trial. Every silver lining has a cloud.

But Tom Twersky had stayed out of trouble since his win with me last year. I liked him. In his own twisted way, he was a man of principle. He'd never hurt anyone, much less shot anyone during a job. He placed great emphasis on the fact that his gun was never loaded during a stickup. It was purely a theatrical prop, used to gain compliance. It was, in fact, inherently risky to run around pointing an unloaded gun at people, since if the victim was armed, and pulled in self-defense, Tom could easily get shot. This meant that he had to be very careful in his selection of victims, almost always choosing obviously unarmed women.

"Mr. Gold, what you got for me? Nothing?"

I shook my head.

"Mr. Gold, I know you got connections. You know people. Find me some real work. I don't wanna stick people up no more. It's getting old."

"What kind of work are you thinking of, Tom?"

He did have his upstate BA. But finding skilled work

for an ex-con is tough in this city. If Tom wanted to do demolition work, or haul garbage at night, no one would care about his colorful past. But office work was a different matter. And Tom was a frail little guy. He was going gray at the fringes of his short brown hair. He had a beak for a nose and always had a cigarette dangling out of his mouth. He looked like a bird. He wasn't meant for physical labor.

"I got good people skills. I was thinking some kind of management position."

CHAPTER 12

"THANK YOU for agreeing to meet me," I said to Harriet King.

She looked about sixty-five years old. Her face was gray with grief, her expression lifeless. She was a small woman, with a prim self-contained look. Her hair was pulled back in a bun. She wore reading glasses. She sat, hands crossed in her lap, on the edge of an oversized white couch. We were in the living room of her brick two-bedroom ranch house in Saybrook, Long Island, a town about an hour's commute from Penn Station that went from being a quaint fishing village to a hideous suburban tract in less than a decade after World War II.

It was actually quite unusual. Almost unheard of. Why would a mother agree to meet with the attorney defending the alleged killer of her only daughter? All I knew was this: If Damon hadn't insisted that I "investigate" Charlotte King, I wouldn't have even made the call. Now here I was, having a face-to-face with Mom, who, surprisingly, had taken my call and then agreed to see me, without much discussion.

She leaned over and picked up a photo album from the coffee table.

"Have a look."

I leafed through the photos. Charlotte King, birth to early death thirty-one years later. From the beginning, she was stunning. Blond. Perfect girl-next-door features, trim but curvy build, which came through loud and clear in a couple of beach shots. You could melt looking at her. But this was more than the perfect girl-next-door look. There was also something knowing, something conspiratorial about her, as if she and the photographer were sharing a guilty secret.

Two things jumped out at me. First, no dad anywhere. Second, in not a single goddamn photo was she smiling. Not even a trace of a smile. Seductive—very—but not a happy person.

I closed the album after a few minutes.

"I'm very sorry, Ms. King. She was beautiful."

Harriet King shook her head.

"It's not just that she's gone. I can't stop thinking about how she died. Shot on the street by a mugger, bleeding to death, realizing she was dying there, for no reason. All alone except for some young cop holding her hand."

She shuddered.

This was hard. The woman's pain was like a wind in the room. I couldn't get out of its way.

"You don't have children, do you?"

It was an accusation, as though I were about to confess to a character flaw.

"Not yet."

"You have no idea, then, do you? Well, it doesn't matter."

She started to cry, prim little tears, tiny squeaks coming out of her, like a little animal with asthma.

"I'm so sorry, Ms. King."

"I wouldn't speak to the reporters, the TV people, no one. No publicity for me. So I spill my guts to you, I guess because you'll listen without filing a story somewhere. That's why I let you come out here. You're the first human being to call me since Charlotte was killed, other than a reporter of some kind."

She was still crying.

"I'm all alone. I was all alone when she was alive, and I'm still all alone. She bought me this couch last month. Nicest thing she ever bought me. But she didn't bother to come out here and see it. Just had it delivered. She was always distant. Called every Sunday. Dutifully checked in. But really, she checked out, as soon as she could, years ago."

This woman had wounds that ran deep, hurts and deprivations from way before her daughter's murder. Now the wounds would never heal. The hurt would be frozen in time. She would carry it with her to her grave.

I knew what she meant about Charlotte. Girls of a certain beauty develop a frozen pleasant gaze. They learn how to look through and past you. This is the only way they can avoid acknowledging the rapt attention of every single guy, in every conceivable setting, twenty-four, seven. It ends up too isolating for some, and they ice over for good, inside and out. I wondered if that had happened to Charlotte King.

"What about Charlotte's father, Ms. King?"

"Died when she was one year old. Heart attack."

"I'm sorry."

"Ah, what's it to you? To me, well. My life ended that day. I had no skills. No ambitions. No desires. Just to be a mom and a housewife and lead our little suburban existence. It never happened. With my husband's life insurance, I bought a candy shop. It made a little money. We survived. My daughter was always ashamed of it. It was across the street from her high school. She would pretend she didn't know me when she came in with her friends."

"You never remarried?"

"I'm too bitter for any man, Mr. Gold. I have a checklist a mile long. None of the men I ever encountered made the cut. Whose loss was that? I don't even think about it anymore."

This woman was so brutally honest with me, I saw no point in beating around the bush with her. I got right to the point.

"Ms. King, can you think of anyone who might have wanted to harm your daughter?"

"Didn't the black boy do it?"

I smiled. "Look, Ms. King, I'm defense counsel. It's my job to look for alternative theories, even in a case like this."

I find that if I characterize my work this way—just doing my duty, but not expecting results—people feel less threatened, and they talk. Ms. King looked relieved to discover that I was just going through the motions and didn't *really* think Damon was innocent. Now she could follow her inclination and speak to me honestly.

"Well, you know, she was sleeping with that Yates fellow."

"Really!"

This was starting to get interesting.

"How do you know that?"

"She told me. Said she was seeing the boss. Career move. Romance with her was always for a reason."

She sighed.

"I suppose I could have been, I don't know. More loving. More available. But I always felt she didn't like me, that she couldn't wait to leave me and my little life behind."

"Was she still seeing Yates, ah, right up to the end?"

"That's a nice way of putting it, isn't it? I don't know."

"Did she have any friends at work, beside Yates?"

"One woman she mentioned occasionally, I think her name was Renee. Renee Albertson, something like that."

She seemed to think for a moment.

"One thing I can tell you is, a few months ago, in the fall, I noticed she seemed to have more money."

She absentmindedly rubbed her hand on the new couch.

"Nicest thing she ever got me."

She appeared to be thinking. After a while she spoke. "When Charlotte died, you know, she was looking for art in some fancy gallery. That was new. She never used to do that."

"Do you think she got a big raise, or a bonus?"

"I don't know. She never mentioned it."

Was Charlotte King blackmailing Yates? Did he have some reason to kill her? Well, at least I had the beginning of a hint of a theory. Mostly it was just my vivid imagination. Charlotte King, the sexy ice queen, blackmailing Yates about their affair. Was he married? I didn't recall any mention of a family in any of the articles I'd read. If he wasn't, where was the problem? Did Charlotte know something else, something about Yates Associates, something that would be a problem for Yates?

Harriet King stood up, signaling that it was time for me to leave. She walked me to my car. She looked up into my face.

"My daughter never had a lot of friends. She always

had a man—at least one. A few months before she died, she told me she'd met someone she really cared for, not Yates."

"Do you know who that guy was?" I asked, as lightly as I could.

"No. She never told me a thing about him. That was her way. I was glad, though. I thought maybe she was growing up, learning to love somebody. People do change, you know."

On the way back to the my office, I put in a call to Dr. Stern, Charlotte's therapist. You never know, he might pick up, if he was between patients or eating lunch.

He picked up. I identified myself and asked if he would mind speaking to me about Charlotte King.

"You represent the accused boy?" he demanded, in a German accent that sounded like grinding machinery.

"That's correct."

"You are not the government in this case?"

"No. I'm the guy going up against the government."

"Zat is okay wit me."

His German accent suddenly signified victim, not oppressor. I guessed the doctor was a German Jew, who didn't trust any government or any prosecutor working for it.

He sighed. "Look, I can't talk to you about her. That's all there is to it. I'm sorry."

He hung up. He sounded like a parody of Sigmund Freud, but he probably knew everything there was to know about Charlotte King.

It was only noon. Plenty of time to pay a call on Yates Associates.

CHAPTER 13

"SHE DIDN'T EXACTLY OPEN up to people. Certainly not guys. She was so beautiful, she never felt comfortable around guys, cuz they were all trying to go to bed with her, or already in love with her from a distance and acting weird, whatever. But she talked to me."

Renee Albertson's eyes misted up as she said this last sentence. She swiped at a tear and looked right at me. We were sitting in her sleek office at Yates Associates, on the forty-third floor of a Midtown high-rise that cost more per square foot than I spent in a week on food.

"I shouldn't be talking to you at all."

"I really appreciate it."

Knowing what I now knew about Yates, that was no lie. The guy was a big-time player in the corporate world. I'd checked him out online back in my office before meeting with Ms. Albertson. In the early 1960s he'd opened a new kind of PI firm, relying on a phone line, a modem, and a computer before most Americans knew what they were. As his reputation and his roster of corporate clients grew, he took on more and more investigative staff, now called "managing directors," who'd had long careers in law enforcement at all levels. He had ex-cops, ex-prosecutors, ex–IRS agents, ex–FBI agents, ex–corporate executives. All of these guys kept up their connections and were rumored to have access to a huge array of confidential data banks. His outfit took in over a hundred million bucks a year. A new kind of PI firm. Computerized. Corporate. Respectable.

"Why are you here? Isn't it obvious that black kid shot her?"

"Not if you know all the details."

"What could you possibly be talking about?"

I didn't respond.

"What's your job here?" I asked.

"Same as hers. Encryption. Recovery. That's how we got close."

I tried to imagine getting close through encryption and recovery.

"She was shot in a mugging. Why are you messing around in her life? Her life's over."

"Because maybe it wasn't a mugging."

"And who wanted her dead?"

"Well, let's see. I guess you knew she was sleeping with Yates. She broke it off just before she died, didn't she?"

"That doesn't usually lead to murder."

"Maybe she knew something."

Renee gave me a long hard look.

"Listen to me, don't mess with this place. Let it be. Believe me. You don't want to fuck with Yates. Not if you don't have to. This kid Tucker looks guilty. Do what you gotta do, as defense counsel must, but don't start with Yates."

She lowered her voice. She looked nervous as she went on.

"You know, word is he's taking this outfit public. He's going to make millions for himself. He sure doesn't want anyone stirring up trouble."

There was a knock on the door. Two big men in suits came in and stood over me. One of them spoke, quite pleasantly.

"Mr. Gold, sir, would you mind coming with us? Mr. Yates heard you were here in his offices, and he'd like to see you. Right this way."

They motioned as if there were no alternative, and I decided there wasn't. I shuffled along.

"Ms. Albertson, take care of yourself."

She was laughing, and shaking her head. I wasn't sure I got the joke.

I followed the goon squad boys in suits down a couple of nicely carpeted hallways, with recessed lighting and framed shit on the walls, until we got to an antechamber, leading to the big man's mammoth corner office. A power office. The guy's phone looked like the controls for the space shuttle. He had four different monitors staring at him, as well as a three TV consoles against the wall. There were photos of him with a lot of movers and shakers, next to the obligatory primitive art that showed you that this executive had multiculture.

Yates was sitting behind his desk, which faced the door. He was a very handsome man, with a finely wrought face, even features, thin lips, a square but lean face, with an almost unnaturally deep tan. Gray hair beautifully cut. Impeccably tailored suit. Woven gold necktie. Gold cuff links. I took it all in with a glance.

"Sit down, Mr. Gold. I'm amazed you have the balls to come into my offices, without speaking to me about it first. But since you're here, we might as well talk."

"Come on, Yates. I wasn't here to see you. Does every one of your employees clear every visitor with you personally? I doubt it. Ms. Albertson was gracious enough to meet with me, even though she didn't tell me a goddamn thing, once I got in her office. But you were monitoring it, so you don't need me to tell you that."

"Nice tongue, Gold. I like that. Guess you're a good lawyer. Why you poking around here? Do you have any idea who the fuck you're dealing with?"

"The way you strong-armed me in here, I'm not so sure."

He got up and walked over to the window, which looked out over Midtown.

"See that big city out there? I got it wired. I got data coming in from every goddamn direction. I got a file on everybody. I got more information at my fingertips than any private citizen on this planet. I can track you, asshole, from my desk, with a level of detail that would knock your socks off."

He stopped, turned, and looked at me, speaking in even tones.

"Ease off. I'm sure Charlotte King was mugged by this black kid Tucker. How else the prints? So why you poking around here?"

"Just to get a feel for her life, her background. Since I'm sure the DA will try to bring it out as much as he can."

He wandered back to his desk.

"What's the defense, Gold? Another black kid, the real mugger, who got away?"

"Bingo. You must've gone to law school."

"Only long enough to figure out I'd rather *not* play by the rules."

"I guess that includes sleeping with the help, huh?"

"You *are* a wiseass. That must be why you work at a job where your clients can't fire you. Hold this kid's hand. Damon Whatsisname. Do your defense lawyer thing in court. But don't poke around my outfit, okay? Now get the fuck outa here."

I left without saying a word. The guy was scary, and I didn't feel like continuing this verbal pissing match. Right now, words were all I had in my arsenal. He obviously had a whole lot more. The guy looked like a banker, and his offices looked like an investment bank, but he talked like a gangster. All of a sudden, I wasn't sure playing by the rules was going to be enough for Damon. Playing by the rules might just get him life without parole at the age of eighteen.

Walking back to the office, his words echoed in my head. "Hold this kid's hand." Was that all I was, as a public defender? The system's hand holder, the guy who gave the appearance of effective assistance for all those defendants streaming through the system day in and day out, year in and year out, on their way upstate for a decade or two?

"Fuck it," I said out loud. I needed to find out what Charlotte King knew about Yates.

The five o'clock support staff exodus had just occurred. The street was full of secretaries and clerks going home. No one heard me.

CHAPTER 14

AROUND SIX, six-thirty, every evening, a migration of young white men in suits begins. They appear from subway entrances on the Upper East Side of Manhattan and walk several blocks past elegant shops to their high-rise luxury condominiums, where they stride through plush lobbies, manned by uniformed attendants, and then into elevators, which whisk them up into their cookie-cutter units.

I slid through the lobby of the Dorsley, on East Seventy-fourth Street, with a faint nod to the doorman, who was dressed in a waistcoat, top hat, and white gloves, and who nodded back politely, with apparent recognition. I looked the part of a young executive, even if I couldn't play it for real. I headed knowingly for the elevators.

I was alone in the elevator, which zoomed up to the twenty-second floor, Charlotte King's floor, in less than a minute. The adrenaline from my forced visit with Yates was still pumping through me. The guy thought he owned the world.

I'd stopped back in my office to pick up one small item before coming over to her apartment, to see what I could find. I felt the thin plastic shank in my pants pocket. About six inches long, the width of a ruler, it was perfectly designed to open most doors that were not actually bolted—the sort of doors with locks that luxury high-rises provided as basic issue, and which many tenants didn't bother adding to, given the appearance of such tight security in the lobby below. Some professional burglar years earlier had passed me the thing through the bars behind arraignments just as he was being taken out to see the judge. He was afraid he'd be found with it on the Rock and would pick up a new charge—possession of burglars' tools, which this thing surely was. I'd shoved it in my desk drawer and forgotten about it, until now.

I stepped out into a long hallway stretching off to my right and left, lined with indistinguishable doors to indistinguishable apartments. From the sign by the elevators, I learned that number 22E, Charlotte King's apartment, was somewhere down the hall to my left.

I FOUND HER DOOR and felt my heartbeat pick up a beat. It didn't have a double lock. The hallway was empty. I put on a pair of latex surgical gloves, slid my shank right around the door where the spring-loaded lock sat, and popped it back easily. I stepped in quietly and closed the door behind me. Burglary in progress.

The place was white everywhere, white walls, white

couches, white table, white bookcases. The few bits of color—books, pillows, rugs—splashed up out of the white and got your attention. It was nicely done. By a decorator, no doubt. No clutter. No accumulation of personal crap all over the place that many of us experience in our homes. Come to think of it, no photos at all, not a one.

I looked around for something revealing—some file cabinet, or pile of papers, or checkbook, or records. Nothing at all. Then it hit me, as I went into the bedroom, which continued the white theme. Charlotte King kept every detail of her life on her computer, just like me. We were the same generation, and that was how we managed things. No paper trail. Just a hard drive that was a window into our lives. Her computer was in the corner of the bedroom. I turned it on.

I was glad I'd remembered to buy the gloves at a hardware store on the way to her place. Arch Gold was never here. I'd do everything I could to help Damon, but getting arrested for trespass or burglary didn't advance the cause.

The computer seemed to work. But when I looked for files, something personal, some sign of use, I got nothing. I went into the root directory of the hard drive and checked out the install date, which records automatically in Windows computers. December 4, at 5:48 P.M. Less than one hour after she'd been killed someone had come in here and taken out her old hard drive, with a life's worth of data on it, and replaced it with this brand-new empty one. I checked out the CPU. Four screws, and the cover slid off. If you knew what you were doing, you could extract a hard drive and replace it with another in a matter of minutes. No need to leave with the whole computer, which would require a pass in a building like this.

I looked over the rest of the apartment, wondering who

might want the information on Charlotte King's hard drive, now that she was dead and buried. What was the big secret? Was she killed because she knew something? If she was the type to work for Yates, she was probably the sort whose hard drive was full of stuff. Who was so hot to get it within an hour after her murder? How could this possibly be a coincidence? If it wasn't, could someone, other than the killer, have found out she died, and immediately felt the need to take the hard drive out of her computer? It didn't seem likely. It all pointed to one thing—Damon had to be innocent. I felt a seismic shift in my gut. I'm not used to the pressure of defending innocent clients.

I left quickly. I closed the door quietly, wondering what the hell I could do with this little fact I'd just illegally uncovered.

"Oh, hi! You must be the boyfriend. I'm so sorry."

I feigned a deep sigh.

"Neighbor?" I asked in my saddest voice, casually plunging my hands into my coat pockets. Regrettably, I still had on the latex surgical gloves.

"Yes. I didn't know her at all. You don't tend to know your neighbors in these buildings, do you? Not like where I'm from."

I didn't ask where that might be. I dared to look at her for the first time. I guessed she was in fashion, a buyer for one of the big department stores. Nice-looking, overdressed, not a deep thinker.

"Take care."

I shuffled off down the hall, hands still in my pockets, hoping she hadn't been watching the news enough lately to recognize me. Fleeting fame had its drawbacks.

I'd soon see who else might happen to recognize me. That morning I'd made an appointment for Ted Silver, depressed, and in need of an initial consultation with Dr. Hans Stern.

CHAPTER 15

I WAS SITTING in the good doctor's waiting room. I was Ted Silver, possible patient, depressed and anxious, referred by Dr. Whatsisname, in for a consultation. Two hundred bucks' worth of consultation. Two hundred bucks to tell a guy why you thought you needed to pay him two hundred bucks an hour to listen to your problems several hours a week. You either have to be very miserable, or very rich, or both, to get into this kind of therapy. I wondered which had applied to Charlotte King.

The door to his office opened, and Dr. Stern came out. He was about seventy, slight, lean face, sharp angles behind a carefully trimmed gray beard. He had an expensive suit and a delicate manner. Whoever had been in with him appeared to have left from another exit in his inner office. Very old-fashioned. Total confidentiality. No possibility of encountering another patient. It all dated back to when therapy was a real stigma.

"Come in, Mr. . . . ah . . . Silver. Nice to meet you. Make yourself comfortable over there." He gestured expansively toward an upholstered swivel chair, a modern thing, but perfectly comfortable, and one of two a few feet apart in the center of the room, a nice setting for therapy, therapist and patient equally seated, equally comfortable, equally able to swivel away with a small gesture.

"I'll be right back," he said. He went out into the hall, I assumed to the bathroom.

I sat down in the comfortable swivel chair and spun around. Now I was facing the doctor's lovely antique desk, cluttered with articles, receipts, envelopes—the paper my generation relied on less and less. Peeking out of the pile was a black IBM floppy disk, with a Post-it attached that said, "Ask me for password. CK."

She'd been dead four days, and old Dr. Stern still wasn't sure what to do with this disk. Maybe he didn't have a computer. Maybe he didn't know who to ask for help. Maybe he just didn't want to think about it at all. But whatever the reason, there it was, sitting on his desk.

To my utter amazement, with a quick motion, Ted Silver put the disk in his suit pocket and swiveled around just as Dr. Stern was coming back in.

"Looking around?"

"Yes, just curiosity."

"I understand."

The good doctor did indeed appear to understand. He was a professional understander. I felt a pang of jealously for those with the time and the money to see Dr. Stern, who sat down in the unoccupied swivel chair, spinning himself so that he was facing his prospective new patient directly.

"What brings you here?" he asked gently.

"I'm not Ted Silver, I'm Arch Gold."

His face lost all color. He swallowed hard. I saw fear, but it didn't seem to weaken his resolve.

"We spoke on the phone, didn't we? When you came in, I thought you looked familiar. I've seen you on the news. Did you really think seeing me face-to-face would make a difference? I believe what I believe. I'm not going to discuss her with you."

He paused and looked at me anxiously.

"It is my sworn oath as a doctor not to reveal my patients'

confidences. I cannot violate that oath. No matter how much I want to, no matter how compelling the reason."

I started to open my mouth. He put up his hand again.

"Look, I can give you my opinion on something, without violating any confidences."

"What's that?"

"I doubt that young black boy killed Charlotte King. Much as I would like to, I can't tell you more than that."

"Doctor, I really appreciate your seeing me, and giving me your opinion, but you have to tell me more. I don't think my client did it either. But our opinions don't count for much. We need evidence."

"I've wrestled with this a great deal. I can't tell you more. But you should fight for that young man. Fight hard."

"Doctor, an innocent man may go to jail for life because you won't come forward. You seem like a very moral man. How can you live with that?"

I was almost shouting.

"My first duty is to my patients. Nothing can change that view."

"Are you afraid for your safety, if you come forward with information? Is that it?"

Maybe this guy was just too terrified of Yates to go out on a limb for his dead patient.

"Mr. Gold, I lived through the Nazis. I'm an old man. I'm not afraid of anything. My next patient is coming in. I must ask you to leave. And Mr. Gold?"

He looked intently at me, to make sure he had my attention.

"Please be careful. You may be in danger, if you push too much."

CHAPTER 16

NEXT MORNING, I took the disk straight to my friend Goodman, who was just getting ready for bed, at 9:00 A.M., when the rest of us are starting the day. He was a thick little man—with a big nose, shaved head, and rimless glasses that magnified his eyes. He was born with talent, all kinds of talent. He was a bass player, a really sensitive jazz bass, which he played from a high stool, bent way over. He was also a hacker, online and off, one of those guys who could always fix whatever computer problems you had, could load unloadable software, get kinks out of any system, download, upload, offload, backup, even open the thing up and move shit around. He just seemed to be born knowing how to make a computer hum, and how to play the bass. Probably connected skills. He was uninterested in hauling himself out of bed before noon, so conventional work was impossible. He made a living playing in a variety of jazz acts and consulting on computer systems in the late afternoons, and early evenings, when he didn't have enough gigs to pay his few bills.

"It's not like you, stealing evidence. I'm surprised, counselor."

Goodman grinned at me, but there was a serious undertone as he exhaled the smoke of his umpteenth cigarette of the day.

"By any means necessary when your guy's innocent, and looking at life."

Goodman put in the disk. There was only one file in its

directory, a file called "Yates."

He tried to open it up, but a box popped up, demanding a password.

"Shit. It *is* locked."

"Fuck it," I said. "How do we get in?"

I was still trying to digest the fact that I'd gotten into Dr. Stern's offices under false pretenses and then stolen evidence like some kind of CIA agent working for Nixon. Now, on top of all that, I wasn't going to get to see what I'd actually stolen. Things didn't work out, even when you didn't play by the rules.

Goodman was shaking his head. "It could be any six numbers or letters. Millions of possibilities. There's a program that will try every possibility. But it could take months to hit."

"There's no other way?"

"Sorry, counselor. Secure really does mean pretty secure."

"Let's get started right away, then. Download that shit right now."

"Yes, sir, right away. And who's paying my fee?"

"You're doing this one for Damon. To prevent an innocent man from being convicted of a murder he didn't commit. Mere money couldn't compare."

"Yeah, mere money just buys mere food and pays mere rent."

CHAPTER 17

Sitting in the counsel visit room on Rikers, waiting for Damon to be brought out, I puzzled over how to explain to anyone exactly how and why I knew that Charlotte's hard drive had been taken out of her computer forty-five minutes after her murder, or that I had a disk, which I believed was hers, which I couldn't open, because it had a password I didn't know. For the first time in my career, I'd crossed the line into guerrilla warfare. Whatever happened to Damon's case, it would be a miracle if I didn't get disciplined by the State Bar Committee somewhere down the road, maybe even disbarred. Right now, I couldn't care less.

Damon came in. My heart was pounding, because this wasn't just helping another guilty guy navigate through the system. That's what I did on most of my cases. I did it well, and I'd gotten a few guilty guys off, but this was different. This was life without parole for an eighteen-year-old kid, for a crime he did not commit. By incredibly bad luck, he'd been in the wrong place at the wrong time. He was the victim of several amazing coincidences.

"There've been some interesting developments, Damon. Let me tell you about them."

He was listening, restraining his anger, trying to give me a chance.

"There's a couple of things I want to cover. First, I think I know why your fingerprints were on the money. You're paid by check?"

"Yes."

"At arraignments, you told me you'd just cashed your paycheck at the video store, right?"

"Every Friday. Boss cashes it for me."

"And after he gives you the money, you count it out, right?"

"Yeah."

"So your prints get on every bill."

"Yeah," he said, more like a question than an answer.

"Now, on Friday, December 4, I believe a woman came into your store who bought a copy of *Fatal Attraction.* You handled the purchase. You scanned the video that she handed you, and then you took three ten-dollar bills from her and gave her change. That woman was Charlotte King."

Damon was looking at me like he'd just seen a ghost. I hoped it was the ghost of Charlotte King. I went on.

"Later that day, you cashed your check with Taback, the boss. He gave you eighteen ten-dollar bills, including the three that Charlotte King gave you when she bought *Fatal Attraction.* That's how your prints and Charlotte's prints got on the same money."

"Unfuckingbelievable."

I sat back while he digested it. After a while he started to smile.

"You're good, Gold, you're good. Matter of fact, you're more than good, you're right. I *do* remember this woman. So *that* was Charlotte King! My fucking God. Isn't that unbelievable? Chick comes in the store, I take care of her purchase, and now they say I killed her."

"Now, everything I've just told you, we can back up, with receipts, with data in the computer at the video store, and with testimony from Taback, and Ms. Ringle, your coworker there. And I bet we'll find out that your prints are on the video in her purse."

Damon nodded. I continued.

"So that explains away the prosecution's physical evidence."

"And the ID. What we gonna do about that?"

"Don't worry, kid. That ID was shit. We both know it. I'll take care of those cops. That's my specialty."

He looked just slightly impressed.

"I'm looking forward to that."

"Now, there's a lot of other stuff I've discovered. About forty-five minutes after Charlotte King was shot, someone went into her apartment and replaced her hard drive on her computer, took all her data. That's got to be the person who killed her. It just makes sense."

"Holy shit. How'd you find that out?"

"No comment. You know what else I found out? She'd been sleeping with her boss, David Yates. The guy runs the biggest PI firm in the world, a man with a lot of access and power. The kind of guy who could easily get into her place and take the insides of her computer if he thought she had information dangerous to him, or his business. The kind of guy who would know how to hire a hit man. Plus, a month or so before she was killed, according to her mom, she was seeing a new guy. So he had lots of reasons to kill her."

Damon took this in. After a few moments, he spoke.

"So it was just an accident that I got arrested. Some kind of coincidence. This guy Yates didn't go out and frame me, did he?"

"No. I don't think he expected an arrest. Maybe he hired a big black kid like you, and Charlotte King's description was accurate. I don't know. But no one set out to frame you. You just got very unlucky. And now we have to get you out of it."

Damon looked up. Finally, he felt I might be on his side. He sounded weary.

"How we gonna do that, Mr. Gold?"

"Our problem right now is that we don't have enough proof. Our alternative theory, that Yates did it, is too speculative. A judge, with what we have, won't let us get it in front of a jury."

Damon looked incredulous. "What are you talking about, man? How can they prevent us? This is evidence.

It shows I'm innocent."

"I know that. But what do we really have? We have that someone tampered with her computer. And that she'd been sleeping with the boss. That's all we have. Nothing more. That's not enough. You gotta take my word on that."

"I don't fucking believe it. I thought I was presumed innocent. How can they stop me from presenting evidence that someone else did it?"

"They can if it's too speculative. That's the law. We need a sufficient offer of proof."

Damon looked at me like I was crazy. To a layperson, it did seem like a harsh rule. But there it was. The Court of Appeals, in *People v. Primo*, a few years back, had laid it all out. In a criminal trial, when you're going ID, you can't just make some wild claim that someone else in particular did it. You need something more than vaguely circumstantial evidence.

Damon was angry again, and I couldn't blame him. I tried to calm him down.

"Look, we're proceeding on two tracks. The stuff we can use, which explains away the prosecutor's case, and the stuff we can't use, which explains who else did it. But if we find more of that stuff, maybe we can use it."

"But for now, we just gonna say it wasn't me and explain away their evidence?"

"That ain't bad, Damon. That should be an acquittal."

He went ballisitic. You couldn't predict what would set this kid off.

"The hell with this legal bullshit! Why can't we just take our story to the *Daily News*?"

"For about three reasons. One, because it will tip Yates off and make it harder to dig anything else up, and right now we don't have enough. Two, it'll tip the prosecutor off and give 'em months to prepare a rebuttal case. Yates'll cooperate with them, I'm sure. Three, as criminal defense counsel, I have to adhere to the Local Rules of New York Court, which prohibit me from talking about the case in a way that might affect potential jurors. And that's no joke. Gotti's lawyer, Bruce Cutler, almost went to jail for talking to the press. They held him in contempt, suspended his license for a year, and put him under house arrest for six months."

"Yikes, don't scare me. Let's see, life without parole, or six months' house arrest. Whose problems should I worry about, yours or mine?"

"That's not the way to analyze it, Damon, and you know it. I've already risked my whole goddamn career for you, and I'll do it again if I can help you. The point is, a press conference won't do you any good at this point."

He didn't say anything. At least he wasn't cursing at me. I assume that meant I finally had some credibility with him. Still, his temper made him a wild card. If he blew up in the courtroom, we'd be in big trouble. Jurors do not believe, ever, that a defendant's anger is evidence of innocence. Jurors want defendants to sit quietly and act respectfully. They want to acquit *nice* guys, not scary assholes. They want to *lock up* scary assholes. Damon was going to have to control himself, however justified his anger.

I decided this wasn't the time for a lecture. For the first time we actually shook hands as we parted.

CHAPTER 18

DRIVING BACK TO THE CITY, I was thinking about Yates's operation and what Charlotte King could have known about it after going to bed with the boss. The radio was playing.

"Give us twenty-two minutes, we'll give you the world."

Right now, the radio was trying to tell me that a Dr. Hans Stern had been murdered on the Upper East Side. Someone had broken into the doctor's town house, which served as both home and office. The doctor was divorced and lived alone. Police believed it was a burglary. The place was trashed. The doctor had been shot and killed. His body was discovered by a patient, name withheld. Naturally. People don't tell their closest friends that they're in therapy. Certainly the police were not giving out a lot of details yet. Par for the course early in a case when no arrest had been made.

I almost drove off the road.

Gentle, delicate Dr. Stern was killed, because of something he knew that Charlotte King had told him in therapy. Or maybe he was killed because of whatever Charlotte put on that disk. Maybe someone had gone to Dr. Stern's office to get that disk and had killed Dr. Stern when he wouldn't cough it up. Trouble is, he couldn't. It was gone. I had just stolen it and, at the same time perhaps, sentenced Dr. Stern to death.

Back in the office, I got right on the phone to McSwayne. I wanted to see if he'd made the connection between Charlotte King and Dr. Stern, or cared.

McSwayne laughed off any connection.

"Gold. Listen. This is a nasty city, and shit happens, as you well know from the work you do. Sometimes shit happens to *people* who are connected. It doesn't mean the *shit* is connected. I'll get you the police reports on it, just to make you happy."

Could the Stern killing not be connected? It was

possible, but if so, it was one hell of a coincidence. If Charlotte King knew something that Yates wanted buried, and he knew she was in therapy, he couldn't just kill her, he had to kill her shrink, too.

A good theory. A good and paranoid theory, with not a shred of evidence yet to back it up, except the fact that he was sleeping with her, and her hard drive was stolen after she died. All circumstantial, and entirely speculative.

McSwayne called me back.

"Gold. My friend."

He always started this way when he was giving me some news that hurt my case. Just to remind me that it was nothing personal.

"I spoke to the detective on the Stern killing. Looks like a burglary. Electronics and computers missing, as well as jewelry, cash, etc. Apparently security in this guy's town house sucked. He basically left the door open, so his patients could get in and out. A trusting soul. One of those Austrian Freudian types who survived the Nazis as a kid and figured this country was safe. He was right about the country, but not this city. Kind of too bad. A guy survives Hitler and gets killed on the Upper East Side in his town house. It's a crazy world, Gold. Oh, and by the way, Damon's prints were on that video, a new copy of *Fatal Attraction*. Unopened. His prints were on the plastic shrink-wrapping. Thumb and four digits. Like he'd handled it. Maybe he thought about keeping it."

"Really," I said. "McSwayne, how do you explain my client's prints on the money, and the video, but not on the gun, wallet, or purse? If he was wearing gloves, there shouldn't be any prints at all, on anything. If he wasn't, then how come no prints on the gun, or on the wallet or purse, just these particular items inside?"

I wanted to know if McSwayne was hip to my theory

explaining Damon's and Charlotte's prints. I doubted it. When cops think they've solved a case, they stop. Dead in their tracks. That's how it works in the NYPD. Too many unsolved cases to keep working the ones you've solved. This case was no exception.

"How the fuck would I know, Gold? Maybe your guy wiped some things off and forgot others. Half the guys I send away can barely remember to wipe their asses."

I had a strong urge to tell McSwayne about the hard drive, and the disk I'd taken from the dead doctor's office. Was I obstructing justice by holding on to the disk, instead of turning it over? It might nail Yates not for one, but now for two murders, if the DA's office could quickly crack the disk. I got on the phone to Goodman. He told me there really was no faster way to do it, that the DA's office wouldn't do things any differently than him, that not even Microsoft could crack the thing any other way. I felt better. I told myself I wasn't slowing anything down. Plus, I wanted to keep that disk just because I didn't know where this all was going to come out. I liked having something Yates wanted.

I walked down to Layden's office, unsure how much I wanted to tell him. The lights were low. He appeared to be sitting at his desk, leaning back, doing nothing. At best he was thinking deeply. More likely he was snoozing, or groveling in his own depression.

"You won't believe the shit I've found out, Kevin."

"What?"

He stirred himself and turned toward me.

"Charlotte King was sleeping around. With Yates, and also with persons unknown. That's what her mom told me."

"Interesting."

He was paying attention now. That was a good sign.

"When was this happening?"

"She wasn't sure. Probably right up until Charlotte King was killed. Maybe he killed her."

"Now, Arch. Don't let your imagination run away on you. Sleeping around doesn't usually lead to murder. I'll admit, it's certainly a nice piece of information. I don't know if you'll ever be able to use it, though, without something more."

"Okay, Mr. Cynical Know It All, try this one on for size. Dr. Hans Stern, Charlotte King's psychotherapist, was killed yesterday. Isn't that an amazing coincidence?"

"No shit! What does McSwayne say?"

"He says, this is a nasty city, and shit happens. Sometimes shit happens to *people* who are connected. It doesn't mean the *shit* is connected."

Layden laughed. "Those Irish prosecutors sure do have a way with words. I'm afraid he's right. Arch, I sound like a broken record, but this is a one-witness ID case. You can check Charlotte King out all you want, that's not going to change."

I decided not to tell him the rest. I didn't want him figuring out I'd broken into Charlotte King's apartment or stolen a disk from the recently murdered Dr. Stern. I felt lonely, now that I'd crossed that invisible line that separates the lawyers who follow the rules from the ones who decide it's just a free-for-all. I suddenly felt a new kinship with all those clients of mine who lived in that shadowy place somewhere outside the regular world of rules and regulations.

CHAPTER 19

THE CRIMINAL JUSTICE SYSTEM in Gotham is a game of roulette. The truth does matter, but often less than who is prosecuting, or who is the defense attorney, or what was the quality of the police work. The weather can trump all. After every big snowstorm, several hundred prisoners must be released, even those accused of violent crimes. This is because every case must be indicted within 144 hours of arrest, exactly six days. Naturally, everything is so backed up that most cases aren't presented until the last day. If the heavens drop a foot of snow, and no cops or victims make it in to 100 Centre Street, then that day a whole lot of fellas are walking out of jail, RORed, released on their own recognizance, for crimes petty and grand, from shoplifting to murder. Their cases aren't over, but they're free.

Weather aside, no single factor is bigger than the judge. There are approximately twenty-five felony trial judges in Manhattan. The path by which you end up in front of any one of them for trial is random. The differences between them are vast, at every step of the way, from the amount of bail they're likely to set, to the kind of offers they demand from the prosecutor, to their interpretation of probable cause, their views on police credibility, and finally, of course, the amount of time they give out at sentencing, if you blow trial. So which of the many "Your Honors" you end up in front of matters.

Right now, I was in the chambers of Judge Bernice

Stoddard. Damon's case was on her calendar today for a probable cause hearing. It was three days before Christmas. The DA's office was moving the case quickly, a departure from their usual tactics. The trial date would still be a couple months from now.

Judge Stoddard was a black woman, early forties, very smart, very friendly, who had overcome all the odds. She was a pleasant-looking woman, with fine features and a big frame. She looked like a musical star of the 1940s, ready to burst into song, instead of sentence your client to state time. She grew up in the projects uptown and fought her way out, step by step, scholarship by scholarship, through college, law school, and the DA's office, where she'd put in her obligatory ten years of service, and then, to no one's surprise, had been appointed a judge by the mayor.

She defied all the stereotypes. She handed down very tough sentences, but unlike most judges with such leanings, she wasn't looking to rig the game procedurally. Everybody was treated with respect, including defense counsel and defendants. You got a fair trial from her, but if you went down, when all the dust settled, she would whack your client, often with the max.

And she was publicly in favor of the death penalty. I had watched her over the years and handled dozens of cases in front of her, including several jury trials. I personally don't believe that in her heart, she wants it. I think she has made a political decision, a calculation. The decision fits her personality, because it is her nature to go against type, to feel boxed in by an unspoken rule that black judges and prosecutors be uniformly unwilling to impose the death penalty, no matter the crime or evidence.

Her solicitous manner was often a total disaster to the newcomer attorney in her courtroom, who might fail to comprehend the absolute steel within her or might mistakenly think that her personal attention, her demands to see pictures of the kids, her schmoozing up at the bench, or in chambers off the record was anything but part of a very serious larger plan, that being the conviction of the defendant.

She was out to show the world that just because she was a black judge didn't mean she couldn't be tough on her own people, and just because she was a woman judge didn't mean she couldn't be a heavy hitter on the sentencing charts. What she couldn't influence directly on the record, she would try to control off the record. She made prosecutors go over their entire case with her in her chambers, in the presence of defense counsel, of course. Although the more intelligent prosecutors resented having to lay things out at so early a stage, the process was tremendously helpful to the less able ones, to whom she pointed out flaws in their thinking or, even more insidiously, demanded to know defense counsel's view, so as to smoke out any argument she might not have thought of herself, all in the guise of trying to avoid any surprises in front of the jury.

Right now, McSwayne, the judge, and I were together around a conference table in the robing room behind her courtroom. Damon was still in the pens one flight down. They hadn't brought him up yet.

"Gold, what is a talented lawyer like you still doing at the PD's office? You should be running the place by now."

"That's way too political for me, Judge. I'm a trial attorney; I don't want to manage a budget and have to fire people because I piss off one of the mayor's underlings."

She smiled.

"All right, counsel, what we have here today is a pretrial

hearing. With a few rather untypical wrinkles, starting with the death of the identifying witness." She paused for a moment.

"By the way, Gold, tell your client, when you go back to see him, that he's lucky I'm not the DA in this county, or he'd be getting ready to fry. Maybe that'll give him a clue about how I feel about this case."

She turned to McSwayne.

"Let me start by asking Mr. McSwayne here how he intends to get all this hearsay identification testimony from these cops into evidence at the trial, assuming I find probable cause, and no constitutional defect in the show-up."

"Dying declaration, Judge," crowed McSwayne, right on cue.

"I was hoping you'd say that," said the judge, smiling delightedly. "I assume you know the ins and outs of the law in that regard."

"I believe I do."

"Your officers are prepared to make the appropriate record?"

"I certainly hope so."

"I assume you are calling the two officers who were with the victim, rather than the two who made the arrest, since they have the closest thing to the victim's perspective in a case like this."

She was thorough. She was making sure the prosecutor was going to call only the officers absolutely necessary to win the hearing, and no more. The judge understood the value of not mucking up the trial record with officers' prior statements. She knew, as well as any regular observer of any New York courtroom, that no two cops could ever tell the same story the same, and the fewer versions out there, the better for the prosecutor in just about every case.

Here, she had the awkward additional fact that one of the arresting cops had thrown the defendant's Walkman into the gutter. His credibility was certainly something she would prefer not to put into play. If the judge had any sway over things, he'd be kept entirely out of this hearing.

"So, looks like we're all set. This is a very serious case, involving a shocking crime, but this hearing still shouldn't take very long, should it, gentlemen?"

"No, Judge," I said, "so I'm sure you won't object if I spend a few minutes before we begin, meeting with my client. I'd like him brought up to the counsel visit room."

"Must we, Gold? That takes so long. Just speak to him in the courtroom when he gets here."

"Judge, I can't discuss trial strategy in open court, much as you'd like me to."

The judge rolled her eyes. "All right. See you in court in fifteen minutes. Don't keep me waiting, Mr. Gold."

THE COUNSEL VISIT ROOM on the twelfth floor of 100 Centre Street didn't allow for "contact" visits. The room used to be one big open space, with lots of desks and chairs, space for a dozen lawyers to meet with their clients. The first time I saw it, in my early days as a public defender, I'd been shocked at how relaxed the whole setup was. It seemed like a recipe for a riot—fifteen inmates and their lawyers, with no barriers, no guards, nothing but the long-held assumption that lawyers don't need protection from their clients. Then one day several years ago a distraught defendant, dying of AIDS and with nothing to lose, had pulled out a makeshift knife, made from a sharpened piece off a soda can imbedded in a melted-down toothbrush, and held it to the throat of his public defender, a fresh young woman just out of law school. "I want time served," he said. All he got was a lungful of mace and a new felony charge. She left New York and went back to whatever midwestern town had coughed her up into the big city, and the counsel visit room got a makeover. Now I was talking to Damon through a heavy steel grating.

Today, Damon was calm. I sensed his rage was still there, like a powerful current, just below the surface.

"What's happening today?"

"Today, we're doing a pretrial hearing, a suppression hearing."

"What's that?"

"Well, as you know, the cops can't just arrest anybody when they feel like it. They need what's called probable cause. If they arrested you without probable cause, the judge would throw out any physical evidence that the cops found as a result of the illegal arrest. In this case that would be the money they found in your pocket. So today, the People call the cops in a hearing, to testify as to what happened when you got arrested. I get to cross-examine them."

"And then we lose, right?"

"Right and wrong. We go into this knowing that we're not going to win the hearing, because I am sure they'll be prepped to say the magic words to make out probable cause. But we do get to nail them all down, under oath, to a version of events, and that's a big edge at trial. This judge isn't tossing any evidence. But she can't help the record we create here today, and I'm sure we'll get some good stuff."

"I sure hope you know what you're doing, man. I'm sitting here innocent, looking at life without parole, and you're talking 'bout losing the hearing, but that's okay. What the fuck. Don't sugarcoat it. Just tell me I'm going down. Tell me we can't win cuz it's a stacked deck. Style points don't mean shit here."

He shook his head grimly. An officer knocked on the door.

"He's going to court. Judge's orders."

"Before we go, Damon, just remember one thing. This judge is very friendly. You'll like her. But don't get into conversation with her. It's all being taken down, and only one person gets fucked out there if you open your mouth. That's you. Don't say anything."

We snaked our way through the pens out into the huge courtroom, empty save for the three daily papers' reporters, and Damon's mom, who was sitting quietly in the second row.

One of the court officers standing near a rear door behind the judge's elevated "bench" suddenly burst into a medieval courtier's cry: "All rise. All rise. Hear Ye. Hear Ye. All who have business here pay heed, the Honorable Bernice Stoddard now presiding. Please be seated, remove all hats, take all food and conversation outside."

Judge Stoddard swooped in from a rear door, her heels echoing on the hard floor, her black robe swinging behind her.

"Good morning, all."

She flashed a big smile, until her gaze fell on Damon, and her look turned serious.

"Would counsel please approach?"

McSwayne and I dutifully trudged up and huddled with her up at the bench.

"Now, I'm sure there's no possibility of a disposition in this case, but I would like Mr. McSwayne to place on the record the offer the People have made and the fact that the defendant has rejected it."

McSwayne spoke:

"Your Honor is well aware that the 120-day statutory period during which my office may elect to seek either the death penalty or life without parole has not yet run. We are therefore not in a position to make any offer to Mr. Tucker. Just between you and me, I doubt Leventhal's going to decide all of a sudden to seek the death penalty on this case. So Mr. Gold's client is looking at life without parole. I assume he's not going to plead guilty to that."

I shrugged. I truly had nothing to say.

"All right, step back."

An hour later the hearing was over. Stoddard found probable cause, and the case was now moving to trial. The only reason a trial date could not be set was that the DA's office had yet to announce its intentions with respect to the death penalty.

As I left I stopped for a moment to speak to Mrs. Tucker. She sighed.

"With God's help, Mr. Gold, you'll get my son out of this mess."

God's help. I thought of an old joke my father used to tell, about a poor Jewish man on the Lower East Side who found a vacant lot full of broken glass and litter. The man spent many hours cleaning it up, plowing the ground, and planting a beautiful flower garden. When it was in full bloom, the rabbi came up and said to the hardworking man: "See what you can do with God's help!" The man laughed. "God didn't do so good 'til he had me as a partner."

CHAPTER 20

NANCY LEVENTHAL was on the bottom. The DA, in all his wooden splendor, eighty-one years old, and still able, once every few weeks, to enjoy Nancy's slippery pleasures, was on top. She'd met him ten years ago, several years after his first wife had died. She was thirty-nine years his junior and several years younger than his grown children. People had talked, but she didn't regret a thing. At seventy-one, when they'd met, he'd been a vital force; now he was a bit feeble, but she still loved him, still remained awed by him. And she'd gotten to have Alice, their beautiful little girl. With the Leventhal wealth, she and her daughter were set for life. When he went, she'd truly mourn, but her life would also begin again. She could handle it.

Just now, he was breathing hard and getting close to his quiet climax. He was a bit old-fashioned. He was tall, over 6' 3", so when he lay on her, her face was pressed against his chest. There was no eye contact, and no view of each other's bodies. The purest of pure missionary positions. It mattered not. He always appeared to enjoy himself.

This time, when he came he sounded strange, and he lay very still afterward. Afterward, for about thirty seconds, until she screamed and rolled him off of her. He was already dead of a massive coronary.

The call came into the governor as he was finishing his morning workout at the executive mansion. He'd gotten elected on a death penalty platform, beating a liberal Democrat who had made it a moral crusade to veto any death penalty bill that the Republican legislature could throw at him. No one had yet been executed in the state, but several cases were working their way through the endless appeals process. The governor felt sure the law would stand up. It was model stuff in every way, taking into account every recent Supreme Court death penalty decision. The larger problem was getting the county prosecutors to use it. Out in Texas, the governor got a lot of credit for all those executions, but that was really only because he had the local folks willing to carry it out. Here, in New York, the governor had intervened once, with the black DA in the Bronx, but he had sworn he would never do that to Leventhal and now he wouldn't have to. He had the exquisite power of temporary appointment when a county DA died in office, and he already knew just the person to replace Leventhal.

CHAPTER 21

JUDGE STODDARD, now DA Stoddard, was a celebrity the moment she strode up to the microphones, looked into the cameras, and announced that she would be seeking the death penalty for Damon Tucker.

The public expected craggy old white men in dark suits to announce that they would try to use the power of their office to execute A or B. Such announcements maintained an almost bureaucratic aspect, despite the violent subject. But the sight of a beautiful black woman, an ex-judge to boot, with a larger-than-life face, who seemed to radiate human understanding and a desire for real justice, the sight of her staring straight into the mikes and talking about state-authorized killing was something new for everyone. It only got better when she announced she'd be trying the case herself.

I was sitting in Layden's office. He was standing looking out the window, nine stories down to where DA Stoddard was holding her first press conference, right in front of the main entrance to 100 Centre Street, a potent visual location that DA Leventhal had never thought appropriate to use for press conferences. Layden was angry. I was so shocked I just sat there, mute, listening, trying to absorb the fact that everything had changed for Damon, and for me. How quickly random events can change the basic landscape of our lives. Now, all of a sudden, I was in new territory, starting to feel the overwhelming pressure I'd never known before, the weight on the mind and spirit of defending a man in a capital case.

Far away, I heard Layden ranting.

"Why couldn't Leventhal wait another couple months to infarct? Who gets executed in this county is supposed to depend on when one old man's heart finally gives out?"

It was Christmas Eve, or to be precise, the day of Christmas Eve. Most lawyers in the city were heading home early. The holiday spirit didn't seem to deter Stoddard in the slightest.

I was on the couch near the TV. I had two images of Stoddard to choose between—I could see her up close on the television, or out the window. I had a bird's-eye view of the press huddled around her in front of 100 Centre Street, that huge old hunk of courtrooms, jails, and dirty halls where I'd spent most of my professional life. It had all been a dress rehearsal, a dry run, in preparation for the real deal—this fight for Damon's life.

Kevin turned and looked hard at me.

"I assume you wanna stay on the case. Am I right?"

"Fuck, yes."

"I'm gonna transfer all your other files. You'll work on this full-time." There was a pause.

"Gold, I know you're a good trial lawyer, maybe the best in the office, juries love you, and all that shit, but you don't know a damn thing about death penalty litigation. You're about to start learning. You may remember we're in a turf battle with the State Capital Defender's Office. To round up Democratic votes for his death penalty bill, the governor agreed to major league spending on capital counsel. That office up there has some first-rate lawyers, who are up on all this stuff. You're going to have one of 'em as co-counsel. Name's Rob Stephens. A whiz. Clerked for Justice John Paul Stephens. Doesn't have to open his mouth in front of the jury, but you better listen to everything he's got to say about the law. This whole thing could come down to an appeal, and you don't have a clue how to preserve the death penalty issues. That's where this guy comes in. Capeesh?"

"Kevin, you're a WASP. Stop talking like you're in the Mafia."

"So, you're not too upset to give me shit. That's a good sign."

I could only imagine the geeky law review type that I'd be saddled with, some hyper-intellectual fellow who probably stuttered and had never spoken to a jury in his life. My co-counsel was one of the chosen, one of the law's priesthood, who finish at the top of their classes at the two or three best law schools in the country, edit their *Law Reviews*, and go on to clerk for one of the nine United States Supreme Court Justices. At the age of twenty-seven or so, Stephens was drafting Supreme Court opinions. That kind of pedigree intimidated some lawyers. It didn't mean much to me.

One of the things I liked most about my job as a public defender was that I worked alone. I was a solitary warrior on every case, with no one second-guessing me. Most of the time, no one was even watching. Now I'd have to explain every move I made to some guy I'd never met before who'd been way too serious at law school.

As Stoddard's press conference ended, Layden packed up his briefcase.

"You're awfully quiet, counselor," he said to me.

I couldn't speak. Layden let out a big sigh.

"Death penalty or not, it's Christmas Eve, and I'm heading home."

He looked at me sadly.

"Not *really* home, Arch. Can you believe I'm not seeing my kids on Christmas? How did my life get this fucked up? Would somebody please explain it to me?"

"I'm sorry. At least you're not facing execution for something you didn't do."

"That's true. But wait 'til *you* have kids. Then maybe you'll understand that not seeing them, being told you can't watch them grow up, being shut out—it's kind of like dying."

You can't miss what you never had. I took his word for it. I had other things to worry about.

CHAPTER 22

I SAT HOME ALONE on Christmas, trying to figure out my next move for Damon. I was still in shock, still dealing with the feeling of dread working its way through me.

I made myself a vodka tonic, my drink of choice, Ketel One, over a large glass of ice, a twist of lime, and a splash of tonic water. My father drank vodka, as did his father. It's a Slavic character trait, probably embedded in some chromosome they have yet to identify. I was talking to myself, asking why Charlotte King had to come into that particular video store, wondering why fate was frowning so cruelly on Damon Tucker, wondering what Charlotte really knew about the Yates operation, wondering how to make any sense out of it all, when the phone rang.

I screened it and listened to the message. It was Stephens, the death penalty genius from the Capital Defender's Office. Layden and I had both assumed Stephens was a guy, but I was now listening to a message in a clear woman's voice.

"I know you're there, Gold, you fucking monk. Layden gave me your number, and guaranteed me you'd be home alone, and probably drunk by now. Pick up. Come on. It's time to go out."

I picked up. I didn't mind the sound of this Rob Stephens at all.

"Hello," I said, somewhat mournfully.

"Gold. Look, I'm done here at my aunt's house. They're cleaning up and won't let me help. The only thing worse than doing the dishes is watching your aunt and uncle do the dishes. Let's have a drink. You can start filling me in."

An hour later, we were in a bar downtown. She was a very petite woman. She probably didn't get to triple digits on the scale. She had short brown hair cut close around her head, a long nose, and high cheekbones. She was no conventional beauty, but I liked the way she looked. I guessed she was in her midforties, a few years older than me.

"Must be a big brain on top of that little frame of yours. My boss filled me in on your resume," I said.

"Do we have to start by talking physical characteristics? I can't imagine how you could have any real intelligence. Very few men with your looks do, in my experience."

"Why, thanks, I like a backhanded compliment."

We both sipped our drinks.

"Your first death penalty case?" she asked, with just enough condescension to annoy me.

"Oh, yeah."

"It changes you," she said, cryptically.

I didn't ask how.

"Griffin wouldn't go quietly, you know. Did you follow that one?" she was saying.

She was focused, this woman, that was clear.

"Missed it."

"The last execution in Texas. The guy wouldn't go. He wouldn't walk to his death. He fought the guards who came into his cell to take him to the death chamber. He hurt a couple of guys. He fought when they tried to tie him to the gurney. Only the lethal injection stopped him."

"It has a calming effect," I observed.

"They ended up beating him pretty good. But they couldn't go too far. They needed him conscious. Unconstitutional to execute an unconscious man."

She took a sip of her whiskey.

"Did you know it's unconstitutional to execute a psychotic person? Violates due process. But it's okay to forcibly give them antipsychotic medication so they're legally competent and then execute them."

She flashed a drunken smile. She'd already downed a decent-sized Wild Turkey. I like smart women who drink. I was debating whether or not to tell her everything I knew. For the moment I decided against it. I didn't want a lecture on the Canon of Ethics. She might not be the type to give me that lecture, but I wasn't sure yet.

"By the way, Gold, since you asked, I've never tried a case in my life. Never questioned a witness, never opened my mouth in court. But I know the law behind this stuff backward and forward. Better than anyone in the country."

"Congratulations. I'm thinking acquittal. That's how I get juiced up. I'm going for the win. I kinda get the feeling you're thinking appeal from the get-go."

"I assume you're opposed to the death penalty?" she said, ignoring my little jab.

"Yeah, just reflexively," I replied.

"On what grounds?"

"What are my options?"

"Well, let's see. Some people are morally opposed, out of some kind of religious conviction. They just feel it's immoral to take another life. The pope, for example. Others think it can never be fairly applied. That too much depends on capricious factors, like the politics of the prosecutor, or the quality of defense counsel, or the judge, or the jurors, or the jurisdiction, or the race of the defendant or the victim. Others think state-authorized killing can never be okay, not for moral reasons, but for reasons of political philosophy. They believe the state should not be in the business of revenge. Others are just too afraid of mistakes—of the inevitability of executing an innocent man from time to time."

She paused, sucking on an ice cube.

"Did I leave anything out?"

"I think you nailed it."

She ordered another drink.

"Okay, Gold, tell me what you know about this case."

I didn't. I described the People's evidence. I told her about my theory that Charlotte King had come into the store, and my explanation for all those damning fingerprints. I didn't tell her about my breaking into Charlotte's apartment or about my stealing the disk. I left Yates and Dr. Stern out altogether.

"That all sounds pretty good. More than good. Great.

We've got a real shot at an acquittal here."

"You sound awfully surprised."

"The issue isn't usually guilt in these cases. It's usually a question of begging for mercy from a jury that doesn't want to hear from us."

She looked at me with her bright eyes.

"What a terrible coincidence for that poor kid. Wonder if he did it, too. Would that make it more, or less, of a coincidence?"

"I think he's innocent."

She nodded. I wasn't sure what it meant.

"What kind of witness will he be?"

"He's very volatile. He's a wild card."

"A lot of 'em are."

"He's not one of 'them.' He's a little out of control because he's innocent, not because he's a killer. There's a difference."

"I don't give a damn whether he did it or not, believe me," she said with more intensity than I expected.

"How'd you get into this line of work?" I asked, sensing some deep currents behind all this. Most lawyers with her kind of high-speed processor became law professors or made zillions analyzing the tax code for Exxon. Instead, she was out there in the trenches doing unbelievably stressful work, for the lawyers' equivalent of the minimum wage.

"My father was executed when I was twelve years old."

"Wow," I said, shaking my head. "That's a conversation stopper. How did that come to pass?"

"My dad was kind of a gangster. He owned a Ford dealership in Miami. He didn't like the Cuban guy across the street who started a Honda dealership. He hired a hit man and had him killed. They caught the hit man, he flipped, and my father went down. He was guilty as sin." She paused for a moment, and her voice got a little thicker.

"But still, they shouldn't have killed him."

"He was your daddy."

She nodded. It was still a wound for her. She still had a big hole inside of her, because they took her daddy when she was a girl. Now I understood. This was a personal mission for her. They shouldn't take *anyone's* daddy, not for any reason.

I didn't feel the same way right now. Sure, as an abstract proposition I'm deeply and passionately against the death penalty. That's why I give a hundred bucks of my meager salary to the ACLU every year. Right now, though, I was specifically against executing Damon Tucker, not because I was against the death penalty in general, but because he was innocent. I didn't have time to worry about the other couple thousand men and women already on death row.

"We should go visit your client tomorrow," she said. "He's probably not feeling too good right about now."

Maybe she had a heart, to go with those brains.

"You single?" I found myself asking her.

"Where's that coming from?"

I grinned. "Just idle curiosity."

"It's none of your goddamn business, but the answer is yes. I run around the country too much, a few weeks here, a few weeks there. Kinda hard to have a real relationship. You?"

"Single."

She didn't look happy. "Let's keep this strictly professional, counselor. There's no easy come easy go for me, okay? I'm not into casual encounters."

She was an all-or-nothing type. Maybe that's what death penalty work does to you.

CHAPTER 23

THE NEXT MORNING, both of us slightly hungover, Stephens and I were sitting in a waiting room at the Men's House of Detention on Rikers Island. Stephens had been suitably impressed by the vast operation as she saw it unfold below her on the drive out over the bridge. We were quiet. Neither of us relished the prospect of speaking to Damon, who undoubtedly knew by now of the arbitrary hand fate had dealt him. What a Christmas present—to learn that a prosecutor has singled you out for execution.

"How many folks have been executed since '76?" I asked Stephens. That was the year the Supreme Court reinstated the death penalty.

"Oh, somewhere around 650."

I shook my head. "It's just a goddamn lottery. Nothing more. It's random revenge."

"I don't see how you could look at it any other way. But not to the right. They say the only reason we even get to make that argument is that we just don't allow enough executions. That once the numbers climb up a bit it won't seem like lotto."

"Wonderful."

"Oh, and by the way, between 2 and 3 percent of executions in this century are of innocent defendants. So since 1976, probably a dozen or so innocent people have been killed."

A guard was bringing Damon down the hall. I wasn't looking forward to this visit. I turned to Stephens.

"Let me spend a minute with him alone, first. Do you mind?"

She looked surprised, but she didn't object. I could tell she was trying to figure out why, and I wasn't going to tell her.

Damon was yelling as he walked toward us.

"All right! Now that they're trying to kill me, they're giving me two lawyers. Just to make sure it's fair."

I left Stephens in the waiting room and sat down with Damon in one of the drab counsel visit rooms.

"How'd you find out? Your mom call you, or did you see it on TV?"

"I watched it live, dude. How many motherfuckers get to see their own upcoming execution announced live on TV?"

He was putting on a brave face, but he looked crazed.

"I'm so sorry they're trying to do this to you, Damon. I won't stop fighting for you. I promise. They'll execute you over my dead body."

I think he saw that I meant it. He looked at me sadly.

"Thank you, man. I know you're trying."

We sat for a while. He broke the silence.

"It's hard staying strong. Sometimes I wish I could just go to sleep and not wake up. Least nobody would be trying to execute me. Trouble is, I'm scared of my dreams. There's always a jury in my dreams, a bunch of white folks laughing and joking, like they're at a party."

I felt my eyes getting wet. I fought it. I didn't want him to see his lawyer crying.

"Damon, let me tell you something. When I was your age, my parents were killed one day, in a car crash, just a few blocks from here, up on Canal Street. It's true, no one was trying to kill *me*, but I wanted to die. Just like you. I wanted to go to sleep and not wake up. But I kept fighting.

I was all alone, but I pulled myself through it. I came out the other side."

He looked at me. He saw my wet eyes. He listened.

"You'll come out the other side of this. You will. Someday soon we'll be celebrating your freedom."

"Thanks, man," he said. "Anything new on my case, besides the fact that they want to kill me now?"

"I haven't dug up anything new since last time."

"Who's that who was sitting with you out there?" he asked, gesturing toward the waiting room.

"That's one smart cookie, Damon, believe me. I'll introduce you now. She's an expert on death penalty cases. But listen. I haven't told her about Yates, about the hard drive, about Dr. Stern, any of it. I'm not sure how she'll react, and I want to wait 'til I have more, okay?"

He didn't look too happy. On the other hand, he didn't go nuts either. A good sign.

"For now, I guess so. But we gotta try to talk about this shit at the trial, no?"

"We'll try, Damon. Right now, any judge would slap us down. We need more. We need an offer of proof."

He let out a big sigh. I went to get Stephens.

"Damon, let me introduce you to Robin Stephens. She's from the State Capital Defender's Office. She specializes in all the legal issues that are now going to come up."

Damon looked over at Stephens and nodded.

"Nice to meet you, Damon," Stephens said gently. "Arch here is still the trial lawyer, but I'm going to help out with some legal issues. I've worked on a lot of capital cases all over the country."

"Anybody fried?" Damon asked. He had a way of getting right to the heart of the matter.

"Yeah, but let's not talk about that now. Let's talk about your case. Sounds like you have a really good defense."

"Glad you think so. Wanna be on my jury?"

Stephens laughed. Damon didn't.

"What an amazing coincidence that Charlotte King came into the store," she said.

"And put me on death row. Ain't life a bitch."

She didn't respond. Instead, she pulled some papers out of her briefcase. I gathered that she was of the "distract 'em with busy behavior/show 'em how much you know" school of client relations. It worked sometimes. Damon was a tough audience. He looked up, though.

"What's that?"

"That's Section 125.27 of the Penal Code, covering murder in the first degree. And this," Stephens pulled out some more papers, "this is Section 400.27 of the Criminal Procedure Rules, which describes the procedure for imposing a death sentence."

"Great. A little cozy bedtime reading. You got copies for me, or that stuff too complicated for dumb-ass niggers in jail?"

"You're a smart kid, Damon, I can tell from the way you're already busting my balls."

Damon looked a little confused that this intense little woman, who weighed about as much as his left leg, was talking about having her balls busted.

Stephens handed him the papers.

"Let's talk about this stuff for a minute. In New York State, certain crimes qualify for the death penalty. Serial killing, torture, murder for hire, terrorism, and the most common by far, murder during the commission of a violent felony, like robbery, or burglary, or rape. They call it murder in the first degree, rather than old-fashioned murder in the second degree, but the proof at trial is just the same. If you're convicted, that's when the death penalty procedures kick in. Basically, the same jury that heard all the evidence and rendered a guilty verdict now does a sentencing hearing, during which we would present mitigating evidence, as to why you don't deserve the death penalty, but life without parole instead."

Damon suddenly raised his hands and stood up so quickly he knocked over his chair.

"Forget it, man. We ain't talking 'bout this shit. It's bad luck. We ain't talking 'bout me begging for my life for something I didn't do. I don't wanna hear about it."

I decided to jump in.

"Damon, I agree. Sit down. Fuck that mitigation hearing, no disrespect to Stephens here. Let's talk about how we're going to win this trial."

"I'm down."

We stayed for three hours, going over every detail of the trial, and even beginning to prep Damon for direct and cross. If he could keep his rage at bay, and just play the part of the victim of a false accusation, he'd do fine on the stand. He might be an excellent witness. But I was still worried he'd blow up on cross-examination. OJ sliced and diced two people, but he was meek and mild in the courtroom, and it paid off.

After three hours, the guard knocked on the door and gave us the two-minute warning.

"Counts at 4:30, counselors. You know that. Wrap it up. This inmate has to go back to his cell."

Damon was calm now.

"Listen, I'm sorry I got crazy on you guys. I know I have to control myself in the courtroom. Sometimes I just can't help it. I explode."

We nodded.

"When you get caught in this system, it's hard not to think your lawyers are just going through the motions for you, like they do for every other fucking guilty defendant."

He paused to look at both of us, with big sad eyes. His voice got quieter.

"I don't think that anymore," he said.

They took him away.

On the way back into Manhattan, driving on the Brooklyn-Queens Expressway, looking across the East River, we could see a huge storm gathering over Midtown. A gray cloud was gradually engulfing the dozens of skyscrapers. The city was disappearing right before our eyes.

"Have you ever witnessed an execution?" I asked Stephens. The question had been on my mind since I met her. I hoped she hadn't seen her father killed. This was the most indirect way I could think to ask the question.

"Yes, just one. Last year. Lethal injection. Texas."

"What was it like?"

There was silence for a moment, and then she answered the question.

"I'm sure you expect me to say how disgusting, gruesome, painful, and wrenching it was. Truth is, it wasn't. But that just made it worse. It was as easy as turning off a light."

CHAPTER 24

WHEN WE GOT BACK to the office, Kathy Dupont was waiting for me in reception. This time, she didn't look so good. Her hair was a mess, her eyes were red, and her makeup was streaked all over her cheeks.

"Didn't you get my messages? They told me they'd page you."

"No, I didn't."

Stephens looked at me, then at Kathy. "Client?" she asked, with one eyebrow raised.

I nodded.

"Ms. Dupont, this is Robin Stephens."

Kathy looked her over. I answered Kathy's unspoken question.

"Ms. Stephens is a colleague. Working with me on that death penalty case."

"Can we talk?" Kathy said impatiently. Stephens went back to her office. I ushered Kathy into mine.

"It's the asshole, again."

"Mr. Johnson?"

"Yup. I mean, he's got an order of protection saying *I* can't go near *him*, when *he's* the one who's bothering *me*."

She did have a point. Usually the woman gets a TOP, a "temporary order of protection," against the man. It's mighty rare to see the situation reversed, and it usually means some judge has screwed things up. I felt for Kathy. No doubt, this guy *was* stalking her, but since she'd punctured his ass with a pen knife, he was the so-called victim. She was in a tough position, legally speaking.

"Kathy, what you're dealing with right now is really a civil matter, not a criminal case. You need to hire a lawyer to get you an order of protection against Johnson. We can't do it in criminal court, since he's not charged with a crime."

"You're kidding me."

I wasn't kidding. I gave her the name of a private lawyer whom I hoped would handle it honestly, without charging her a fortune. I also gave her my cell phone number, telling her now she couldn't complain about not being able to reach me. She liked that.

Two minutes after she left, Stephens popped into my office.

"She your type? Her left tit is bigger than me."

I laughed. "Stripper. Cut up a boyfriend who wouldn't leave her alone. She's okay, really."

Stephens eyes were wide. "I'd say she's more than okay. I'd say she's got a thing for you."

"What of it?" I demanded.

"Neither here nor there," she said coolly. "Let's get to work. Know anything about jury selection in a capital case?"

"Not much," I had to admit.

"Death qualified," said Stephens. "They get to pick a death-qualified jury. Basically, any prospective jurors who have doubts about their ability to impose the death penalty in any case are prohibited from serving."

It sounded a whole lot different from the jury selection in a typical murder two case, the kind I was used to. The fact is, exactly who ends up on your jury is critical, more important than the details of the case, the quality of counsel, or the attitude of the judge. All trial lawyers know this, but it doesn't mean they can do anything about it when they pick the jury. The way juries work remains deeply mysterious. As in many of life's mysterious processes, the obvious applies, and the rest is just gut instinct or guess.

Unfortunately, in the past few years most exemptions from jury duty had been eliminated, so even lawyers and judges had to serve. Bad news for defense attorneys, believe me. Last year, Layden got called, showed up willing to serve, and almost got on a jury. We all got a kick out of that. Problem was, for every Layden added to the pool, there were hundreds of bankers, lawyers, and doctors looking to clean up the city with our clients, and not terribly worried about "reasonable doubt." Now they'd get to serve as "death-qualified" jurors.

"What other wonderful death-related legal issues can we expect to crop up?"

"Probably not too many. Unfortunately for Damon, New York's death penalty is pretty much a model statute, designed to address every conceivable constitutional problem."

"Doesn't sound like we got much, Ms. Appellate Genius."

"All right, then, counselor, don't bitch and moan. Go out there and come up with some evidence favorable to our client. Right now, *they've* got a defendant who fits the general description on the central dispatch tape, who is positively identified by the lady as she lies dying, and who is found in possession of money with the victim's fingerprints. What have *we* got?"

I decided to tell her what I knew. I filled her in on Yates, his relationship with Charlotte, breaking into Charlotte's apartment and finding the replaced hard drive, Dr. Stern's murder, everything but the stolen disk. I didn't think she could handle that. Plus, it didn't prove a thing, yet.

She was more impressed by my stupidity than by the so-called evidence I'd uncovered.

"You know, Gold, if you don't play by the rules, you just fuck yourself *and* your client. Now, you've gone and done things that could get you disbarred, but you haven't come up with much, really, that we could use at trial. No judge is going to let that bullshit in. Meanwhile, you've committed two crimes and compromised yourself terribly. Not too smart."

"We'll see," I said, trying to hide my anger. "For now, just keep it all to yourself, and try to restrain your urge to turn me in to the Disciplinary Committee, do you mind?"

She left. The intercom went on.

"It's that old fellow Rose to see you, Mr. Gold."

I waited for Hyman Rose. My life was more pressured but much less complicated now that Layden had relieved me of all my cases other than Damon's. But since I had never officially been assigned Hyman, he couldn't be taken away.

The man did not look well. He'd lost weight since I'd last seen him, almost three weeks ago, three days after Damon's arrest. The skin of his face was a pasty white now and stretched thin over his bones. His white hair was a tangled mess. Each breath was labored. He eased into a beat-up office chair and focused his gaze on me. His eyes were still sharp.

He pursed his lips. A solitary tear rolled down the taut skin of his cheek. He was a tough man trying to keep it together.

"Got the big C. They tell me it's gonna be fast. Less than a year. I told my doc don't sugarcoat it for me. I need to know the real deal."

"I'm so sorry, Mr. Rose."

"Aren't we all." He paused. His voice got a little gentler.

"My wife's gone. I watched it take her five years ago. Fought like hell with the doctors. They didn't seem to mind that she was dying in pain."

I nodded sympathetically.

"My son, he's having a hard time right now. His mother gone. Me sick. The DA's office. He's shittin' a brick right now. I'd like to leave him some dough. How we doin' on my case?"

"Truthfully, sir, it's moving rather slowly. Right now, the prosecutor is telling me that if you'll come in and tell them what you know about the whole operation, he'll think about unfreezing your IRAS. So we need to sit and talk about just what you do and don't know, and just what you are and aren't willing to say. Who is the guy with the book? Someone you're willing to talk to the government about to save yourself a hundred grand? That's the bottom line."

"Sonny, I ain't never talking to those fucks. Ever. Got it? I didn't come in here for you to hold my hand while I ratted out guys I've known my whole life. If they wanna fuck me, they're gonna have to hold me down. I ain't givin' 'em a thing."

I sighed. This old guy was as unbending as any street kid I'd ever represented.

"That's fine. Those are decisions you have to make. If we fight it, we may lose. It's a game of chicken. Maybe they'll settle for some of the dough down the road. But it may be too far down the road for you."

"All right, all right, sonny. That's fine. File the papers. Make the motions. Let's make 'em work a little. Even if I'm dead you can fight it, right?"

"Mr. Rose, right now I'm working on that death penalty case. It's really the only thing I'm supposed to be doing. I'm making an exception for you."

"Thanks, kid. Do what you can."

He got up to leave. As he walked out he turned to me.

"Fight like hell for that black boy."

A memory came flooding back to me, of my father talking about the Supreme Court's decision in 1972 outlawing the death penalty, for what would turn out to be just a four-year hiatus.

CHAPTER 25

I WAS TWELVE years old at the time. We were sitting at the kitchen table, eating breakfast. My father was reading the paper and talking about the day's news with my mother, a ritual they shared every day of their lives.

"The government doesn't belong in the killing business." he said. "No just society kills its citizens. Lock them up. Throw away the key. Fine. But don't take a life."

Once again, I found myself thinking about the day *his* life ended, almost twenty years ago.

I spoke with my father a few hours before he and my mother died, their little Honda Civic crushed like a piece of tinfoil when it was hit head-on by a long-distance trucker who'd fallen asleep at the wheel on Canal Street. The cruelest things in this world can happen just because someone's a little tired. At a young age, I came to appreciate the random nature of our lives.

We were in my father's "office," the little room at the back of his store, from which he ran his second, illegal, and more profitable business. It was Thanksgiving 1978. I was home from college for the first time, my eyes opened wider now to the world out there beyond the Lower East Side of Manhattan. I was at Yale, with the sons of bankers and lawyers, scions of families that never bet on anything but the regular arrival of their dividends and coupons, families that didn't know what a "perfecta box" was, and never would.

My father sensed my turmoil. He was a big jovial man,

with a round face, a loud voice, and a sensitive nature. He had the spiritual presence of a rabbi, but he had been denied any formal education by his father, David Gold, who had started selling electrical cable from a pushcart, while also running a small book, shortly after arriving from Lithuania, one step ahead of the pogroms in 1938. After several years the book was big enough to bankroll the purchase of the electrical supply business that became the front for the bookie operation. When my grandfather died, my father took over the businesses, both of which grew, and my father became something of a figure in our community, a moral man running an illegal operation with strict rules of its own.

His greatest desire in life was that his only child be "legit," part of the educated intelligentsia, the keys to which his own father had lacked the vision or desire to provide for him. This meant private school for me, even if it was just the local yeshiva, and the best college Arch could get into. Well, Arch turned out to be one hell of a student. I didn't really care about grades. I was not really an intellectual. I loved baseball as much as I loved Shakespeare. But I wrote well, thought clearly, and spoke with authority at a young age, a trait I've always assumed I inherited from Noah. I'm not sure which, my lefty swing or my grades, got me into Yale, but there I was, one step closer to the "legit" world my father had never been allowed to join.

"How they treating you up there in New Haven, Arch?"

My father was so shocked that I had actually managed to get into Yale that he still had trouble uttering the word.

"Okay, Dad. Really okay. A lot of these kids are like nothing I've ever seen before, I'll tell you that much."

"You're the first one in the family, that's never easy. But

repeating your parents' life is harder. Believe me."

He sighed, then he smiled.

"You playing baseball up there?"

I nodded. Baseball was the best thing I had going in the land of Skull and Bones. I didn't have a sports car, and I didn't wear topsiders or LaCoste shirts, but I could hit the hell out of a baseball, and the coach liked that. I wasn't exactly killing myself studying either. In fact, I was barely going to any classes. I didn't see the point. I'd rather read than listen to some pompous professor who was never going to grade my papers anyway, that task being left to some underpaid graduate assistant.

"Studying a little?"

"Now and then."

My father nodded. We were avoiding the real issues, the way only parents and children can, trying to connect emotionally around the stuff that doesn't touch a nerve. That day, though, I really wanted to talk.

"Dad, have you ever had to hurt anyone, being a bookie?"

My father gave me a long look. We'd talked once or twice about the "other" business, but we'd certainly never mentioned the "collection" aspect of it. Generally, the fact that my father was a bookie went unacknowledged. Now that I was up at Yale with kids whose dads went to work in glass towers, and never even raised their voices to their secretaries, I wanted to know, did my father have guys like Rocky Balboa breaking legs for him?

"Arch, I want to tell you something. Whatever I do, I do for you, and your mother. Sure, running a book is illegal. You've known that since you were a little kid. But it will never go away. People want to bet, just like they want to make love, or listen to music, or drink. Gambling is a part of life on this earth, and that will never change."

"What do you do when someone doesn't pay you, Dad?"

"The rules are clear when you place a bet with me, Arch. I'll cut you off if you start to get in too deep. You will never bet with me again. But I'll carry a debt forever before I'll hurt a man who owes me money. I figure, better I should be running this business than a greedy man, or a violent man. I live off people's vices, but I don't punish them for it."

I nodded. I knew my father, I loved him with all my heart, and I believed him. He didn't need to explain further. But I'd moved something in him, and he had more to say.

"When I grew up, I had no options, like you do. Nobody was sending me to good schools. My father was a tough uneducated man, who fought for everything he ever had and trusted no one except his family. I could've given up the book. Your mother still wants me to. But how will I pay for our lives?"

I had no ready answer.

"There's two worlds out there, Arch. The legit world, and the world you come from. Now, you're going legit. But never forget, even out there where you're headed, sometimes you have to break the rules to do the right thing."

Three hours later he and my mother were dead. I don't think I've ever really gotten over it. I sold their store and shut down the book. It was enough to pay for college and law school.

At the age of eighteen, I found myself alone in the world.

I missed him so much. I would've liked to talk about life with him right now, about Damon, about Charlotte King, and Dr. Stern, and Yates, about everything I suspected but couldn't prove.

I pulled myself out of my funk and called Goodman. He had nothing to report. Disk still locked. One of his three state-of-the-art desktops was fully occupied. He felt a little deprived but seemed to be willing to let the project go on. I reminded him again that he should never mention it to anyone.

The phone rang. It was Twersky.

"Hey, Arch, you're big time now, huh? Getting ready for the big trial?"

"You bet, Tom."

"Got anything for me?"

I felt a deepened affection for Tom Twersky, now that I had a felony offense under my belt.

"Not right now, Tom, but if something comes up, I'll give you a call."

"Thanks. And, Arch?"

"Yeah?"

"Thanks again for everything you did for me. I'll never forget it."

"Anytime. Now stay out of trouble."

"Well, I hope you don't get a call from arraignments. Know what I mean? I'm starting to get the itch."

"Don't scratch that itch, Tom. You know better."

I hung up and called the detective on the Dr. Stern case, a Bill Blakeman. To my surprise, the detective took my call, probably because he had nothing to report and, therefore, no information to protect. No leads. No prints. No distinctive MO. It had turned pretty quickly into a cold case. Usually more to go on in a burglary. This one looked like the work of real pros, not junkies looking for smack money. But Detective Blakeman saw no reason to think it was anything but a real nasty burglary gone bad.

"What about the ex-wife?" I asked.

"Lives in Boston. She didn't want to talk to us. We've

got no reason to suspect her, but definitely, she's a little strange. Also Austrian. Very suspicious of the police."

"I'd like to talk to her. Do you mind? Have you got her number?"

"So, counselor, your angle here is what again? Remind me."

"Detective, I think it's very strange that Charlotte King and her shrink were both killed within days of each other."

"Coincidence, counselor. I mean, who do you think is gonna orchestrate that kinda shit?"

"That's what I'm trying to figure out."

"Maybe if you had ham, you'd have ham and eggs, if you had eggs. You got yourself a nice imagination, counselor. You got anything to back this up? DA interested in this theory?"

"I haven't gone to the DA with this. Because you're right. I've got nothing to back it up. But I would like to talk to Dr. Stern's ex-wife. What's it to you? All you have right now is a case that got cold real quick. She wouldn't talk to you, maybe she'll talk to me."

"Counselor, give it a shot. Why not. It's 617-875-4939. Boston number. Don't tell her it came from NYPD. Okay?"

"Thanks, Detective."

"Sure, Gold. You're a wacky one, anyone ever tell you that?"

It didn't pan out. Mrs. Stern was a bitter woman. She spoke to me but she couldn't help.

"Mr. Gold," she said, in her heavy Viennese accent, "my husband was a wonderful psychiatrist, but he couldn't function in the world outside his office. He could give advice, but he couldn't follow it. He couldn't maintain any relationships, except with his patients. I'm a therapist, too, you know, but I wanted to live in this world, not in my study, thinking about the human condition. I have no idea why someone would kill him. I assume it was just one of those horrible crimes that happens in New York City from time to time. But I can't help you solve it. My husband's life was a mystery to me, and so, it turns out, is his death. Good-bye."

Layden was right. This case was going to be tried as an ID case, a street crime where the cops arrested the wrong black kid. Right now, that was all I had.

CHAPTER 26

JURY SELECTION in the capital case of *People v. Damon Tucker* began in the second week of February 1999. That morning the sky was a powerful blue presence in the little park across the street from the courthouse, called Collect Pond, named after some eighteenth-century body of water that had long ago been filled in. It was now a square that opened up the canyons of old downtown New York, a spot where the sun shone brightly on the bums and drunks just waking up and stretching on the benches in the little park that was their home, a half-dozen faces as familiar to me as the judges, prosecutors, and lawyers I saw every day inside 100 Centre Street.

Today, the streets around the park were lined with TV trucks, and each of the networks, local and national, had reporters poking around the wide sidewalk in front of the courthouse, trying to decide which angle they should shoot their report from, if their makeup was properly applied, and perhaps, even, considering what they were going to say, as the "People" of the State of New York set about the task of finding twelve citizens to convince beyond a reasonable doubt that Damon Tucker was guilty and should pay with his life for Charlotte King's death.

Stephens and I walked quickly up the courthouse steps as the TV cameras followed us. The cameras were really looking for DA Stoddard, but they would look in vain, since she could go directly from her offices on the ninth floor of 100 Centre Street to the courtroom of Judge Robert Wheeler, where jury selection was scheduled to begin at 10:00 a.m., and where no cameras would be allowed. What's more, Judge Wheeler had issued a gag order, stating that none of the attorneys, neither defense nor prosecution, could speak to the media about the case. So, with no trial to televise, and no attorneys to interview, the talking heads could do no more than talk. But it was still a huge story, even if the judge had shut it down as a television event.

Once inside 100 Centre Street, the press left us alone, since they couldn't interview us.

"I assume you're not going to bring up any of your extralegal activities and whacked-out theories before we pick a jury, are you, counselor?" Stephens asked me.

She was still pissed at me.

"Nope. Maybe never, at this rate. Right now, we don't have enough to get it in, even if I felt like laying it all out, which I don't. So relax."

She didn't look relaxed, even though this would not be a particularly stressful day. Some five hundred prospective jurors would be given a fifteen-page questionnaire to fill out. It might take some of them all day.

It was certainly an anticlimactic day for the news media. Once the reporters found out that the process might take a couple weeks, they lost interest. Worse still, the judge ordered that jurors be referred to only by number, rather than name, until the trial was over, so that the press would not be able to track them down. For two weeks, while we picked a jury, these guys would have nothing to do.

The same was not true for us. The questionnaires presented us with a huge mountain of work. We sorted them every which way, by race, sex, age, occupation, neighborhood, education, and, of course, attitude toward death penalty. It appeared that one in five New Yorkers, 20 percent of our questionnaires, had substantial doubts that they could impose the death penalty in any case. So they were gone, and we were left with another four hundred who claimed to be able to sentence another human being to die, but only on particularly deserving cases. Oh, and of course, none of this death talk would affect their view of reasonable doubt.

What a lot of crap. After a couple of days and evenings sorting through the questionnaires, and watching Stephens input the data into her computer, I got too restless, and I headed out, to Midtown, to Yates Associates's offices. I needed to do something besides guess which citizens of New York City were least likely to want to fry Damon. I decided I'd see if I could find out what Yates did after work. He didn't have a family—no wife or kids to fill up his life. How did he entertain himself? I got lucky. It only took me a couple of nights to find out.

The first evening I sat from six to eight-thirty in a Starbucks across from his building, waiting to see if he came out. I knew he lived in the city, and I bet he liked to walk, perhaps accompanied by a bodyguard. He never appeared.

I came back the next night. At 7:00, he came out, alone, and started going south on Broadway. I followed, half a block behind. He couldn't have noticed me.

He was walking at a brisk pace, dressed, as usual, like the Prince of Wales. When he got to Thirty-fourth Street, he headed west, until he got to the entrance of an elegant-looking club called the Executive Lounge. A large man in a tuxedo, who looked like an All-Pro lineman going to an NFL awards ceremony, was standing on a red carpet, under a heated awning, next to a velvet rope, manning the door. I guessed it was a high-class strip joint.

The bouncer in the tux shook Yates's hand. Yates gave him a tip. The guy held the door open, and Yates ducked inside. I didn't. I'd seen enough. I didn't want to risk another encounter.

So Yates liked to watch girls dance. Big deal. Most men did. Kathy Dupont suddenly popped into my head, and I wondered which club she worked.

CHAPTER 27

PART 63, THE LARGEST COURTROOM in 100 Centre Street, was packed. The press had been given the first ten of the twenty rows of thick old wooden benches, which were usually empty save for the occasional relative or friend of the participants, either victim or accused. Evelyn Tucker sat in the eleventh row, on one side of the center aisle. Harriet King sat on the other side. No one else was on hand for Charlotte King. Just her mom. In some murder trials, the victim's family and friends turned out in droves, reminding everyone that when a life is lost, the living suffer, too. Not in this case. The rest of the people in the audience were simply spectators, who'd waited for hours outside in the hallway for the chance to watch the first death penalty trial in Manhattan since the 1930s, back when Part 63 was brand-new, back when there were fifteen thousand felony arrests a year in Manhattan, not a hundred and fifty thousand.

The jury was, for the first time, now seated in the jury box. It had taken two weeks to select them. We had five black women, two black men, three white women, and two white men. We had three hospital workers, two secretaries, a doctor, a social worker, an insurance agent, a token collector, a city clerk, a mailman, and a flower store owner. All death qualified.

Judge Wheeler was giving his preliminary instructions, reminding the attentive jurors about the basics—reasonable doubt, presumption of innocence—those legal mantras we repeat over and over to ourselves, whose real meaning we are seldom called upon to examine.

He spoke very quietly, leaning forward toward a small microphone that amplified his voice around the courtroom in a way that I still found strange, although most judges had adopted this electronic mode of address. I still preferred the old days, when a judge tried to project his or her voice, instead of using a public address system, which, in Wheeler's case, made him sound like a breathy disc jockey on lite FM, rather than the presiding judge in Manhattan's first death penalty trial.

Judge Wheeler was a mixed blessing. Politically, he leaned toward the defense side. He was opposed to long sentences for nonviolent drug cases. He didn't think every cop spoke the gospel truth. He was a former counsel to the ex-governor, a brilliant policy man who had authored much important legislation, the death penalty statute not being among them. When the governor lost, one of his last acts was to make sure that Wheeler had a lifelong sinecure on the bench. It also happened to be a merit appointment. He was one of the brightest judges in the city, destined for the appellate courts, and maybe even higher, if he didn't screw up.

Only problem was that he didn't have any guts. He was very ambitious and too afraid his name might appear in the headlines for the wrong reasons. More than one liberal judge's career had ended because he or she released some guy in a nothing case who then went out and shot a cop. So Judge Wheeler was always looking over his shoulder. I doubted he was going to take any risks to help Damon. On the other hand, I don't think he was looking to convict Damon. I knew he was privately opposed to the death penalty. Perhaps, despite his lack of courage, he would help us. Judges who push too hard for a conviction, making close rulings in favor of the prosecution, risk reversal on appeal. That is the only thing that constrains many of them from overtly favoring the prosecution. But a judge who wants an acquittal doesn't have to be as careful. In America, an acquittal is unappealable. Badda bing, badda boom. Not guilty is the end of the game. No higher court can throw out an acquittal and order a new trial.

Judge Wheeler—spineless, bright Judge Wheeler—could help us without fear of reversal.

He was finishing his opening instructions to the jury.

"Now, by law, the prosecutor must make an opening statement. Defense counsel may make an opening statement if he chooses but is not required to do so. We will now hear from District Attorney Stoddard."

I stood up. "Your Honor, may we approach?"

The judge looked surprised. His eyebrows shot up quizzically.

"If we must. Come up."

Once up at the bench, I took it a step further.

"Your Honor, this needs to be on the record, but without the jury or the press or public."

He nodded.

"This better be worth it, Gold. All right, then, we'll clear the courtroom. Step back."

"Ladies and gentlemen, we will take a short recess, while the lawyers discuss something with me. I'll ask everyone to leave the courtroom, press and public included."

There were a few howls from the journalists, but they had no choice. They could sue later, for a copy of the transcript.

The courtroom slowly emptied. Finally, the doors were closed.

"To what do we owe this dramatic interruption, just as we were getting under way, Gold?"

"Your Honor, I'd like to make an offer of proof regarding an alternative theory we wish to present to the jury as to the identity of Charlotte King's killer."

Stoddard let out a snort. "I can't imagine what counsel has in mind. Do we really have to waste everybody's time?"

For weeks, Damon had been demanding that I make an offer of proof on the record about our theory that Yates was the killer. Stephens and I had explained to him again and again that we just didn't have enough, that there was no point to it, and that if Yates got wind of it, it would shut down any hope we had of digging up more evidence. Damon couldn't accept this idea. Eventually, I stopped fighting and determined to do what he wanted. There were some good reasons for it, too. Maybe if Damon heard the news directly from the judge, instead of having to take my word for it, maybe then he'd be able to accept the limitations on our case. A judge's ruling might calm him.

There was one other thing I liked about our hopeless

offer of proof. It would confuse Stoddard. I had no intention of mentioning our explanation of the People's fingerprint evidence. I wasn't willing to give away our *real* defense theory before things were even under way. So this lame offer of proof wasn't all bad—it gave me an opportunity to run a little misdirection play on Stoddard and make her think we had less than we did.

The judge, patient as ever, turned to me.

"Let's hear what Mr. Gold has to say."

"Judge, we believe that David Yates, head of Yates Associates, and the victim's employer, killed her. We can establish the following facts: Yates was having an affair with Charlotte King. Her mother will testify to that. Yates is planning to take his firm public sometime next year. He stands to make tens of millions of dollars. Charlotte King knew something about Yates Associates, something that would kill the public offering. Whatever it was she knew, she told it to her therapist, Dr. Hans Stern. He was killed just days after her death. Why? Because someone had a reason to think Dr. Stern might go public with what Charlotte King had told him, now that she was dead. We believe that someone was Yates."

I paused, took a sip of water, let all these allegations sink in. Stoddard looked at me as if I'd lost my mind.

"Further, Your Honor, we have reason to believe that just forty-five minutes after Charlotte King was shot, someone entered her apartment, opened up her computer, and replaced the hard drive. It is our position that whoever did that had to be the real killer. We submit it was Yates. It couldn't have been Damon. He was already in custody. It's too much of a coincidence to ignore. It's powerful evidence that someone besides Damon killed Charlotte King."

"And what do you have to prove *that*, counselor?" asked

the judge.

Now things were getting tricky for Arch Gold, the arch criminal.

"Your Honor, if the court would permit, I ask that we be permitted to subpoena and bring to court Ms. King's home computer."

DA Stoddard laughed out loud. The judge turned to her.

"You'll have your turn in a moment, Ms. Stoddard. Is that all, Mr. Gold?"

I nodded.

The judge continued. "You claim but can't yet prove that the victim's computer was tampered with, you claim she was sleeping with the boss, who is taking his firm public, and her shrink was killed several days after her death. You say this all adds up to some level of proof that Yates killed her or had her killed. Have I summarized your position correctly?"

"Yes, Judge."

Stoddard rose, and cleared her throat. "Your Honor, may I respond?"

"I don't think that will be necessary. Even assuming, *arguendo*, that everything Mr. Gold has asserted is in fact true, it would still not be a sufficient offer of proof to permit him to bring these matters out on his case. The offer of proof is insufficient as a matter of law. Counsel will not be permitted to allude to this highly speculative theory at any time during the trial."

Wheeler turned to Damon.

"Sir, I don't know whether or not you intend to testify. That decision is entirely up to you. But I can tell you this. If you do testify, you are to make no reference to what your attorney has raised here. Are we clear? If you violate my order, I'll declare a mistrial, and we'll just start over.

Pick a new jury, and do it all again. I don't think any of us wants that."

He looked sternly at Damon, who wasn't taking this well at all.

"Fuck this. Fucking fuck this shit. How can you shut me down? This dude had her killed, and you want me to fry for it."

The judge ignored Damon's outburst.

"Are the parties ready for openings?"

We all nodded. The truth was, I hadn't expected our offer of proof to go anywhere, and my opening was unchanged from how I'd prepared it—explaining away the People's evidence and asserting that the real mugger was still out there. It wasn't a bad defense. What's more, Stoddard wasn't hip to it.

If Damon could just keep cool, and not turn the jurors against him with some nasty outburst, on or off the stand, we had a shot at an acquittal.

"Bring in the jury," said the judge.

CHAPTER 28

STODDARD GOT UP from behind the prosecution table and walked to the little podium, a few feet from the jury box, to give the People's opening statement. The only sound in the huge courtroom was the click of her heels on the hard cold floor. I felt my heart start to pound. Stephens, sitting next to me, smiled ever so slightly. Was it a show of confidence? I certainly didn't share it. I'd never faced an adversary so smart, so appealing, so charismatic. Usually, at the start of a trial, I was charged up, amazed anew at the trouble the state went to in protecting a defendant's rights, at the high and heavy burden of proof beyond a reasonable doubt placed on the prosecutor, and the great variety of procedural safeguards the courts of New York State had developed over the generations to make sure no defendant was unfairly convicted. Today, it all seemed to add up to nothing in the face of this celebrity prosecutor, a woman who could have been Damon Tucker's mother, talking now in simple straightforward tones to a death-qualified jury: twelve New Yorkers who had all already declared that if push came to shove, they'd have no problem seeing to it that Damon Tucker's life would end strapped to a gurney somewhere as deadly drugs from a lethal injection flowed through his body.

My gaze shifted from Stoddard to Evelyn Tucker. I remembered Stephens's drunken words last night.

"You will never hear another sound like a mother wailing when she is watching her son be executed. There's no other sound like it. It is just this horrendous wail, and you can't get away from it."

I took Damon's hand and squeezed it. He squeezed back. He was dressed in a black suit, blue Oxford shirt, and tie. His handsome face was solemn, but his eyes were bright as he listened to the district attorney lay out the case against him in simple sentences.

"Good morning, ladies and gentleman. On December 4, 1998, Charlotte King left work at around 4:30 P.M., as she often did on a Friday afternoon. She walked west, into the Chelsea gallery district, looking for art. She went in and out of various galleries. She was alone on foot when this young man, Damon Tucker, confronted her, pointed a gun at her, and demanded her money. She gave him her purse. Then, in an act of cold-blooded terror, this young man shot her in the stomach, mortally wounding her. She fell to the sidewalk and lay there bleeding. She died right there on the street in a policeman's arms several minutes later."

She cradled her arms as she said these words, as if holding the dying woman herself.

"Her final act, before she died, was to identify her killer."

"Objection." I was on my feet. "The DA may give her view as to what the evidence will prove; she can't state these matters as if they are facts."

The judge actually appeared to think for a moment. Then he spoke softly, as usual.

"I'll allow it. Ladies and gentleman, what you are hearing now, no matter how Ms. Stoddard phrases it, is a preview of what she believes the People's evidence will show. Nothing she herself says is evidence or proves anything. Please continue."

She wasn't the slightest bit ruffled.

"Of course, ladies and gentleman, this is not a contest between the lawyers. The only thing you have to think about is the evidence, and there's plenty of it against Damon Tucker."

"Objection, again. This is not summation."

The judge looked almost apologetic. "Sustained. I'll ask both counsel to save their arguments for closing statements."

Stoddard resumed.

"Two plainclothes police officers happened to be cruising in an unmarked car nearby. They heard the radio transmission from central, which went out moments after the officers found Ms. King and which contained the description she'd given them. Black male, black coat. It's not the most specific description you'll ever hear, but as you'll find out, in this case it just doesn't matter. Because when the police stopped this man over here . . ." she gestured over to Damon as if he were just another piece of physical evidence, like the gun or the money, "they found 180 dollars in his pocket, eighteen ten-dollar bills. Each one had his fingerprints, and three of them had Charlotte King's fingerprints. Of course, the police officers didn't, and couldn't, know that at the time. They simply took Tucker back to where Charlotte King was dying and asked her, 'Is this the man who shot you?' She managed to nod, and her lips formed the word 'Yes.' You will hear about this identification from two different officers who witnessed it."

She paused, to let them absorb this damning evidence. Then she wound it up.

"That, ladies and gentleman, is more than proof beyond a reasonable doubt. That all adds up to overwhelming evidence of this defendant's guilt. The evidence will show that he was identified by the victim. The evidence will show that the defendant was running from the scene when he was stopped. The evidence will show that the victim's fingerprints were on the money found in his pocket. Damon Tucker robbed and killed Charlotte King in cold blood. She died a painful horrible death, on Twentieth Street. It is up to you now, to see that justice is done."

She walked back to her seat. Click clack of those high heels. That was it. Very short. Very sweet. Very effective. It was a simple case, and she was keeping it that way.

Surprisingly, she'd made a common rookie mistake, perhaps because she was overconfident. She hadn't talked about any of the problems in her case. This gave me the opportunity to give new information to the jury in *my* opening, which inevitably gave them the impression that the prosecutor was trying to hide the facts in its own case. I expected this kind of stuff from the average run-of-the-mill assistant, but not from the district attorney herself. It just proved to me once again that even the smartest, most experienced lawyers could lose perspective and buy into their own bullshit. I saw it happen all the time to the highest-paid members of the private criminal bar, a pompous, bombastic bunch who tried to make everything complicated, thereby justifying their own big fees. I hadn't expected it from Stoddard.

Now it was my turn.

"Good morning, ladies and gentlemen of the jury."

I paused to look at each of them, to make eye contact where possible. Those who refused to meet my gaze usually didn't want to hear what I had to say.

"Now you've heard the prosecutor's opening statement. And it sure does sound like a simple case, doesn't it. Very clean. Very neat. Well, ladies and gentleman, any story can sound that way when you leave out half the facts. The prosecutor told you all the details that *help* her case. She seems to have forgotten the things that *hurt* her case."

"Objection. Just exactly what is counsel insinuating?"

"Overruled."

I smiled. Took a sip of water. Stepped back from the podium.

"Ladies and gentlemen, on Friday, December 4, 1998, someone committed a terrible crime. Someone shot and killed Charlotte King in cold blood, apparently for a few dollars. Someone took her life. She was only thirty years old. A successful Wall Street executive. And she died a horrible painful death. That is not in dispute here. We're not saying that didn't happen. This is not a 'how'd it happen.' This is a 'whodunnit.' Someone killed Charlotte King by shooting her in the stomach. But it wasn't Damon Tucker."

I paused. They all seemed to be listening.

"Let me tell you some of the facts in this case that you're going to find out soon but that you didn't hear from Ms. Stoddard here. You're going to find out that Damon Tucker worked in a video rental store around the corner from where he was arrested. You're going to find out that on December 4, 1998, he was working behind the cash register at that store, and that he sold a video, *Fatal Attraction*, to the victim. She paid him with three 10 dollar bills. Those very same bills ended up in Damon's pocket not five minutes later, when he cashed his paycheck with the boss, who paid him right out of the register. You'll hear from the store manager, John Taback. He'll tell you that Damon cashes his 180 dollar paycheck every Friday, which is payday. He'll tell you that Damon always counted the money right in front of him. That's why his fingerprints are on each of the eighteen 10 dollar bills found in his jeans pocket, and also on the copy of *Fatal Attraction*, which Ms. King had in her purse when she died.

"So all the overwhelming fingerprint evidence that the prosecutor just described to you doesn't turn out to be so overwhelming after all."

Pause. Sip of water. I was giving them a lot of information, and I wanted to let it sink in before I went on. I glanced over at Stoddard. She was staring straight ahead. An MRI would have shown a total frenzy of brain activity in the sector used to process unbelievable fucking new information. I knew that expression. I could see Stoddard's mind racing along, testing each permutation and possibility, thinking about how to deal with this new twist.

Some defense attorneys didn't believe in making opening statements at all. There was always the danger that things would come out differently when real live witnesses got on the stand, or that you would get locked into a theory of the case that you would then have to alter in the middle of the trial, the kind of maneuvering that was usually fatal and led to a swift conviction. But years of experience had led me to believe it was worth taking the risk. The worst moment in the trial was usually right after the DA had just laid out the People's case, and if the defense attorney didn't counter with something, didn't hit the ground running, sometimes the whole fight was over before it began. The conservative old-style approach was not to open, not to put your client on the stand, and just to pick away at the prosecution's case, hoping to kick up some dust, and possibly a little "reasonable doubt." I didn't buy it. No matter how many times a judge instructed a jury that the defendant had no burden, had nothing to prove, and that they couldn't hold it against the defendant if he or she didn't testify, juries did hold it against defendants, did assume either that they had a record or had committed the crime and didn't want to lie about it on the stand. So I like to hit the ground running in most of my cases, and unless my client has a record a mile long, I put him on the stand.

"You're going to find out that when Damon was stopped, sure, he was running, but he was also wearing a Walkman, listening to music. Ask yourself, as you hear this evidence, does a fleeing gunman put on a Walkman? And if, theoretically, he's trying to blend in by putting on the Walkman, does he run? What's more, the cops must have realized the same thing, because you're going to find out that one of the police officers who stopped Damon took his Walkman and threw it down through a grate into the gutter. The only reason we know this is that the defense discovered it, down there in the sewer. It had Damon's prints on it, and also the prints of the officer who threw it there.

"Now, there will be no testimony that gloves were recovered on Damon or found anywhere near the scene. Yet no prints were found on the wallet, purse, or gun. Why, if Damon's prints were on the money and the video, weren't they also on those other items, the wallet, the purse, or the gun? Why? Because the real killer either wiped them clean or wore gloves. The real killer still has Charlotte King's money. The money found on Damon was his. Sure it had her prints, because she'd come into the store, but he didn't take it from her on the street. It came from the cash register at the video store.

"Now, the prosecutor claims that Damon was identified by Ms. King shortly before she died. We will present expert medical evidence to you that she was in no condition to identify anyone, and that in fact, she simply had a spasm and died just as Damon was brought in front of her. These officers who will testify that she ID'd him are either lying, or exaggerating."

"Objection," said Stoddard, in her most insulted tone. "This is not summation."

"Overruled," said Judge Wheeler quietly. "Jurors, as I mentioned during the prosecutor's opening, nothing that either counsel says to you is evidence. It's simply a preview of what they believe the evidence will show. Continue, Mr. Gold."

"Ladies and gentlemen, you have a heavy, heavy responsibility in this case. An unspeakably horrible crime has been committed. A life has been taken. A young woman has been killed in cold blood. Nothing we do here can bring her back. But now, you must keep all the promises you made when you were selected as jurors. You must look only at the evidence. You must not let your passion, your compassion, or your desire for justice blind you to the reality before you, which is this: The police in this case arrested the wrong man. Damon Tucker did not commit this crime. He was in the wrong place at the wrong time, and because of a series of remarkable coincidences, he now stands before you with his very life at stake."

"Objection!" Stoddard was yelling. "Defense counsel knows very well he is forbidden from mentioning punishment at this phase of the trial."

I knew the rules, and as usual, I was intentionally breaking them. In most trials, it truly was a significant transgression to mention punishment during the trial, since the jury had no idea how many years a defendant might or might not be facing, particularly if he'd sold a small amount of drugs, in which case the jury assumed he'd be doing a small amount of time, and had no idea that he'd do a minimum of four and a half to nine years if convicted, the same penalty as rape, attempted murder, or a gunpoint robbery. Here, of course, everyone in the courtroom knew that Damon's life was on the line. Not mentioning it at this point in the trial was a contrivance, a fiction, nothing more. I liked watching Stoddard's face get twisted in anger over something so obviously silly to the jury, who could not, for one single moment, forget about the death penalty. It was in the air they breathed, it weighted every word spoken in that courtroom. For Stoddard to get up and howl because I was stating the obvious smacked of "Big Brother," of the state stupidly attempting to enforce some kind of impossible thought control on twelve perfectly intelligent people.

The judge saw all this immediately. He nodded knowingly and spoke in his usual low breathy tones.

"Jurors, we all know the stakes in this trial. None of us can forget them at any point. However, Ms. Stoddard is technically correct that the lawyers are not supposed to mention punishment until after you have reached a verdict.

Obviously, if you acquit, none of us need think about it again. If you convict, then we will formally consider the issue in a new phase of these proceedings. Continue, Mr. Gold."

"Thank you, Your Honor."

I finished up.

"Ladies and gentlemen, none of you wanted this difficult job. Now you are doing the hardest work a citizen can do. You are being called upon to judge the fate of another human being. After you've heard all the evidence, after you've weighed it all, discussed it among yourselves in the privacy of the jury room, you will conclude that Damon Tucker is innocent. Nothing any of us do can bring Charlotte King back. But convicting an innocent man will only compound this tragedy."

I'd definitely gotten their attention.

CHAPTER 29

THE PEOPLE'S FIRST WITNESS was Officer Dave Newman, the cop who had found Charlotte King lying on the pavement, bleeding to death. Stoddard's plan was for him to jump on the stand and glibly announce that Charlotte King had identified Damon as her killer. Before Stoddard could get away with this, she had a few legal hurdles to get over, and I wasn't planning to make it easy for her. If the judge ruled against me, okay, we'd have our first big appealable issue for Stephens down the road.

At a trial here in America, no one can testify as to what someone else said. Hearsay just isn't allowed. The Constitution says you have the right to confront the witnesses against you, the right to cross-examine your accusers, to question them in open court, in front of the jury. If cops are allowed to get up there on the stand and say what someone else said to them, the whole right of confrontation goes out the window. All the accused could do would be to question the cop, a professional witness who has been trained and coached as to what is required to get a conviction. So the law says no, if the person who actually said something isn't available, that statement is hearsay, and it isn't admissible evidence. Otherwise, one cop could just get up there and basically file a report to the jury. Maybe that's how it works in China, but not here. Not in most cases.

Of course, like every rock-solid rule in our world, there are big exceptions, all of which were carved out three centuries ago, in England, and all of which rely on some indicia of truth. For example, one person testifying that she overheard another person say "I robbed a bank last week" would be allowed, since it is unlikely someone would falsely admit guilt. Similarly, sometime in the eighteenth century, way back when the average bloke on his deathbed was totally preoccupied with thoughts of heaven and hell, and which one would be his final resting place for eternity, the courts developed the notion that no one would lie if they knew they were dying, since the fear of eternal damnation would be heavy upon them.

As the twentieth century draws to a close, very few folks out there were any more likely to tell the truth as they lay dying than at any other time in their lives. Still, there are a large number of homicides where the courts are looking for some reasoned basis to let in a dying identification witnessed only by the police. The most common stumbling block is the victim's lack of awareness that he or she is actually dying. The fact that the victim does in fact die is not sufficient basis to invoke the "dying declaration" exception to the "no hearsay" rule. The victim has to in fact *know* that he or she is about to die, since otherwise the original, and by now meaningless, basis for the rule— fear of eternal damnation resulting from a deathbed fib— would not apply.

Stoddard knew that she would have to get in King's deathbed ID as a dying declaration. Without a dying declaration, the case was immeasurably tougher for the People. If these cops couldn't testify to the fact that King identified Damon, the evidence linking Damon to the crime, including fingerprints, would be purely circumstantial and wouldn't prove that he was the shooter. Whether the cops would come through with the right magic phrases remained to be seen. I certainly didn't want to let the so-called ID come out in front of the jury, where it could never really be taken back, without first getting a ruling from the judge. Rest assured, when the judge says "disregard that last statement" or "strike that from the record," it just gets more ingrained in the jury's mind.

We were up at the bench, talking in muted but strained tones. Lawyers in criminal cases develop a strident whisper that allows them to go quietly crazy two feet from the judge, without alerting the jurors to anything.

"Your Honor, obviously the DA would like nothing better than for this rookie cop to get up and tell the jury, in violation of all of the rules of evidence, what he thinks Charlotte King said before she died. How convenient, since she's dead and can't be cross-examined. Unfortunately, the rules of evidence just don't allow it. How exactly does Madame DA expect to get this deeply damaging but very questionable testimony into evidence?"

"Dying declaration, Your Honor. This is a textbook case. Officer Newman will testify that Ms. King was dying, she knew she was dying, and with her last breath, seeking justice for herself, she identified her killer. That's a classic fact pattern for admission of a dying declaration. I believe I've made a sufficient offer of proof. I'd ask you to permit us to go forward. And I would just like to ask, if Mr. Gold was so concerned about this issue, why didn't he raise it before openings?"

The judge turned his gaze on me.

"Your Honor, that's the DA's problem, not mine. She shouldn't open on inadmissible evidence. If she does, she runs a risk. May I propose a hearing on this issue, without the jury? Once we let the genie out of the bottle, we can't put it back. We need to hear what this officer will say. I'm making a motion *in limine*."

"Gold, thank you for the right Latin phrase. That's exactly what we're not going to do. I don't see the need. If the DA has misrepresented this officer's testimony, her case will suffer dire consequences. Believe me. Counsel, step back."

Not bad. Judge Wheeler was basically telling Stoddard that since she failed to raise this issue when she should have, before the trial began, she was now flying naked. If Newman didn't come through, the judge would instruct the jury to disregard all ID testimony, notwithstanding her opening to the contrary. I could certainly live with that.

Newman hopped up on the stand like an eager young puppy and swore to tell the truth.

Since the rapid expansion of the NYC police force several years ago the average age of cops was getting lower and lower. This Officer Newman looked barely old enough to drink or drive, let alone carry around an automatic pistol and attempt to evenhandedly enforce the laws. He had blond hair, cut in a fashionable fade around the edges, an earring, and a nervous smirk. He was two years out of the police academy, no college, and this was the first homicide he'd encountered on the job.

Stoddard was easing him into the narrative.

"And what if anything did you see on Twentieth Street that day?"

"I saw a female lying on the sidewalk in a pool of blood."

"And what if anything did you do at that time?"

"At that time I approached the female and checked to see where she was injured, and if she could speak."

"Go on."

"She could barely talk, but she was trying to say something."

I objected, loudly. "Objection to any characterization as to what she was trying to do."

The judge looked over at me with amusement. "Sustained. Officer, just tell us what you saw and heard."

Newman nodded. "Sure, Judge.

"She was lying on her back. She wasn't moving. She was bleeding from a wound in her abdomen. I could see the blood gushing out from her blouse."

"Did you speak to her?" asked Stoddard, trying to get Newman focused on the heart of the matter, the goddamn description.

"Objection," I said again. "Leading the witness."

"Sustained," said the judge, turning his sleepy eyes toward the young cop. "Officer Newman, just tell us what happened, as best you can. Okay?"

"Sure, Judge. I leaned over this female, and she whispered something to me. She said, 'Black male. He shot me. Don't let me die. Help me.' I said, 'We'll help you. What did he look like?' Then she whispered something I couldn't understand."

"Did you ask her anything else?"

"Yes. I asked her what the black male was wearing. She said, 'black coat.' "

"And then?"

"I pulled out my radio and put out that description, black male, black coat, armed."

"And then what did you do?"

"I stayed with the female vic. She wasn't, like, doin' too good. She was losing a lot of blood."

The cop stared straight ahead, like he was giving a report in the military. In the old days, a lot of police officers came from the military and fit well into the essentially military organization of the thirty-five thousand New York City police officers, a force larger and without doubt better trained and armed than many a country's entire army. But this kid was just playacting; this didn't come from military service, this came from too many hours in front of the TV as a kid, watching *Hill Street Blues.*"

"And then?"

"And then I waited for the bus and the boss."

"By that you mean an ambulance and Sergeant Speazel, right?"

"Yes. The ambulance got there quick, actually, uh, before my sergeant. They put a line in her and tried to bandage the bullet wound. But she was losing it fast."

"Did she say anything to you while you were waiting?"

"The victim was moaning weakly. She said, 'Don't let me die. I feel like I'm dying.' "

"Did there come a time when some other officers arrived on the scene with a suspect?"

"Yes. After a while two other cops showed up with Mr. Tucker here. They pulled him out of the squad car, uncuffed him, and brought him over to where the victim was on a stretcher. They were about to load her in."

"And then?"

"One of the officers said, 'Is this the man who shot you?' She didn't say nothing, but she nodded her head up and down, like a yes, a few times."

"Then what happened?"

"Then she let out a big sigh, and it looked like she died."

"Did she in fact die?"

"Yes, she did."

"What was Damon Tucker wearing when Ms. King identified him?"

"Objection, whether or not that was an identification is a matter of opinion."

"Overruled," said the judge.

"He was wearing a black down jacket. That's all I remember."

"Nothing further."

Now it was my turn. Cross-examination is like surgery. You know ahead of time what you're going to go in and get. If you don't have a plan, if it's just "exploratory," then your case, like the surgery patient, is in trouble. You only ask questions to which you know the answer or questions where the answer, whatever it is, can't hurt you. The tricky part is getting the witness to give up the answer you want, understanding how to box him in with questions so that ultimately, you got your answer, your little factoid, whatever it might be, to be used later on summation.

"Good morning, Officer. Other than this morning, you and I have never met, have we?"

"Uh, no."

"But you did meet with the prosecutor concerning this case, did you not?"

"Uh, yes."

"In fact, you went over the questions you would be

asked, and the answers you would give, correct?"

"Not exactly."

"What did you talk about, then?"

"We talked about the case."

"But you didn't go over what questions you'd be asked, and what answers you'd give?"

"Yeah, I guess we did."

"By the way, you did discuss this case with the other officers involved, correct?"

"Yeah, sure."

"With Armstrong?"

"Yeah."

"With Smith?"

"Yeah."

"With Barnett?"

"Yeah."

This was all just a little warm-up drill, to get me loose, to ask a few easy questions, and sometimes, to create some problematic answers for the prosecutor, who might have forgotten to tell her cops to admit the obvious—that they had been prepared by the prosecutor to give their testimony and that, of course, they had discussed the whole thing with their fellow officers. Jurors hated this kind of dishonesty, hated the idea that a cop wouldn't admit that he'd discussed a case before testifying. It heightened their suspicion that the whole thing was scripted, a programmed performance that nobody was willing to acknowledge.

"Officer, where were you when you first saw Ms. King?"

"I was in my squad car, with my partner, Armstrong, when a civilian ran up to our car shouting that a lady was lying in the street bleeding."

"So at that point, you drove over to Twentieth Street, where Ms. King was lying on the sidewalk, correct?"

"Yes, sir."

"Officer, is this the first case with a shooting victim you'd ever handled?"

"Yes."

"Were you nervous?"

Stoddard jumped up. "Objection. Irrelevant."

"Nonsense," I said. "The officer's state of mind affects his ability to observe. His level of experience is clearly relevant to the jury's assessment of his credibility and reliability."

"Overruled. You may answer the question."

"Yeah, I was real nervous. I'd never seen anyone shot before."

"Never seen anyone dying before, either, had you?"

"No."

"Now, Officer, you say you heard her say 'Black male. He shot me.' Black male, black coat, correct?"

"That's right."

"Did she say anything else?"

"No."

"Where was your partner while you were leaning over her?"

"He was standing a little behind me as I leaned over her. He was calling for an ambulance."

"How much time elapsed until Mr. Tucker was brought in front of Ms. King?"

"I don't know, maybe six or seven minutes."

"And that was after the ambulance arrived?"

"That's right."

"How quickly did the ambulance arrive?"

"Pretty quick. Maybe two or three minutes. Pretty fast."

"Was Damon cuffed or uncuffed when these other cops brought him in front of Ms. King?"

"I believe he was uncuffed."

"Was he cuffed when they brought him out of the squad car?"

"I believe so. I think they uncuffed him after pulling him out of the car, and then they brought him over."

I knew he was lying about the cuffs. I expected the other officers to do the same. I didn't doubt Damon's claim that he was cuffed when he was hauled in front of Charlotte King. Even if he was guilty, he didn't know enough about criminal law to understand the significance of a cuffed show-up, and lie about it.

But even though I knew Newman was lying about the cuffs, I wouldn't be able to do much about it right now. It's generally not effective to call a cop a liar unless you have something to back it up other than the word of the defendant, something like a contradiction in the paperwork, or conflicting testimony from another cop, or a civilian witness. I needed something other than Damon's angry words to discredit Newman about the cuffs, and I didn't have it. I went on to more fertile ground.

"Now, you say, after nodding her head up and down, Ms. King let out a sigh and died—is that your testimony?"

"Yes."

"Did she move at all at that point? Did her head move, other than up and down?"

"She might have had a little spasm."

"A little spasm?"

"Yes."

"And which way did her head move when she had that little spasm?"

"Kinda all over."

"So that would include back and forth?"

"If you think so."

"I don't think anything. I'm asking you. If her head

moved 'kinda all over,' wouldn't that include from side to side?"

"Sure."

He was starting to get testy, when I wasn't really being nasty at all, just trying to unpack his way too tight testimony. His attitude was bound to offend the jury. He was a lousy witness.

"Now, you already stated, Officer, that this woman nodding her head up and down to you indicated a 'yes,' correct?"

"Oh, yeah. Definitely."

"So I take it that if she had nodded her head from side to side, you would have taken that to be a 'no.' Correct?"

"Sure. I didn't know what she was gonna do."

"But isn't it your testimony that just a second after she nodded her head up and down she started nodding it side to side?"

"Objection. Counsel is mischaracterizing what the officer said."

Stoddard didn't like the way this was coming out. I didn't blame her. This officer's ID testimony was shit.

"Overruled. Answer the question."

Naturally, the not-too-bright officer had already forgotten the question, but after the court reporter dutifully read it back in a monotone, he answered with a muted "yes."

"Now, again, how long after she nodded her head up and down did she have that spasm that included back and forth head movement?"

"Maybe just a couple of seconds."

"So it's your testimony that she nods her head up and down, indicating, in your view, a positive identification, and then just a couple seconds later, she starts moving her head in other directions, like back and forth. Is that your testimony?"

"Yes."

"What makes you so sure any part of those head movements was a positive identification?"

"It just seemed that way to me."

"Are you aware of the seriousness of this case?"

He nodded.

"Are you aware that your testimony is absolutely critical here?"

"Yes."

"You don't want to embellish or exaggerate?"

"No."

"So what you're saying to this jury now is that it 'seemed' to you that she ID'd him. I take that to mean that you're not positive."

"You can take it any way you want."

"Officer, you're here only to answer questions, not to make statements to me. Do you understand that?"

Grudging yes.

"Where was your partner at this time?"

"He was canvassing the area, looking for other evidence. He's the one who found her wallet down the street."

"How far was Damon from Ms. King when she saw him?"

"Maybe ten feet."

"Where were Barnett and Smith, the two cops who stopped him?"

"They were standing on either side of him."

"And they were in plainclothes?"

"Yes, sir."

"And exactly where were you?"

"I was kneeling down right next to the victim. I didn't think she was going to last much longer."

"At any time did you hear the victim actually use words to identify Damon Tucker as the shooter?"

"No."

"Nothing further."

Judge Wheeler called the lawyers up to the bench, and in hushed tones, ruled against Damon on the dying declaration issue.

"The evidence is obviously admissible. The woman believed she was dying, and she was in fact dying. Whatever the quality of that ID, it's up to the jury to decide. It's a classic dying declaration."

I protested in muted tones.

"Judge, it wasn't an ID at all. It was just a spasm. Dying declaration is two words. Dying and declaration. Here we have the dying part, but we don't have the declaration part."

"That's good, Gold, but I've ruled. You can sit down. You've got your record. You'll have a nice little issue on appeal."

I'd lost the battle, but the war was looking tougher for the People. This cop was locked into very unconvincing ID testimony. There was definitely reasonable doubt as to Charlotte King's ID of Damon. I'd been right from the beginning. It wasn't an ID. It was a dying spasm that proved nothing at all.

We broke for lunch. The press rushed out to file their latest stories. Nowadays, it wasn't just some evening deadline they had to meet. They had to get their stuff out and online immediately. The *New York Times* website was updated every five minutes. At lunch, my colleagues in the office were reading accounts of the morning on the *Times* website. Today's news, twenty minutes after it had happened.

CHAPTER 30

AFTER LUNCH the next witness was Officer Barnett, one of the two cops who'd received the radio run about the shooting and stopped Damon. Up on the stand he was a world apart from Newman. His face was a little beefy, but his eyes were intelligent, and his expression was a kind of sad sack tolerance, conveying an air of resignation that he'd have to repeat the truth so many times. Stoddard was humming right along.

"And so, Officer, did there come a time when you received a radio transmission connected to this case?"

"Yes, there did."

"What was that transmission?"

"Robbery shooting on Twentieth Street. Large black male, black coat, armed."

"Where were you when you received this transmission?"

"Turning the corner of Twenty-second and Twelfth."

"As you turned that corner, what if anything did you see?"

More tortured questioning, designed not to lead while leading. I love the phrase "what, if anything, did you see?" What did it mean? You always saw *something*. You couldn't turn the corner and see *nothing*.

"I saw a black youth, who I later learned to be Damon Tucker, running down the street."

"What was he wearing?"

"A black down coat."

"Did you stop him?"

"Yes, we did. We stopped him, we told him he was a suspect in a robbery, and we searched him. We found the 180 dollars in his pocket, and 13 in his wallet."

"Who actually recovered that money?"

"Well, actually, it was my partner at the time, Officer Smith. He searched the suspect and first found the 180 loose cash in the front jeans pocket. He pulled it out and handed it to me. I pocketed it for eventual vouchering."

"What is vouchering, Officer?"

"Vouchering is when we fill out forms and turn evidence we've recovered over to the property clerk's office for safekeeping."

"So you vouchered the 180 dollars?"

"Yes."

"And what about the other money?"

"That money was in his wallet, which we also vouchered."

"Was anything else taken from the defendant?"

"Yes. My partner took a Walkman from the defendant and threw it in the gutter."

"Why did he do that?"

"I guess he was angry. I don't know. He shouldn't have done it."

"Do you know if that Walkman was eventually recovered?"

"I believe it was. I believe defense counsel found it."

"Now, did you fill out any forms requesting that these items be tested for fingerprints?"

"Yes, I did."

"Which items?"

"The money, both sets of money. And also the purse, and its contents, and the wallet."

"Turning your attention back to the afternoon of the

murder, sir, once you stopped Damon Tucker and found the cash on him, what did you then do?"

"We took him back to the vic, the victim, who was on a gurney, getting ready to go into a bus. An ambulance, that is."

"And what happened there?"

"We took the defendant out of the car and brought him right in front of the woman."

"Was he handcuffed at that point?"

"No. We took off the cuffs when we got outa the car."

Big surprise. Barnett was lying about the cuffs, just like Newman.

Stoddard continued.

"What happened next?"

"I said, 'Is this the guy who shot you?' but I don't think she heard me. Then Officer Newman kinda leant over and said something right into her ear. I couldn't hear it. Then she kinda nodded, and Newman gave like a thumbs-up. He said, 'That's him.'"

"So you didn't hear the victim identify Damon?"

"No, I did not. Only Newman did. But he let us know right away."

"Nothing further."

I popped up, ready for action.

"Good morning, Officer. Now, on December 4, 1998, you and your partner, Smith, stopped my client Damon Tucker on the street, correct?"

"Correct."

"At the time he was running, wasn't he?"

"Yes, he was."

"And he was wearing a Walkman, which he was listening to, correct?"

"I believe so, yes, sir."

"Now, your partner, Officer Lorenzo Smith, he took

that Walkman off of Damon Tucker, didn't he?"

"Yes."

"He took that Walkman, and headphones, and he threw them in the gutter, down through the grating into that dark space below the street where no one ever looks. Right?"

"Well, sir, you looked there."

"And what did I find?"

"You found the Walkman that Smith threw down there."

"Officer, you've been a cop for eight years, right?"

"Uh-huh."

"Went to the police academy?"

"Yes, sir."

"One of the things they taught you is the importance of preserving evidence, correct?"

"Yes."

"That Walkman was evidence, wasn't it?"

"Yes."

"Were you intending to hide the fact that Damon Tucker was running with a Walkman on? Did you think that hurt your case against him?"

"Objection," squealed Stoddard. "Objection."

"I'll allow it," said the judge. He was enjoying this.

"Honestly, I didn't have time to think about it before Smith chucked it in the gutter."

"Did you report that to anyone?"

"No, sir."

"Is it not your obligation to let your superiors know if your partner has destroyed evidence in a murder case?"

"I should have."

"When did you finally decide to tell the truth?"

"Must have been after you found the Walkman, and it came back with Officer Smith's and Damon Tucker's prints on it."

"You had no choice then, did you?"

"No, sir."

"Were you prepared just to let the Walkman sit down in that gutter forever?"

"I guess I was."

"So it didn't matter to you that evidence in a murder case, what turned out to be evidence favorable to the defense, was being concealed?"

"Objection, argumentative."

"Sustained. You've made your point, counselor, now please move along."

Even Judge Wheeler, who had been more than fair, wasn't going to let me torture this poor cop forever on the stand. Most judges will sit back and let a defendant self-destruct totally on the stand, but they will usually jump in at some point to rescue a cop who's being pulverized by defense counsel.

"Now, when you brought Damon back to the crime scene, you hauled him in front of Ms. King, correct?"

"Yes. Sure."

"How far was Damon from Ms. King when she supposedly looked at him?"

"Maybe five feet."

"When you got out of your car, where was Officer Newman?"

"He was kneeling down next to the woman. He may have been holding her hand. He had his ear close to her mouth."

"Did you ever hear anything he said?"

"Actually, no, I couldn't hear nothing."

"Did you hear anything Ms. King said?"

"No."

"So you yourself don't know if Ms. King actually ID'd Mr. Tucker here, do you?"

"Yeah, sure she did."

"You didn't personally witness that, did you?"

"No. Newman did that."

The next witness was Officer Armstrong. He testified about finding the purse, the wallet, and the gun, and sending them all off for fingerprints. He, too, claimed not to have actually heard poor Charlotte King say a thing. I didn't need to cross him on all that. But I asked a few questions anyway. Juries like to see defense lawyers defend. Not asking a question leaves the impression of inaction or defeat. So I asked him about the ID, nailing down that he hadn't seen or heard a thing.

I had only one real question that mattered. He agreed that he hadn't found any gloves anywhere near the scene.

The identification was all going to come down to the word of Newman, the eager young humpster of a cop. No other cop could say a thing about this mythical identification. And Newman's testimony was shaky. Things were on an uptick right now. They would look good right up until we got to the goddamn fingerprint evidence. That would kill us.

But, first, we had the comic relief of the medical examiner. He was an Indian doctor named Singh Perm, which sounded like some kind of hairdresser problem but was apparently just his name. He was a small delicate man, who didn't look like he'd spent much time outside of his grotesque laboratory.

I will never understand why a doctor would choose to become a medical examiner. If you have spent ten seconds at the morgue, you will wonder about the sanity of anyone who goes all the way through medical school and then chooses to spend his or her life cutting up brutalized scarred and charred bodies, which smell like the worst rotting things you could ever imagine. The things they do to these dead bodies are beyond description, starting with peeling off the face, and removing the brain. The one time I visited the morgue I vomited. My goal now was to avoid any gruesome testimony. But a couple of points had to be made.

On direct, Dr. Perm was succinct, unemotional, and also pretty much unintelligible. His English was sophisticated, but his accent was so thick that you just had to guess what he was saying. Perhaps he became a medical examiner here in America because he was incapable of communicating with living people anywhere but in Bangladesh. The court reporter's brow furrowed deeply, but he must have heard this doctor before on the stand, because he appeared to take it all down. Stoddard was trying to ignore the problem, but the jurors were confused. Some were suppressing grins. I guess the only way you could laugh about an autopsy is to hear it described by a guy you can't understand.

"Doctor, what in your opinion was the cause of death?"

"Thengyu, yes, missive wind in cheskafty."

"And what was the cause of this massive wound in the chest cavity?"

"Yes, thengyu, Ideed nodree covear a booleet."

"I see. But what caused the wound?"

Eventually, the DA established that the wound was caused by a single gunshot from a large-caliber pistol, that it punctured the aorta, and the victim bled to death in a matter of minutes.

My turn. I had only one point to make, but it was important.

"Now, doctor, you just testified that the victim bled to death, or 'bled out' in medical parlance, in a matter of minutes. Correct?"

"Yis."

"Now, isn't it a fact, sir, that once she suffered this wound, her blood pressure would drop very very quickly?"

"Tees psible?"

"Likely, isn't it?"

"Ikud nodsay."

"Doctor, isn't it a fact she went into shock?"

"I was not adseen, Icon nodno." His voice got singsongy when he got defensive.

"Doctor, come on, if someone is shot in the aorta and bleeds to death in a matter of minutes, don't they first go into shock, into another state of consciousness?"

"Objection."

"Sustained."

I sat down. I'd made my point.

It was 4:45 in the afternoon. Golden sunlight was spilling through the high windows of the courtroom. The beam came through twenty-five feet up in the air and shed a soft light across the room onto the jury, as Judge Wheeler turned to look at them.

"Ladies and gentlemen, you've had a full first day. We'll break a little early today, but be here at nine sharp tomorrow, so we can get a good workday in. Remember, don't talk about the case with anyone, and please try to avoid all news accounts of this trial. Good night."

What did they think as they filed out past us? Most looked down at the ground, or into the distance. But one juror, number 7, one of the black women who worked as a nurse, looked right at me as she walked by and gave me a little nod. Juror number 11, the social worker, did the same. Stephens noticed it, and when the jury had left, she turned to Damon.

"Did you see, Damon? At least two of these sisters are

already in love with defense counsel here. That's a good first day."

Damon sighed. I realized I had never seen him smile.

CHAPTER 31

STEPHENS LOOKED AT ME as we hurried away from the courthouse toward our offices.

"How about dinner, counselor?"

Her desire to keep things professional was bumping into her general loneliness. I knew the feeling.

"Sure."

We went to a nice quiet sushi place on Twelfth Street.

"So what's your story, Arch?" she asked, sipping on her hot sake.

"I thought you'd never ask."

Her curiosity about my personal life hadn't exactly been overwhelming up to now.

"New Yorker?"

"Yup. I'm just another hairless Jew from the Lower East Side. My father was a bookie. An honest bookie."

She laughed. "Is he still in the business?"

Like many people who've lost parents young, she assumed everybody else her age still had 'em alive. I know. The heart is a lonely hunter.

"My parents died in a car crash. When I was eighteen."

Not an execution, but still, another conversation stopper. After a while she spoke.

"So we're both alone, aren't we, no parents, no siblings. Funny," she said.

"I wish it were funny. I see all these other people, with living parents, whom they fight with, bear grudges against, carry on about. I don't think they know what they have."

"Maybe your parents were really special. Maybe if they were still alive you wouldn't be fighting with them. Not everyone fights with their parents."

"I don't know," I said. "When they died, I was still too young to figure that out."

"Ever been married?"

"Yup. Before I knew I didn't want to be a corporate lawyer, I married one. Big mistake. She didn't think I billed enough, just like the partners in the firm I quit. You?"

"Never. Not 'til I quit this work."

"Keep this up, we'll apply you for sainthood."

"Fuck off, Arch. I don't believe in altruism. We're all driven to do what we do. We can't help ourselves."

The sushi came, and we gobbled it down. Heavy conversation, light food.

We said good night. We gave each other kind of an awkward wave. No kiss. No handshake. The usual rituals didn't seem to fit. I put her in a cab and walked home, as I almost always do, wishing I could take little Robin Stephens with me for the night.

At home, I clicked on the TV. The screen was filled with yet another sketch of me, gesturing during my cross-examination of Officer Newman. I'm in the foreground, in profile. Damon is seated in the center, scowling. Newman is on the stand, looking a little surprised.

The anchorman, a white man in his early forties with perfect features, jabbered on, superimposed over the drawing.

"The trial resumes tomorrow with the People's fingerprint evidence. It should be an important day. You may recall that the victim's fingerprints were found on the money recovered from Damon Tucker's pocket."

The anchorman dipped his head and grimaced slightly, silently saying to the millions of viewers out there that he, too, believed Damon Tucker was guilty.

As he spoke, the pastel sketch disappeared, and there was a clip of me walking out of 100 Centre Street, waving pleasantly.

I recognized the shot. It wasn't from today's proceedings, but from several weeks ago, during jury selection.

I was already file footage. I clicked off the TV and got to work on my cross of the fingerprint cop.

CHAPTER 32

THE NEXT MORNING at nine o'clock we were all back in our positions, ready to let the machinery of justice grind forward in the person of Detective John Boyce of the Police Fingerprint Unit, the People's next witness. I'd dealt with him in prior cases. He was a ruddy-faced man in his late fifties, wearing a suit with his gold badge pinned on the jacket pocket. He had an air of utter matter-of-factness. Listening to him, you got the deep feeling that fingerprints didn't lie, and neither did this guy. The fact that he looked like he took a drink now and then only added to his authenticity.

"Detective, what is fingerprinting?"

"Ma'am, fingerprinting is the process of securing your impression of the so-called papillary ridges of the fingers for the purpose of identification, usually in a criminal matter."

His accent was heavy Archie Bunker. His attitude was "Hey look, there are some long words involved here, but this ain't rocket science." It always played well with the jury.

"How does that work?"

"Well, if I understand your question, ma'am, what we do is, we compare an existing print in our file with a 'latent,' a print lifted from a crime scene, or from some object connected to a crime."

"In this case, sir, what objects did you examine for latent fingerprints?"

"Well, let's see here, we examined cash recovered from the defendant, the purse, the wallet, and the gun found in the street, and the contents of the purse and wallet."

"In layman's terms, what were the results of your work?"

She was keeping it short and simple. Some DAs dragged the details of fingerprinting out for an hour, boring the jury to death with details about the history of this arcane science. Not Ms. Stoddard. She was just homing right in on the damaging evidence.

"I found the defendant Damon Tucker's fingerprints on every one of the bills recovered from him, as well as on the video recovered from the victim's purse."

"And did you find Charlotte King's fingerprints on any of these items?"

"Yes, I did. I found her fingerprints on three of the bills recovered from Damon Tucker's blue jean pants pocket. I believe those there were your ten dollar denomination."

"How can you be certain about this information?"

"That's easy, ma'am. All fingerprints have distinct characteristics, or patterns, called arches, loops, and whorls. You've got your regular arch, your tented arch, your radial loop, your ulnar loop, your plain whorl, your central pocket loop, your double loop, and what we call your accidental."

"I see. And what is the significance of those different patterns?"

"Simple, really. The way those different types of characteristics exist on any particular fingerprint makes it absolutely unique. No two fingerprints in the world are alike. Even a portion of a print is unique. So we can compare the prints we took from Damon Tucker and Charlotte King's dead body to any print or partial print we recover from the crime scene. That's it."

It really was that simple. Fingerprints, to jurors, are like God speaking the gospel truth. Nevertheless, because overkill is the style of New York County prosecutors, Stoddard put into evidence the big blown-up photos of Damon's and Charlotte's loops, whorls, and ridges, to show just what this fellow was talking about. It wasn't necessary. I wasn't about to call him a liar. My cross would focus not on the prints this guy found, but on what he didn't find.

"Good morning, Detective. Let's talk for a moment about how you lift prints off an object."

I liked to start off, when questioning an expert, with a little demonstration of my own knowledge, however superficial it was in fact. And I like starting with a statement, a road map, instead of a question. It makes clear that I'm setting the agenda and tells the jury where I'm going.

"Now, when lifting prints off a smooth nonabsorbent surface, such as a gun, you typically dust the object, correct?"

"Yes."

"That's because the oil from the human finger stays on the surface of a nonabsorbent object, and the dusting material sticks to it, creating an image of the latent print. Correct?"

"Yes."

"But when lifting prints off paper, or other absorbent materials, you use reactive chemicals rather than nonreactive dust, right?"

"You got it right, counselor." He shrugged, as if to say "Yeah, yeah, yeah, but your client is still guilty."

"Typically, you would dip the specimen in a solution of silver nitrate, or ninhydrin, right?"

"You've done your homework, counselor."

"Thank you, Detective, I appreciate that. Now, you did in fact test the gun recovered in this case for prints, didn't you?"

"Yes, I did."

"What prints did you find?"

"Only the prints of the officer who recovered the gun. His name escapes me."

"No other prints?"

"No, sir."

"That would mean that the shooter either wore gloves when he or she handled the gun, or wiped it down afterward, correct?"

"Fair assumptions, counselor."

"So if, as the People claim, Damon Tucker was the shooter, he either had to be wearing gloves when he used the gun, or he wiped it down after the shooting."

"I'll buy that."

"Now, no gloves were recovered in this case, isn't that true?"

"I believe that's true."

"No cloth that could have wiped down a gun, or a purse or a wallet, was ever recovered in this case, isn't that true?"

"Counselor, you can wipe down a gun or a purse or a wallet on your shirt. Money's a little tougher to clean."

Zing. Zap. He was a real counterpuncher.

Boyce's answer told a story, much more than I had ever wanted to emerge from his testimony. The jurors could now picture Damon running a couple of blocks away, and then quickly wiping off and discarding the gun, the purse, and the wallet.

You didn't need to be Sherlock Holmes to conclude that Damon wouldn't wipe the money because he expected to keep it, and spend it, far away from Twentieth Street. The other stuff, since it was being discarded, had to be print free so it couldn't be connected to him when it was inevitably recovered near the scene.

"Detective, the plastic wrap surface of the video, that would've been easy to clean also, wouldn't it?"

"I guess he forgot that, counselor."

"Sir, you have no way of knowing when those prints got on the money, do you? Could've been minutes, hours, days, or even months, right?"

"True."

It wasn't much of a recovery. I'd been burned, like a rookie, asking one too many questions. Damon himself was going to testify about how his prints and Charlotte King's got on that money. I wanted the story coming out of his mouth first. I certainly didn't want the entirely credible detective giving his theory of the case, when his testimony could've simply been confined to prints, and nothing else.

"Nothing further."

I sat back down, trying not to slump too much.

That was the end of the People's case. Two days. A fraction of the time it took to pick the jury. The fact is, it was a simple and powerful case.

For the first time, I felt doubt creeping into my psyche, that self-defensive doubt that pops up when we've fucked something up and are looking for a way to blame someone else. Sure, I'd just made a slight tactical goof in crossing this cop, but so what? Damon was probably guilty. Was I really thinking this? I banished the thought from my mind. The pressure of dealing with death was playing tricks on my thinking. I'd done dozens of trials. In most of them, the evidence was not overwhelming against my clients, which was why we were going to trial in the first place. I'd always managed to believe in my own case right up until the jury's verdict, to buy into my own bullshit, whatever it was.

Was the pressure too much for me now? Because Damon's life was at stake, was I looking for a way to let myself off the hook?

My dark reverie was interrupted by the judge.

"Ladies and gentlemen, that concludes the People's case. Tomorrow is Friday, my regular calendar day, when I handle all the other cases on my docket. You will have the day off. We will resume on Monday, with the defense case. Have a good weekend. Do not talk among yourselves about this trial, and avoid all media accounts. Thank you."

As I was leaving, Stoddard tugged on my sleeve and pulled me into the clerk's office, which gave us a little privacy.

"Gold, I just wanted to let you know, we had the mother let my detective into the victim's apartment last night. We checked out her computer. The hard drive was installed last summer, not the day she died."

She looked at me with a little pity, as if she felt sorry that I was grasping at straws for my poor doomed client.

I wasn't surprised at this news. Whoever had done the job for Yates had screwed it up. Yates must've figured that out and had someone go back to clean it up. They'd substituted an entirely different computer, with an older hard drive. Tracks covered. Evidence gone.

CHAPTER 33

"WHAT ARE YOU DOING WITH THIS DAY OFF, ROB?" I asked Stephens on Friday morning.

Right now, she was mostly a spectator at the trial. Her first big job—jury selection—was over. Her second big job—appeal—had yet to rear its ugly head, and might never. So she wasn't exactly overwhelmed with work on Damon's case.

"Actually, I'm reading the papers in a case that's about to go to trial upstate, in Buffalo."

"That your next stop?"

"You bet, counselor. And you? Today?"

"Me? I don't know. I'm thinking of heading up to Pittsfield, in Massachusetts, where Yates grew up. I haven't seen much on his childhood in the press, and I'm curious. Maybe I'll find something in the local papers up there."

"Wow, you *are* desperate, aren't you?"

She was blunt as ever. I wasn't feeling particularly tactful myself.

"Well, you've already convicted Damon, haven't you? You're just sitting around waiting for transcript to read."

"And *you're* dreaming. So what if Yates was screwing her. So what if her shrink got mugged four days later. So what if you *say* but can't *prove* that someone messed with her computer. You don't have shit. Not a thing on this guy. I'm more likely to find help for Damon in his goddamn trial transcript than you are out there playing Dick Tracy with Yates. The guy is the most powerful private investigator in the world. I mean, let's face it, Yates is so insulated, so connected, so protected, that you can't get to him in the present, so you're going into the past. Good luck, Arch. I think you're wasting your time."

I stormed out. I didn't hold it against her personally. I still wanted to take her home with me. But she was an *appellate* lawyer. She couldn't help assuming that Damon would be convicted. That was her job.

I poked my head into Layden's office, to tell him where I was going. He shook his head grimly.

"Arch, stay out of trouble, okay? You should be focusing on this trial, not running around New England. Do you really think you're going to turn up anything on this guy Yates? Come on! You're in the middle of a trial going ID, and you're out there looking for more evidence *during the trial*? That's some wacky shit, Arch."

An hour later, I was on the highway, heading to the town of Pittsfield, Massachusetts, in the heart of western New England, 150 miles north of New York City, but a world away, where, according to the clippings I'd found online, Yates had grown up. Details of Yates's early life were scant. There'd been a fair amount of publicity about him in the last decade, most of it quite favorable. But no article talked about his youth. They all just said he'd left Pittsfield to go to college in 1962.

Pittsfield was an old New England city, population sixty thousand, the biggest town in Berkshire County. The place had been transformed early in the twentieth century when General Electric built a huge manufacturing plant, acres and acres of redbrick factory buildings, which provided a good living for fifteen thousand able-bodied men who built the appliances that became standard issue in most American homes: the radio, the dishwasher, the washing machine, the dryer, and, later, the television. Then, in the 1980s, GE closed the whole thing. Like many big manufacturing companies, GE found it was more economical to send most of its production operations overseas, leaving behind only a high-tech plastics division, which employed a few hundred computer operators.

Now, in the 1990s, the downtown looked like a ghost town. There was plenty of material for a Bruce Springsteen song in the closed movie theaters, empty storefronts, and old men sitting in little parks and on the benches that ran along Main Street. The town still had plenty of people in it, but half of them were retired, and the rest didn't have much more to do than drink and drive, hunt, fish, smash up their cars, fix up their cars, and smash them up again. Those were the men. The women tried to stay married to these men, and to raise children with enough education to leave.

Of course, when the weather got warm, all the rich folks from New York City came up to the Berkshires to spend time in their summer houses. A kind of two-tier economy had developed in the county. There were plenty of upscale restaurants and gourmet food shops that the locals couldn't afford, places that slowed or shut down during the long cold winters. But these summer folks avoided Pittsfield. It was too depressing. They went to the picturesque towns nearby that hadn't industrialized. Pittsfield was a town to leave if you possibly could, whether you were born there or just passing through.

I was sitting in a dumpy diner on Main Street, eating a tuna sandwich and reading a copy of the *Berkshire Eagle,* the local daily paper that tried to emulate the *New York Times* by carrying the *Times*'s lead articles as its own on the front page, but also served as the bible of local

affairs. The local news included births, deaths, high
school graduations, arrests, car accidents, anniversaries,
birthdays, just about every goddamn little detail of life in a
town where nothing much mattered, because nothing was
going on, so all the little things mattered instead. Nobody
here was concerned with world events, or consumed with
their careers, or how much dough they made, or how much
their house looked like it cost. The monotonous rhythm of
life in Pittsfield was written in black and white, in this
quaint local paper. I decided to make the *Berkshire Eagle*
archives my first stop.

Mrs. Santoro, the white-haired women who was the
keeper of the records, up on the fourth floor of the *Eagle*
building, a beautiful old art deco structure right on Main
Street, didn't seem terribly interested in the details of
my research project. She set me up in the records room,
showed me how to use the index, and happily retrieved
the particular rolls of microfilm I'd requested.

The paper had been meticulous in its indexing. Every
individual whose name appeared in the paper was part
of the General Index, modeled after the *New York Times*
General Index. Recently the paper had been sold to a huge
national chain, but prior to that, and since its founding in
the nineteenth century, it had been in the same family,
and it had tried to model itself as a mini *New York Times*,
including its archival system. For anyone looking to check
out life in the second half of the twentieth century, this was a
treasure trove. Unlike the online news services, microfilm
was an actual edition of the paper, layout, photos, and all.
It sucked you right back into that time.

I didn't actually know Yates's date of birth. I assumed
it was in the mid-1940s, just as World War II was ending,
since according to the information I already had, he'd
gone off to Boston University on a scholarship in 1962.

Trouble was, there was no mention at all of Yates in the index. None.

Time to talk to Mrs. Santoro. I went over to her desk and cleared my throat.

"Excuse me, ma'am, but I'm striking out over here. I wondered if you might have any suggestions."

She looked up at me through thick glasses that magnified her eyes, revealing every detail of her wrinkled skin. She was an old-timer.

"Who are you looking for, young man?"

"Looking for details on a fellow named David Yates. Birth announcement. Anything else I can find. I know he was born in Pittsfield, left here to go to college in 1962, and never came back, but I'm not finding any Yates in the index that matches up to him. Just more recent stuff. Yateses who aren't connected to him. Any suggestions?"

"Which Yates you looking for? The one that runs that big outfit down in New York City?"

"How'd you know?"

"Well, you're not the first person to come poking around about him. I guess he's a big shot down there. Don't think he ever made it into our paper."

"Funny you should know about him. I mean, to the general public, he's not that famous. Who else came up here checking him out?"

"Couple of magazine reporters several years back. Didn't like 'em. Real snotty city folks. I like you a little better."

"Thank you, ma'am."

"Are you another journalist?"

"Actually, no. I'm a lawyer. I'm working on a case involving an employee of his. I'm doing a little research on his background. Truth is, I'm finding it a little strange there's no record of him as a child here in Pittsfield."

The woman shook her head.

"You won't find David Yates in this paper. He changed his name when he turned eighteen. Used to be Norton Gorham."

I looked at her with obvious disbelief.

"Really!"

"Don't take my word for it. Go down to the county clerk's office and check out name changes. It's a legal proceeding, and they keep nice records of it. They don't want anyone totally slipping through the cracks, you know."

I did as I was told. The county clerk's office was in the town hall, a beautiful granite four-story Florentine number, built a hundred years ago. Through a second-floor door, I found the county clerk's office.

Mr. Trevor was the blandest of the bland, a middle-aged white man in a cardigan sweater, humming to himself, happy to be of civil service. I told him I was looking for a record of legal name changes, and he disappeared through a back door, emerging five minutes later with a huge bound leather volume that looked to be at least a century old.

"We don't pull this out too often. People don't even know it exists. I'm sure there are a lot of stories behind the names in here, believe me. This particular volume dates back to 1879."

I opened the big book. Name change wasn't the most common occurrence in Berkshire County, maybe twenty to thirty per year, but each was carefully entered into the leather-bound book and available for public inspection. It didn't take me long to find Yates's name.

On October 23, 1962, just five days after his eighteenth birthday, a fellow named Norton Gorham, in a proceeding before the county court, had legally changed his name to David Yates. The judge's order was neatly entered by hand into the big leather ledger, noting the date, the old name, and the new name. Thank you, Mrs. Santoro. I went racing back to the *Berkshire Eagle* record room.

The first mention of Norton Gorham was a birth announcement. October 20, 1944. Judith and Charles Gorham announced the birth of their son, Norton, at Berkshire Medical Center. The baby weighed six pounds five ounces.

The next mention of Norton Gorham was five years later, on December 26, 1949, and it was on the front page.

MAN SLAIN BY WIFE AS SON LOOKS ON

Local police were called to 245 North Road in Chester this afternoon after a neighbor who came over to borrow some sugar found a gruesome sight, a five-year-old boy, who told police that a day earlier, he had seen his mother shoot and kill his father in the family's kitchen. According to Detective Broder of the Pittsfield Police Department, the boy, Norton Gorham Jr., saw his mother, Judy Gorham, shoot Norton Gorham Sr., in the head with a shotgun. The woman then fled in the family pickup. She remains at large and is considered armed and dangerous. The boy, who was being treated for psychological shock, told police he stayed with the body because he was hoping his father would "get better." The boy was covered with his father's blood when police came to the remotely located house. The nearest neighbors are half a mile away.

Norton Gorham Sr. worked at the GE plant, on the dishwasher assembly line. His wife, Judith Gorham, formerly Judith Reston, reportedly was employed as a dancer at a local club, the Pussycat Lounge. According to police records, she had three recent arrests for prostitution. The family pickup is missing, and she is presumed to have fled in the vehicle. The boy has been placed with relatives. Although he was a witness to the killing, his young age makes it doubtful the prosecution could call him as a witness, according to local authorities.

Holy Shit. My heart was pounding. Smooth and slick-looking Yates, sitting at the top of the corporate espionage world, he'd had a pretty rough start in the world. Right out of a horror movie. Watching your Pussycat Lounge mom shoot the head off your factory worker dad, and then leave you with Daddy's bloody body, where you stayed for a day, doing God knows what. I couldn't even imagine the damage to the poor kid.

The next mention of the Gorham case was a month later. A prostitute had been found dead near the West Side Highway, in New York City. Heroin overdose. Relatives in Pittsfield had gone down to the city and identified the body. Judith Gorham. Possible suicide, possible accidental overdose. Her son, Norton Gorham Jr., would remain with his paternal grandmother and grandfather.

I found no more articles on the case. It had faded from public consciousness, and Norton Gorham had grown up with his grandparents. A check of the death notices revealed that they had died in the 1960s, one in 1964 and one in 1965, after Norton Gorham had left home, changed himself into David Yates, and started a new life for himself away from the horrors of his early years.

What had made Judith kill her husband? Was he a good man, or a bad man? Did she kill him because he wanted her to stop dancing, to stop turning tricks, to stop drinking and drugging? Did she kill him because he was going to leave her and take the kid with him? Had *he* harmed the boy? Was it an accident? Was it self-defense? It didn't matter after all these years, but I wanted to know.

I heard someone clear their throat behind me. I'd been so engrossed, I hadn't heard Mrs. Santoro approach. She was looking at the microfilm screen over my shoulder.

"That was quite a case, young man. I do remember it well. One of the worst crimes ever happened 'round here."

"Actually, Mrs. Santoro, I didn't know a thing about it until you gave me a little guidance and sent me over to the county clerk's office. How'd you know?"

"I followed the case. I felt for that boy. Did you see the byline on that second article. I wrote it. Back when I was the only woman reporter on this paper. I remember that boy well. He was a tough, smart little kid. But he had a look in his eyes that told me he'd never trust a soul on this earth again. I always wondered what would become of him. I'm one of the few folks here who knew that he changed his name. His grandparents were friends of mine. They told me. It broke their hearts. They raised him like their own son, and he just blew out of here with a new name as soon as he could. I felt sorry for them. But I couldn't blame him. Life had been too cruel to him. He wanted at least the illusion of starting over. Now he's a big success, isn't he? I doubt he's happy."

Driving back to the city, I turned the whole hideous story over and over again in my mind. It didn't prove a damn thing about Damon's case, that was for sure. And where did Charlotte King fit into all of this? Was she some kind of payback for Judith Gorham's sins a half century ago?

I shook my head in disgust. I was so goddamn sure

Yates had killed Charlotte King, but I still had nothing but my gut and my wild imagination to back it up.

On the way back to Manhattan, Kathy Dupont called me on my cell phone.

"Hi, cutie." she said. "Listen, I just wanted to thank you for all your help. I got that TOP, and the asshole's been leaving me alone. So that's good."

"Glad to hear it, Kathy."

"You working on that big death penalty case?"

"I sure am."

"Yeah, I saw it on TV. Just a drawing of you. You look better in person."

"Thanks."

"Listen, why don't you come and see my show?"

"Kathy, that's not really my thing, know what I mean?"

"Not really. What kinda guy doesn't like a hot strip club?"

I didn't really have an answer. The reality was, I just found it a bit too much. Was it a puritanical streak in me? Or was I just a slave to political correctness? Who knew? I knew how I felt, but not why. So I made up an excuse.

"Look, your case is still pending, isn't it?"

"Yeah, I guess so. I go back to court next week when it's gonna be dismissed."

"That's great. But 'til then, I just don't think it would be appropriate for me to come see you . . . dance."

She laughed.

"You're definitely different, Gold, but I like that. Bye."

I called Goodman. No news.

CHAPTER 34

"WHEN DID DAMON TUCKER begin working at Video Edge?"

"Must've been about eighteen months ago."

"What were his duties there?"

"General stuff. A clerk. Retrieving videos from the back. Ringing up rentals and purchases. Familiarity with the computer system. Restocking. The usual routine."

John Taback, the manager of Video Edge, with his thin pasty face, and salt-and-pepper ponytail, was our first witness.

Taback's face told the jury he'd tried every drug available since Woodstock. He'd put on a thrift-shop shirt and tie for the occasion, but he still looked like the bass player in a bad rock band entering rehab for the tenth time.

"How much was Damon paid?" I asked.

"He was part-time. No benefits. He got nine dollars per hour, and he worked twenty hours a week. He was paid weekly, by check."

"What day of the week was he paid?"

"Fridays. The day he got arrested, he'd been paid."

"Now, you said he was paid by check. Did you generally cash the checks for him?"

"Yes, I did."

"On December 4, 1998, did you cash Damon's paycheck?"

"Yes, I did."

"How much was that check for?"

"One hundred eighty dollars."

I picked up the actual check, which I had taken from the video store, and I handed it to Taback.

"Sir, is this the check that you cashed for Damon?"

"Yes, it is."

"How do you know?"

"Well, it's made out to him. It's a check from our store. It has the date on it, December 4, 1998. And it's endorsed by Damon on the back, to Video Edge."

"I ask that this document be entered into evidence."

The judge turned to Stoddard, who was looking just a wee bit surprised.

"No objection."

"Please mark the document as Defense Exhibit A."

"Where did you get the cash to give him?"

"From the cash register."

"What time was that?"

"That would have been around five o'clock, when Damon's shift ended."

"What if anything did you see him do with those bills when you gave them to him?"

"He counted them out, one by one, to make sure he'd gotten the full 180 dollars. I believe he was paid with eighteen 10 dollar bills."

"You're certain about that?"

"Yes, I am."

"Why is it you remember that?"

"Because when he got arrested, I thought about that whole day many times."

"Where did those bills come from again, Mr. Taback?"

"They came from the cash register."

I paused and gave everybody a few seconds to digest this new information.

"Do you have a safe in the store?"

"Yes, we do. But it's only opened at the end of the night, around ten o'clock, when we close. At that point, I put all the cash remaining in the register into the safe, for safekeeping overnight. Twice a week, a Brinks truck comes, picks up the cash, and takes it to the bank. Other than that, no money is taken out of the safe."

"So all employees who want to cash their checks with you get their cash from the register?"

"That's correct."

"There's enough cash in the register for that purpose?"

"Yes. We do a good business."

"Mr. Taback, let's talk about your computer system at the store for a moment."

It was a statement, not a question, but since it told everyone in the courtroom where we were going next, no one objected.

"Now, every time there's a sale or a rental, the bar code on that particular video gets scanned into the computer, is that right?"

"Yes."

"Does that generate a customer receipt?"

"Yes, it does."

"What is printed on that receipt?"

"Date, time, form of payment, item purchased or rented, and code of employee making the sale."

"After this information is printed out and given to the customer, does it remain in the computer?"

"Yes."

"So, by reviewing your computer, you can see that a copy of a particular video was sold at a particular time?"

"Yes, that's right."

"Was a copy of *Fatal Attraction* sold on December 4, 1998?"

"Yes, according to our computer, at 4:58 P.M."

"According to the code in the computer, who made that sale?"

"We can see from the computer that Damon Tucker made the sale."

"By the way, are those codes a secret?"

"No, not really. But everybody wants credit for their own sales, so I can't see why anyone would punch in a code other than their own."

"Is there anything stopping them from actually doing so?"

"Nothing other than that they might get fired if I found out."

I was conducting my direct examination a little like a cross, bringing out the weaknesses in his testimony, as well as the strengths. Layden taught me that. It adds to our credibility with the jury and takes some of the wind out of the DA's cross.

"Can the computer print out all this information that is contained on the customer receipt?"

"Yes, it can."

I handed him a document.

"What is that, sir?"

"That is a printout of the receipt generated by the sale of *Fatal Attraction* on December 4, 1998. It says the time, 4:58, the date, that cash was paid, and that Damon Tucker made the sale."

"I ask that this document be moved into evidence as Defense Exhibit B."

Again, Stoddard looked a little worse for wear, but she offered no objection.

"So moved."

I took the check and the receipt. Holding them up, I addressed the judge.

"Your Honor, I'd ask that these documents be published to the jury at this time."

The judge nodded. A court officer took the receipt and the check from me and handed them to juror number one, who solemnly examined them, and then passed them along. All twelve jurors and four alternates did the same. The courtroom was quiet. It was one of those rare moments when no lawyers were talking, and the jurors themselves, for a few moments, dictated the pace of things.

It seemed to last much longer than six minutes. This is real drama, when the jurors get to handle evidence that has just been revealed for the first time and that didn't come from the prosecution. I looked over at Stoddard. She was staring straight ahead.

The last juror had finished examining the stuff. The judge turned to me.

"Anything further from this witness, Mr. Gold?"

"Nothing further."

Stoddard's cross was brilliant. She really knew how to think on her feet. Plus, she knew something I didn't know, even though I'd asked Taback about it over and over again. He had a drug conviction, for selling LSD, ten years ago. He'd lied to me about it. Looking at him, I'd suspected as much, but when I'd asked him directly, on Saturday, in my office, he'd denied it. Unfortunately, defense counsel has no way to check a witness's record. Only the DA and the police have access to New York State's data bank of everyone's arrest and conviction history. I had to take his word for it. Stoddard didn't. With his date of birth, which I was obliged to give her at the beginning of the trial, she could easily check his criminal record.

Still, she was on tricky terrain. Technically speaking, she couldn't introduce into evidence the fact of his drug-dealing conviction. If she asked him, "Sir, do you have a conviction for dealing drugs?" and he lied, and said, "No, I don't," she was bound by his answer. That's because she was getting into what's called "collateral extrinsic" evidence. It sounds complicated, but it isn't.

The basic point is that when cross-examining witnesses, other than the defendant, you ask questions about their past at your own risk. If they won't admit the truth, or give you the answer you want, too bad. You can't introduce extrinsic evidence to prove that they're lying. If the rule were any other way, then every trial would digress into a series of minitrials, with each side trying to prove that the other side's witnesses had gotten parking tickets, or failed to pay their rent, or bounced a check, or smoked a joint, all with the goal of discrediting their testimony regarding the evidence they were giving at the trial. The courts across America have simply said, sorry, but no way. Unless the issue goes directly to the case on trial, counsel has to live with the answer he or she gets. Proceed at your own risk. So if Stoddard asked Taback about his drug conviction, and he had the balls just to lie about it, she was stuck.

Instead, she did something very goddamn sneaky. Even though she knew she couldn't introduce his rap sheet, she went over to her table, picked it up, and then, looking at it, and appearing to read from it, she asked Taback the big question.

"Sir, isn't it a fact that you have a criminal record, a conviction for dealing LSD in 1988?"

He went white as a sheet. He shot me a look, like, Oh shit, I can't believe this is happening. And then he admitted that yes, ten years ago he'd sold an undercover cop enough LSD to kill an elephant, even though he didn't have to, even though, if he'd only told me that he had a drug conviction, I would have told him to deny it on the stand if he was asked, since his denial couldn't be contradicted.

"So, Mr. Taback, when you take LSD, you hallucinate, is that correct?"

"Well, yeah, I guess it depends how much you take."

"When did you last take LSD?"

"I dunno, maybe a couple years ago."

"Did *you* take enough to hallucinate?"

He laughed nervously.

"Objection! Objection!"

I was yelling. There wasn't much else I could do.

"Your Honor, may we approach?"

"Yes," said Judge Wheeler, although we both knew the damage had already been done.

Up at the bench, I went ballistic, in a whisper, of course.

"Judge, let the record reflect that the DA deceived this witness into admitting a criminal conviction by waving around his rap sheet, as if it were admissible, when she knows that it is not. It's one of the cheapest, sleaziest tricks I've ever seen in my career. I'd expect more from the district attorney herself, in this county's first death penalty case. I'm moving for a mistrial. My client's rights have been violated!"

Judge Wheeler let out a sigh.

"I'm afraid I can't do that, Mr. Gold. The fact is, the witness does have the conviction, and he admitted it. There just isn't enough, on this record, for me to do a thing. Ms. Stoddard, that wasn't pretty. Matter of fact, it was ugly. But you've gotten away with it."

She was defensive, as she should have been.

"It's nothing defense counsel doesn't do every day in this building. We all know it."

The judge gave her a withering look.

"No more LSD questions, Ms. Stoddard. Now, counsel, step back."

What a mess. It didn't get much better.

Stoddard continued.

"Now, Mr. Taback, you say the cash you gave Damon, those eighteen 10 dollar bills, came from the cash register, correct?"

"Yes, yes," said Taback, grateful to leave the LSD fiasco behind.

"But you do have a safe in the store?"

"Yes, we do."

"You keep money there as well?"

"Yes."

"How can you be positive those bills came from the cash register, and not from the safe?"

"Because I remember taking them from the cash register. That's how I always do it, to pay employees."

"Are you sure your memory wasn't clouded by anything?"

"Objection."

"Overruled."

"Yes, I'm sure."

If he had denied his LSD conviction, this little bit of cross wouldn't have hurt us at all. Now I wasn't so sure.

"Sir, each employee has a code that they punch in the register when they make a sale, right?"

"That's right."

"Are the codes secret?"

"Not really."

"Is there anything to prevent one employee from punching in another employee's code?"

"I suppose not, if they knew that particular code."

"So, if another employee used Damon's code, it would appear that he had handled the sale, when in fact he hadn't, isn't that right?"

"I suppose so, but I instruct each employee not to give out their code to anyone else."

"But you have no way of knowing whether they follow your instructions or not, do you?"

"Actually, I regularly check receipts to see if they match up. So far, we haven't had any problems."

"Would you call the fact that Damon Tucker murdered Charlotte King a problem?"

"Objection!" I thundered.

"Sustained," said the judge.

"Nothing further," said Stoddard, and sat down.

She was good, no question about it.

NEXT WAS Damon's fellow worker, Debbie Ringle, the punk girl with the purple hair. Not much about her had changed since I'd first interviewed her months ago. She was wearing a little less metal on her face, perhaps out of deference to the judicial process, but she didn't inspire confidence or respect. Her voice was unexpected, gentle, and intelligent, in complete contrast to her scary look.

"Ms. Ringle, on December 4, 1998, did Charlotte King come into the video store?"

"Yes, she did."

"How do you know?"

"Well, at the time, I didn't know who she was. I just remember this attractive woman coming in and buying a copy of *Fatal Attraction*. Damon was at the register, and when she paid, and he gave her change, he said, 'Be careful out there, sister.' "

She giggled nervously. Her hand went up to her mouth. She had a nice smile. She was obviously nervous, and also obviously telling the truth. I liked the way she was coming across.

"I'm going to show you what has been marked as People's Exhibit 6."

I handed her the video, inside the police plastic sealed bag. She turned it over a few times.

"Do you recognize that video?"

"Well, it's a copy of *Fatal Attraction*, and it came from our store."

"How do you know it came from your store?"

"It still has the sticker on it from our system."

"Is that unique to your store?"

"Actually, it is."

"By the way, how do you know it was Charlotte King whom Damon sold the video to that day?"

"I know because the next day you came into the store and interviewed me."

"Go on."

"Yeah. You showed me a picture of Charlotte King from the paper, and I said, Bingo, that's the women who came into the store yesterday."

"Do you have any doubt about the fact that Charlotte King came into the store that Friday?"

"No."

"About what time was it when she came in?"

"Late afternoon. Around five. I remember because she was Damon's last sale of the day. Then he closed out his register, cashed his paycheck with the boss, and left, like he did every Friday."

"Now, when you say she was Damon's sale, what do you mean?"

"Oh, I mean she gave him the video and the money at the register. He scanned in the video, and he took the bills, put 'em in the register, and gave her change."

"That's what happens in every purchase, right?"

"Yes."

"How do you happen to remember December 4, 1998, so well?"

"Well, everybody read about Damon's arrest in the paper the next day and saw the story on TV. At the store we, yunno, like reconstructed what happened the previous afternoon, cuz, like, we just couldn't believe that he could've done this crime."

She put her hand up to her mouth again, this time with no giggle.

"Was I not supposed to say that?"

There was an uncomfortable moment before the judge piped up.

"Ms. Ringle, please just answer the questions as best you can." He turned his gaze to me.

"Anything further, Mr. Gold?"

"Yes, Judge, one more question." I turned toward the purple-haired witness.

"Ms. Ringle, are you friends with Damon Tucker?"

"Not really. Like, we've never socialized outside of the video store, really, like, ever."

"Nothing further."

It was Stoddard's turn.

"Now, Ms. Ringle, Damon's code is on every receipt he rings up, correct?"

"Yes."

"So it's not exactly a secret."

"No, I guess not."

"Yes or no, ma'am?"

"No, it's not a secret."

"So nothing's to prevent you, if you wanted to, from using his code when you rang up a sale, correct?"

"I would never do that."

Stoddard looked at the judge.

"I'll ask that the answer be stricken as nonresponsive."

Judge Wheeler was getting tired of Stoddard.

"Ms. Stoddard, just ask your next question, please. We'll leave it up to the jury to judge the credibility of all the testimony."

"Whether or not you now say you would never do that, Ms. Ringle, if you wanted to, there's nothing to stop you?"

"Except that if I got caught I'd get in trouble. I like my job. I don't wanna lose it."

Stoddard had made her point, but she wasn't demolishing Ringle the same way she'd dispensed with Taback. She tried with no success to get Ringle to admit that she wanted to help Damon. It didn't fly. This purple-haired girl wasn't looking to help anybody. Period.

The fact is, Stoddard couldn't really deny, at this point, that Damon had sold the video to Charlotte King. How else did his fingerprints get on the video? She'd made some headway discrediting our theory about the eighteen 10 dollar bills, that was true. The jury could decide that Taback was not a reliable witness. But she hadn't really made a case as to why Taback or Ringle would lie for Damon. After all, the date and time on the receipt were not in dispute. Unless they'd both known that Damon was about to go out and rob then shoot Charlotte King, which was a ridiculous idea, they'd have no reason to help him cover up his actions ahead of time. She'd kicked up a lot of dust, but that's what happens in trials. Stoddard was going to have to incorporate the fact that Damon sold the video to Charlotte King into her version of events.

CHAPTER 35

DR. WUN HO LU was a whole lot easier to understand than Dr. Singh Perm. Dr. Lu was the medical examiner for New Haven, Connecticut, and a professor at Yale Medical School. We'd hired him to look over the ME's report, and to actually reexamine Charlotte King's body, so he could reach his own conclusions regarding her mortal wounds.

"Good morning, Dr. Lu."

"Good morning, Mr. Gold."

"Dr. Lu, did you have an opportunity to examine the body of Charlotte King in the morgue?"

"Yes, I did."

"And did you also review the official autopsy report?"

"Yes, I did."

"Dr. Lu, in layman's terms, can you describe the wound that Ms. King suffered?"

"Yes, she was shot in abdomen. Based on nature of wound, kind of damage done, it was high-caliber bullet. I understand gun recovered at scene was .45 caliber automatic."

"Objection."

"Sustained."

Who cared if Dr. Lu wasn't supposed to testify about the gun? Who cared if it was hearsay? We were just trying to make things clear to the jury, and the point was made—high-caliber bullet.

"What was the nature of the wound, Doctor?"

"Bullet sliced though abdominal wall, lacerated liver,

and ruptured aorta, causing immediate massive loss of blood into abdominal cavity. Massive amount."

This guy didn't use articles or pronouns, but he was otherwise perfectly straightforward.

"Tell the jury, what is the aorta?"

"Aorta is main artery leading from heart. It is largest single artery in human body, and under greatest pressure."

"What does that mean, in layman's terms?"

"That means if severed or ruptured, massive internal bleeding occurs, blood pressure drops dramatically, person goes into immediate end-stage shock, and dies within minutes."

It didn't sound good.

"What would be the mental condition of a person minutes after such a wound?"

"That person would be severely impaired, unable to see clearly, or speak. They would be in highly altered dream state."

"In your opinion, was Charlotte King in such a state?"

"No doubt, yes."

"In your opinion, Doctor, would she be able to make the sort of identification the People claim she made in this case?"

"Absolutely impossible. By the time the police brought Mr. Tucker in front of her she was no longer able to see in the normal sense. Her blood pressure would be so low after a few minutes of internal bleeding that she would be in massive shock. When a person goes into shock, one of first things affected is vision. People in shock suffer a reversal of positive and negative, sort of like seeing the world as a photographic negative. They also cannot hear. Sounds become remote and distorted. Low blood pressure basically distorts vision and hearing. That is what happened to Charlotte King."

"Do you disagree with the findings of Dr. Singh Perm?"

"Well, Dr. Perm's autopsy report is entirely accurate. However, conclusions he draws as to victim's ability to make an identification are to me way off base. Way off base. They are not credible."

"Thank you, Doctor. Nothing further."

Stoddard popped up. She knew she had to damage Dr. Lu one way or another. Sure, she had the fingerprints, and they were turning out to be the centerpiece of her case, but she couldn't just let the good Dr. Lu blow her identification testimony right out of the water.

"Dr. Lu, the massive internal bleeding, which you claim led to shock in Ms. King, that was because of the wound to the aorta, correct?"

"Yes. There was bleeding from other wounds, in muscle, in liver, but nothing compared to flow from aorta."

"Doctor, Ms. King's aorta was not completely severed, was it?"

"No, it was not."

"In fact, it was still at least 50 percent intact at the point of contact with the bullet, yes or no?"

"Yes, but—"

"All I want, sir, is a yes or a no. Thank you."

"Objection. She can't put words in this witness's mouth. He has to be allowed to answer the question."

"Overruled."

"Yes or no, sir, Ms. King's aorta was at least 50 percent intact?"

"Yes."

"Now, a fully severed aorta would lead to almost immediate death, correct?"

"Yes."

"But Ms. King did not die immediately, did she?"

"No. It took her several minutes to bleed to death."

"And the smaller the wound to the aorta, the less the level of shock, as well, correct?"

"Yes, I suppose up to a point."

"Now, you did not personally observe Ms. King, did you?"

"No."

"You are speculating as to her mental state, correct?"

"I have no doubt about her condition."

"Isn't it a fact that patients in hospitals suffer aortic damage, such as aortic aneurusms, and survive for hours or days?"

"Yes, it is."

"So not all damage to the aorta leads to immediate shock or death?"

"True."

"Nothing further."

We broke for the day. That night, Stephens and I worked some more with Damon. He was scheduled to take the stand the next morning. We sat in a tiny cage behind the courtroom, with Damon separated from us by heavy-gauge chicken wire. The place stank of sweat and piss. It was hard to breathe, let alone concentrate or think.

I knew Damon had to testify, but I still wasn't very confident that he could do it without exploding in some damaging way I couldn't even foresee. So far, he'd been a model defendant in the courtroom. No outbursts. No explosions. But I could feel the pressure building.

We went over his direct testimony again and again, honing each answer, trying to get his deep anger to recede just a little so that he would be more sympathetic and less threatening to the jury.

It was uphill work.

We practiced cross-examination, so he'd see what it was like to have a hostile prosecutor right in your face. He didn't take it well.

"Look, Damon, your life is going to depend on your performance tomorrow. Remember, it's a performance. The fact that you feel indignant, angry, that you feel that you're being framed, none of those emotions matter to the jury. You've chosen to go to trial. You've got to convince them it's not all just a big con. The way to do that is not to be angry, but to be sad, to appear to be the second victim, not the murderer who's trying to get off."

He might have exploded at this speech, but he didn't. That was a good sign.

Stephens jumped in.

"Damon. Archie's just trying to get you into the right frame of mind. You know all this, because we've been repeating it like a broken record. You can't be angry. It doesn't work with this jury. You've got to be quiet, sad, another victim. We all know what you're going to say. That's not the issue. It's how you say it that's going to determine what this jury decides."

We all paused. Nobody wanted to hear what Stephens was going to say next.

"Look, Damon, God forbid you're convicted. Then, we've got to save your life. And if the jury hates you, they're not going to want to let you live. They have to emotionally connect to you, as a fellow human being. That's what they have to do."

"A fellow human being," he repeated. "A fucking fellow human being."

Suddenly he exploded. He slammed his fist into the steel door. The door dented. His hand broke. We could all hear it. The guards came running. I jumped out from the booth.

"It's cool, guys, it's cool. He just banged the door. That's all. He's gonna need medical attention. I think he broke his hand."

They took him away. We could hear his sobs echoing down the hallway.

I hoped and prayed he'd gotten something out of his system, that he could play the role he had to play tomorrow, the role of a lifetime.

CHAPTER 36

"THE DEFENSE CALLS Damon Tucker."

Damon stood up and walked to the witness box. Big guy. Big fucking guy. It didn't help the case that Damon was physically intimidating. The charge, a shooting, did not require physical strength, yet I knew that Damon's size somehow made it more likely to the jury that he was able to pull the trigger.

He took his seat in the box, and placed his hand, which was in a white plaster cast, on the Bible.

"Yes, I do," he intoned seriously, beginning the defense of his life. I knew he was in a lot of pain, although he didn't seem to be showing it. Physical pain and anger fuel each other. I don't know if he was nervous. I was. For him.

"Good morning, Damon."

"Good morning."

"How old are you?"

"I am eighteen years old."

"I'm sure the jury has noticed that cast on your hand.

Would you tell them how you got that?"

"Sure. I punched the door in jail back there last night."

Damon gestured behind himself. He looked at the jury.

"I was frustrated. Because I am innocent. I didn't do this crime. That's why I broke my hand, out of frustration at being locked up for something I didn't do."

"Where did you grow up?"

"On One hundred thirty-second and Lenox Avenue. I live with my mom. She's a nurse's aide at Harlem Hospital."

"Any brothers or sisters?"

"Nope. Just me and my mom."

"Is that where you've always lived?"

"Yes. That's my home."

"Have you ever been convicted of a crime?"

"No."

"Are you a high school graduate?"

"Yes, I am. I graduated in '97. I'm enrolled at City College. I was, that is, 'til they locked me up for this."

"Have you worked since high school?"

"Yes, I was working on the day I got arrested. At the Video Edge. Eleventh Avenue and Twenty-second Street. I'd been working twenty hours a week there for a year and a half."

"What were your duties?"

"Cashier, restocking, inventory."

"What was your pay?"

"Nine bucks an hour. No benefits."

"How were you paid?"

"By check."

"What did you usually do with the check?"

"Cash it with the boss right after he gave it to me."

"That was your regular routine?"

"Yeah. Every Friday."

"On Friday, December 4, of last year, is that what you did?"

"Yes."

"About what time was that?"

"Around five o'clock."

"When you left Video Edge, what did you do?"

"I headed over to the Circuit City on Fourteenth Street. I was going to buy my moms a DVD player. I'd already checked out the model."

"Were you walking?"

"Actually, I was running. With my Walkman on. I run a lot. After eight hours in that video store, I feel like movin' around."

"Did you have money on you?"

"Yes, I had 13 dollars in my wallet, and 180 bucks, my paycheck, loose in my jeans pocket."

"Where did that cash come from?"

"Register at Video Edge. Boss took the bills right outa the register and handed them to me."

"What happened while you were running down the street?"

"Two cops stopped me. With guns drawn. Scared the shit outa me, pardon my French. Threw me up against the wall. Smashed my face into a brick wall. I needed five stitches to close the gash. Still got the scar."

He leaned forward a little and pointed up to his eyebrow. We'd argued about this, among other things. I didn't want him to go into it at all. I didn't want too much indignation. I wanted the jury to like him, not feel afraid of him. But some things he just had to get off his chest. He was so angry, he couldn't think strategically.

"Stole my Walkman. Threw it in the gutter."

"Then what happened?"

"They put me in their unmarked car and drove me a

couple blocks to where this lady was lying on a stretcher, being loaded into an ambulance."

"Go on."

"They took me outa the car and brought me right up close to this woman. She didn't look good. She was white as a sheet. One of the cops said, 'Is this the guy?' She didn't say nothing at all. She just started to shake a whole lot, and then she was still. She died."

"Did she identify you?"

"No."

"Did you rob or shoot her?"

"Hell, no."

I paused. It amazes me every time anew how quickly you can get a story out in front of the jury, if you're not trying to stretch it for one reason or another. We were almost done. It had only taken a few minutes.

"Was that the first time you had ever seen Charlotte King?"

"No. I sold her a tape just a few minutes earlier. To be honest, I don't actually remember her face in the store. I do remember saying to a white woman who was very cute, 'Be careful out there, sister.' Now I know that was Charlotte King."

"How did she pay for the videocassette?"

"With three 10 dollar bills."

"How do you know?"

"Well, because my fingerprints are on three of the bills that the boss gave me when he cashed my check. That's how money with her prints on it ended up in my pants pocket."

"So when your boss cashed your check, and paid you, he took out eighteen 10 dollar bills, and three of them had not minutes earlier been handed to you by Charlotte King?"

"Correct."

"How did your fingerprints get on the video in Charlotte King's purse?"

"I handled it when I scanned it. The customer picks out the video on the floor, and hands it to the cashier to be scanned. Happens on every sale. That's how my prints got on the video."

That was it. I keep direct examination tight. Just presenting the simple facts seems very quick, but believe me, it's okay, because the DA's going to make the defendant repeat the whole thing endlessly, and from every angle. I'd seen it happen over and over again. Guys who were nervous and clipped on direct loosened up when the DA got in their face. Defendants won the jury over on cross as often as on direct.

Stoddard began her cross-examination.

"Mr. Tucker, you saw Officer Newman testify here, did you not?"

"Yes, I did."

"Are you telling this jury that he lied on the stand, to frame you for something you didn't do?"

"Whether he's lying or mistaken, I don't know. I can't read his mind. But that woman never said anything to him. Her head started shaking, and then she died. So Newman got it wrong. Whether it was deliberate or not, I don't know."

"So he's mistaken?"

"Yes."

"And the fingerprint detective, is he also mistaken?"

"No."

"So, it's just an amazing coincidence that you came to have money in your pocket with Charlotte King's prints on it."

"You can call it anything you like. It's the truth."

"If it's the truth, it involves one heck of a coincidence, doesn't it?"

"You bet it does." Damon let out a bitter laugh. "I still can't believe it!"

"Isn't it a fact, Mr. Tucker, that you decided to rob someone, and when you walked up to Ms. King with your gun out, you realized, when you got right in front of her, that you had just sold her a video in the store moments earlier, and she could identify you? Isn't that why you shot her?"

So this was how Stoddard was going to use the new facts in the case. Motive! How goddamn clever. She was turning it around, using *our* evidence to explain why Damon *had* to shoot Charlotte King—because she *recognized* him. Stoddard was using our proof to help the jury make sense of this senseless murder. Now they had a reason for Damon to shoot Charlotte King. We'd given it to them.

"No and no. I didn't rob that woman, and I didn't shoot her. I was just running down the street, wearing a black coat. That's why I got arrested. That's all I'm guilty of, being black and running down the street in a black coat."

"So you're being framed because you're black?"

"Maybe it don't look like it to you, cuz you're the DA, and that's your job, but that's how it feels to me. Y'all are framing me. I'm innocent! Why me?"

He was yelling now. His voice had gotten higher and higher and was now totally out of control. She wasn't letting up.

"You were caught running two blocks from where this shooting occurred, you had the victim's money in your pants pocket, and you expect this jury to believe anything you're saying?"

"Fuck, yes."

Big mistake. Juries just don't like big men swearing on the stand. It turns them right off. It shows a lack of respect. In Damon's case, it wasn't a lack of respect, it was just pure rage, plain and bitter. He just could not control it. He had to speak with emphasis, and the only way he knew how was to throw in a "fuck" here and there.

Unfortunately for Damon, in a close case like this, where it was a question of whose version you believed, personalities could decide it. If the jury didn't like Damon, he was finished. And if the whole thing turned on whether they liked him, that certainly didn't bode well for the penalty phase.

Stoddard was doing damage. Lots of it. She was just damn good. She was incredulous, but not obnoxious. She could be sarcastic without being irritating. Stephens was looking a little grim for the first time. I didn't like that either. Stoddard was making Damon look mean and bad.

Damon wasn't done.

"There's a lot of stuff these jurors don't even know about. They don't know about the real killer, David Yates. They don't know he was sleeping with Charlotte King, and she dumped him. They don't know he was taking his outfit public. She knew something. She had some dirt on him. Her shrink was killed, too. A few days later."

I couldn't believe it. We'd gotten through most of the whole trial without a fatal blowup by Damon, and now he was screwing it all up with one outburst.

The judge interrupted.

"Stop right now, Mr. Tucker. Step up, counsel."

We approached. Stoddard had a sly look on her face.

"If the People request it, I'll grant a mistrial."

"Your Honor, we don't want a mistrial. We don't want to do this all again. We would just like the opportunity to put on a rebuttal case. We might need a short adjournment."

"Who might you be calling?"

She was playing it coy. "I guess we'll all find out tomorrow, won't we?"

This was turning into a nightmare. The law is pretty clear that when the defendant makes factual claims during his testimony that are totally new to the case, the prosecution has the right to put on kind of a second minicase—called the "rebuttal" case—to show that these claims aren't true. They don't usually do it. But when they can blow you right out of the water, well, then they kind of like that old rebuttal case.

CHAPTER 37

YATES LOOKED the perfect executive up there on the stand. He was beautifully turned out, as usual, totally relaxed, pleased, it seemed, to have this opportunity to clear up these silly claims against his respected name.

"Mr. Yates, tell the jury what you do, sir."

"I am the chief executive officer of Yates Associates, a Wall Street firm."

"What kind of organization is that?"

"We are private investigators."

"Was Charlotte King an employee of your firm?"

"Yes, she was."

"Was your relationship with her anything but professional?"

"I respected her a great deal. She was also very beautiful. But our corporate rules forbid any type of interaction of that sort. No, I wasn't having an affair with her."

He had just the right tone. The jurors were eating it

up.

"Sir, where were you, if you remember, on December 4 of last year, in the late afternoon?"

"I was on an airplane, flying to Hong Kong. The flight took off at noon on the fourth, and arrived in Hong Kong nineteen hours later. Yes, I was on an airplane."

"Thank you. Nothing further."

Now it was my turn to cross the motherfucker. I knew it was useless. I had a few riffs, but nothing to nail the guy. I'd just be floundering around for a few minutes. But I gave it a shot.

"Sir, you are about to take your organization public, correct?"

"That's true."

"You stand to make millions and millions of dollars personally, don't you?"

"Perhaps. You never know, on Wall Street. But I've built my business up over many years. We're now the most respected organization of our kind in the world."

"Negative information about your firm could threaten the value of that public offering, couldn't it?"

"Objection. Hypothetical."

"Sustained."

This wasn't going to be easy. I got specific.

"Isn't it a fact, Yates, that Charlotte King knew some dirt about your outfit? That's why you ordered her killed, and her therapist, too?"

"Objection," wailed Stoddard.

"I'll allow it," said the judge coolly.

Yates smiled. "No. That's silly stuff. First of all, my firm has nothing to hide. We're squeaky clean. For goodness sake, when the U.S. government wanted to track Iran's assets in the United States, who'd they hire to do it? Yates Associates."

I wanted to ask him about Norton Gorham. I wanted to ask him what it was like to see his mommy blow his daddy's head off when he was five years old. I wanted to ask him why he still went to strip clubs, like the one where his mom worked.

But it was all inadmissible. I'd get shut down by the judge after each question, Yates wouldn't even have to answer, and I'd look like a fucking lunatic.

"Isn't it a fact, sir, that if you wanted someone killed, you wouldn't have to do it personally? You could be in Hong Kong, or on the moon, for that matter, while someone else did your dirty work right here in New York?"

"Objection."

"Sustained."

Yates was frowning, like I was some kind of fucking lunatic. The jurors were with him on this one, not me. I gave it up.

"No further questions."

Finally, just to nail it down, Stoddard called some cute Asian clerk from Japan Airlines, who testified that yes, indeed, Yates was on that flight to Hong Kong. The clerk pulled out the ticket records, and the flight manifest, to prove it.

We were in trouble. Now we were in a pissing match, and we were going to lose it.

That was the problem with putting on an affirmative case, instead of just poking holes and going for a general sense of reasonable doubt. You ended up shifting the burden of proof onto yourself, instead of leaving it solidly where the law puts it, on the prosecution. Instead of the People having to prove their case, the thing turned into a contest between competing versions of the "truth." It had seemed worth the risk, because our explanation of the fingerprint evidence defense was so solidly grounded on incontrovertible evidence. But now, after Damon had announced that Yates was the killer, and the prosecution had effectively obliterated that notion, the risks, the equation, were all out of whack. This jury might now convict Damon just because they didn't believe that Yates was the killer. The fact that the prosecution had not proved its case beyond a reasonable doubt was getting lost in the shuffle.

CHAPTER 38

THAT NIGHT, I WORKED at home, preparing my summation. Unlike a lot of public defenders, I don't get up in front of the jury and ad-lib from notes. When I get up in front of those twelve jurors, I want to be more than the thirteenth juror, just thinking things through out loud with the folks. That casual approach works well for some lawyers, but it's not my style. I don't want to leave any phrase or thought to chance. I want my summation to be perfect. I don't just make an outline. I write out every goddamn word, carefully thinking about every point I'm making, and how I'm making it. Of course, I try to deliver it in a spontaneous style, stepping back from the text, so it doesn't look like I'm reading a speech, but a speech it is, nevertheless. It's usually very effective, or so I've been told.

I have always believed in the system. I have always believed that innocent people are acquitted, and most guilty people are convicted. The price of raising the bar high enough not to convict innocent people, is, of course, that some guilty people are also acquitted. This seems to be a price we're all willing to pay. I am one of those people who would rather let ten guilty people go than convict one innocent person.

Ask any criminal defense attorney, and they will tell you that they hate defending an innocent client. If your client is guilty, and you lose, well okay, nobody's getting anything they don't deserve. But actual innocence? It's a terrifying thought. In my ten-year career as a public defender I have never had an innocent person convicted after trial. I have gone to trial on thirty-four felonies. Of those thirty-four trials, my clients were guilty in all but two cases. I won those two cases. Out of the other thirty-two trials, twenty-four were also acquittals, not because my clients were innocent, but because the People's case was weak, or their witnesses had problems, or the assistant DA handling the case was inept, or I did a great job turning shit into gold, or any combination of the above.

I have never lost a trial for an innocent man. Sitting at home, working on my summation, I realized that I was terribly afraid because Damon was innocent. This was more pressure than I wanted to handle. If this jury convicted Damon, the system would have failed in its most critical test, a death penalty trial, and I would have been part of the failure.

My father always talked about me going "legit." That was a word he always used. Was this "legit," shepherding a man who might be innocent to his death at the hands of the government?

The buzzer rang. It was Stephens, who'd come over to see how I was doing.

"Playing lawyer, for a change?" she said gently. "No investigations tonight."

I laughed, though I wanted to cry.

"I gotta give a good summation tomorrow. If we go down, I'll have plenty of time to figure out a way to get

Yates. Can't do it tonight."

We were both tense. She came up behind me, as I was hunched over my computer keyboard typing away. She started to massage my shoulders.

"That's nice," I said.

She kept it up for a few minutes. It felt awfully good.

Why, I asked myself, do women always wait for just the moment when there is absolutely no possibility of things progressing—for example, tonight, when I had to write my summation in this death penalty trial—to show a little physical affection? Of course, I knew the answer. She was giving me a massage right now precisely because she knew it couldn't go further.

CHAPTER 39

SUMMATION IS SUPPOSED to be the peak moment for a criminal defense lawyer in a trial. It's when you put it all together for the jury, when you hope that all those little points you racked up during your cross-examination of various witnesses can be strung together, bound up into a tide of logic, law, and emotion, leading inexorably to unanimous acceptance of that great god of the accused: Reasonable Doubt.

It doesn't always work out. I labored for twenty-four hours straight on my summation, and I could never get it right. The double-fisted combination of Charlotte King's supposed identification, coupled with her prints on the money in Damon's pocket, was just too much to explain away. Prints but no ID. Maybe. ID but no prints. Perhaps. But each served to validate the other, and to make any explanation negating both was mere convenience, and nothing more. Of course, the fact that Damon hadn't come across particularly vulnerable or likable didn't help matters. Nor did the obvious tilt of this death-qualified jury. It's hard to read a jury, but you didn't need to be Clarence Darrow to see that these folks just weren't really listening to me. This is the worst fate, the nightmare of defense counsel. That you've already been written off.

They didn't seem impressed when I suggested to them that nobody robs someone at gunpoint after waiting on them at a store. Nobody walks up to someone with whom they have just conducted a business transaction, whom they recognize, and who recognizes them, and robs them. Nobody could be that stupid, I said.

They weren't really paying much attention when I told them that they couldn't convict Damon for being loud, or angry, or making an accusation against Yates that didn't make a lot of sense, that "not guilty" wasn't a civic award, that they didn't have to invite him over to dinner afterward.

They all seemed to look away when I said that the judge would instruct them that if there were two inferences to be drawn from the evidence, one consistent with innocence, and one consistent with guilt, that the law required them to adopt the inference consistent with innocence, in other words, *our* explanation of the fingerprint evidence, rather than the prosecution's explanation. No sir. No way.

This was "death qualification" coming back to bite me in the ass. They had already decided Damon was guilty.

Stoddard was fine. She didn't go on too long. She was very sarcastic, but not inappropriate. "How convenient," she kept saying, "how convenient" that Damon just happened to have taken money from Charlotte King in the store. "How convenient" an explanation for the prints of a woman who also just happened to identify this killer before she died.

"Ladies and gentlemen, Damon Tucker's story is a lie, a lie tailored to explain all the evidence that he can't make go away. He's lying because he doesn't want to pay for his crimes. That's why he's lying.

"Sure, Charlotte King came into his video store. That's why he had to shoot her. Because she recognized him when he walked up to her to rob her. He shot her because he knew if he didn't, she'd identify him, and he didn't want to go to jail.

"Now, defense counsel has asked you to acquit Damon Tucker because he says no one would be so stupid as to rob someone they just saw, who recognizes them. Where does he get that idea? Murder is a terribly stupid thing. But it happens one thousand times a year in this city.

"Maybe Damon only realized who she was after he'd pulled his gun and confronted her. Maybe he didn't recognize her from behind, or the side, and after he jumped in front of her, it was too late.

"Damon's not stupid. He's smart. He realized she recognized him. He knew the sales slip with the video in her purse had his name on it, for heaven's sake. He made a calculated, cold-blooded decision to shoot her, so he wouldn't have to go to jail.

"Well, now it's time for you to hold him responsible for what he's done. Make him pay for the murder he committed."

CHAPTER 40

THEY DELIBERATED for ten hours, over two days. On a Thursday morning, at 11:05, they sent out a note that said simply, "Verdict."

Stephens and I had been back in my office, a phone call away, waiting. Damon was in the pens behind the courthouse, pacing his small cell like one of the polar bears at the zoo, proving to himself a thousand times over that his jail wasn't changing size or shape. His mother sat quietly in the courtroom. I couldn't tell if she was actually praying.

The note from the jury got everybody's heart thumping. I cannot describe to you the adrenaline rush of a jury verdict. You've fought your heart and soul out to win for your client, and finally, there's nothing more you can do except listen for the first and last time to the soft-spoken words of the jury foreperson.

"What say you, madame, as to the first count of the indictment, murder in the first degree."

"Guilty."

The first sound was Evelyn Tucker letting out a howl. Damon exhaled and then banged his good fist down on the table. The guards closed in on him, saying, "Easy, easy, kid," very quietly. They didn't want to have to subdue him in front of the jury, this same group of citizens who were now going to decide whether Damon lived or died. But he wasn't causing any more trouble. He was just crying. Weeping. I cried, too. Tears for Damon, who'd gone down

on my watch, who'd blown trial with Arch Gold. I heard
the faraway voice of the judge excusing the jury, thanking
them for their efforts, and asking them to return in four
days for the sentencing phase.

The guards took Damon back. Stephens and I followed.
We stood in the little hall behind the courtroom, next to
Damon, waiting for the prison elevator to take us down to
the pens. Damon turned around toward us. His face was
a sneer.

"Thanks for nothing. Get the fuck outa my face."

CHAPTER 41

WE WERE in the judge's robing room, a sparse room,
empty but for a desk, several chairs, and a phone. Some
judges do a lot of work in their robing rooms. Others,
like Judge Wheeler, just pass through to grab their robes
and throw them on as they head into the courtroom. This
morning, the day after the verdict, Judge Wheeler had
called Stoddard and me in for a conference. Neither of us
knew why. Probably he wanted to discuss something way
off the record, without court officers or court reporters to
leak it out.

Wheeler wasn't yet in his robes. He looked like just
another lawyer with problems he couldn't solve.

"This is why I'm opposed to the death penalty," he said,
staring right at Stoddard.

"This kid might be innocent," he went on. "They
convicted him because they didn't like him. I guess you
never know what a death-qualified jury's going to do.
They certainly didn't seem overwhelmed by the concept

of reasonable doubt."

"Judge, you could've thrown it out after the close of evidence. You didn't have to let it get to the jury."

"Mind your manners, Gold."

There was silence for a moment. Many truths hung in the air, unspoken. We all knew that if Wheeler was really convinced of Damon's innocence, and if he had the inclination, and the guts, he could take matters into his own hands. When a judge believes there is not proof beyond a reasonable doubt against a defendant, he can dismiss the case before letting it go to the jury. This is called a trial order of dismissal. It has the same legal effect as an acquittal by the jury. It cannot be appealed by the prosecution. The case is over, forever over, and the defendant goes free.

But Judge Wheeler hadn't done that, and now he was in trouble. Now, if he threw out the verdict, a higher court could simply reinstate it.

He turned toward Stoddard. Just a few months ago, they'd been colleagues on the bench. Now they were glaring at each other with intense dislike.

"Bernice, why don't you just go for life without parole. I have to tell you, I am considering throwing the whole thing out."

Her brow furrowed, her eyes blazed, her voice got deeper, rather than louder. She leaned over toward Wheeler. She got right in his face.

"Wheeler, you don't have the balls to throw this out, and we both know it. If you did have balls, you'd have done it before it got to the jury. But you didn't. You were hoping the jury would bail you out with an acquittal. Now, if you throw it out and the court of appeals reinstates it, your career's over. And they might. But even if they don't, you don't want to be the judge who let Damon Tucker off the hook. I know you. So don't try to bargain with me. If you want to set it aside, go ahead. I say you don't have the guts. I'm seeking death."

He looked away. If human beings had tails, his would be between his legs.

CHAPTER 42

"YOU GUYS had your turn, now it's mine. Things didn't come out so good for you. Maybe I'll do better. It's my life, so I'm gonna do the talking."

It was the morning after the verdict. We were on Rikers, in the counsel visit room.

"Damon, are you saying you want to take the stand at your mitigation hearing?"

"No, I'm saying I wanna represent myself."

Damon wanted to go *pro se*, to serve as his own lawyer. It is every person's right, a constitutional right, which cannot easily be denied. It is usually a mistake to exercise this particular constitutional right. This particular right does not need exercise. If I were charged with a crime tomorrow, I would call Layden. I would never dream of attempting to represent myself, whether I was guilty as charged or innocent as the fallen snow.

I felt sorry, very sorry, for Damon. I couldn't blame him, either, although I knew he was making the wrong decision and screwing himself. But he was going to pay the penalty, not me. Why shouldn't he speak his heart and make the arguments?

"I wanna walk up and down in front of that jury box and tell them twelve folks the truth, straight from my mouth, no bullshit. You watch. The judge'll have to let me do it, too."

"I'm sure he will, Damon. Not even the judge can stop you from exercising your constitutional right to fuck yourself."

I couldn't hide that I was pissed off. Every defendant has the right to defend himself. It's always a mistake, and the judge is required to hold a hearing to warn the defendant that it's probably a mistake and make sure he's clearly waiving his rights, but the sort of guys who want to go this route are usually fired up enough to get through it with flying colors. I was sure Damon would be no exception. I turned to Stephens, looking for help.

"What do you think, Stephens, judge going to allow it?"

"Yup."

That was all Damon needed.

"Matter of fact, y'all, I bet you this judge gonna cut me a lotta slack. My life's at stake. What's he gonna say, I can't speak my mind?"

"So what are you going to say, Damon?" Stephens was genuinely curious, even if we'd just been fired.

CHAPTER 43

I WILL NEVER FORGET the sight of Damon, all 6' 4" of him, prowling the floor in front of the jury box, howling for his life, railing, to no avail, against the forces that had mysteriously aligned themselves against him. I watched him up there, scaring the jury with his intensity. No guilty man could be so self-destructive. If he were guilty, and trying to save his life, he'd let his lawyers do the best they could. He wouldn't be so headstrong. If he were guilty, he'd understand that the trial was a show we had to put on, a show that was much more important than the truth itself. If he were guilty, he'd recognize that his own lack of talent had put him into this nearly fatal situation, and he'd see the sense in letting some pros do their best to get him out of it.

But he was innocent. He didn't commit the crime. That was why he couldn't play the game. That was why he seemed so intent on fucking himself. His innocence was driving him crazy. He'd lost any perspective, any traction to grab on to the things that could help him, like moderating his manner, quelling his anger, playing the role of the victim. Even though the stakes had been raised to life or death itself, a capital trial was still a performance, a contest, which in a close case was won or lost on personality and style, not substance. The truth was *not* destined to prevail. Damon was innocent, but because he was too pissed off to put on the right show, he was going down. His innocence was the very reason he'd been convicted. On the same evidence, a different likable guilty defendant might well have been acquitted. After all, this was not a case with overwhelming evidence of guilt. It was what we call "triable," meaning it could be won. Understand, no trial is a sure thing from the defense perspective. It's all too unpredictable and turns on too many variables. All you can ever say is you have a shot at an acquittal. I have never told a client we had better than a 50 percent shot. Well, Damon had blown his shot. Something had tipped in the jurors' perception of him. Early in the trial, they had concluded, viscerally, unconsciously, that he was angry because he'd been caught, not because he was innocent. Once this visceral reaction settled in, it tainted their view of all the evidence.

Poor fucking Damon. The kid's heart was pure. He hadn't done anything wrong.

"Look, y'all, I've decided to speak to you directly because it's my life you hold in your hands, it's me whose life is going to end one day strapped down to a stretcher somewhere far away from this courtroom, if you want it that way. So why shouldn't you deal with me directly, that's what I asked myself, since it's me you're talking 'bout killing."

He paused to drink some water. He certainly had everyone's attention. I had absolutely no idea what he was going to say next. He was waving around the copy of the statute we'd given him weeks ago.

"This here is called a 'mitigation' hearing. You all are supposed to decide if any of the mitigating factors put forth by me outweigh the aggravating factors, which in this case is that I'm supposed to have robbed and shot Charlotte King. If these mitigating factors, like, outweigh the aggravating factors, then I get life instead of death."

He looked down at the photocopy of the sentencing statute.

"The mitigating factor in my case, ladies and gentlemen of the jury, is that I did not commit this crime. I am innocent. That is the mitigating factor."

"Objection." Stoddard was on her feet. God knows why she cared. Damon appeared to be doing himself nothing but damage. Why didn't she just let him continue? I was almost grateful to her for interrupting.

We couldn't have bench conferences any longer, since Damon had to be included as his own counsel, and security just wouldn't allow him uncuffed up at the bench. So the jury was led out, and we all went at it. I was now Damon's "legal adviser." I wasn't allowed to speak to the jury, that

was his sole province, but I could continue to argue law
for him in front of the judge.

Stoddard was livid.

"Judge, you know the defendant can't relitigate his guilt
at this proceeding. It's deemed established. It's beyond the
scope."

Damon didn't miss a beat. He had a litigator's pacing.

"Your Honor, fuck the scope. Y'all can't shut me down
at this stage of the proceedings. Y'all can't. My life is at
stake."

The judge looked at Damon like he'd just stated some
well-established legal principle.

"Thank you, Mr. Tucker. Mr. Gold?"

"Your Honor, Mr. Tucker is facing the death penalty.
Why not just let him say what he wants to say?"

Damon turned toward me.

"Thank you."

There wasn't much else to be said, since the DA was
four squares right on the law. Damon had already been
convicted of an "aggravating factor," murder during
the course of a robbery. It was already proven beyond
a reasonable doubt. So he couldn't really talk about his
innocence. It was inadmissible. The judge could just
shut it down. He looked directly at Damon, not me, as he
made his ruling. He sounded like he was talking about the
weather, not life and death.

"Mr. Tucker, now technically the DA may be right in
her view of the statute, but I am going to take a somewhat
broader view of this hearing, since you have chosen to
represent yourself. As long as you don't curse, or get too
close to the jurors, or shout, you can say just about anything
you want. Your life is at stake, and I'm not going to stop
you from speaking. Just a word of advice. Just because
you now can say something doesn't make it a good idea.

Remember, this jury has already convicted you of first degree murder. It might not improve your prospects to get in their faces too much."

Truer words were never spoken. Damon was deeply unmoved.

"Judge, I ain't going down without a fight."

The poor kid knew he was going down, but he couldn't help himself.

They brought the jury back in. Damon leaned over the podium, not three feet from the front row of jurors. They weren't used to such proximity. Did it humanize, or demonize, Damon? I wasn't sure. From a distance, he could've been a lawyer, a young black lawyer, making his closing arguments. Up close the look frayed at the edges. Nothing fit quite right, the tie was off, the collar wrong, and you could see that this was just a kid in his old church suit, never worn for any other occasion out there in the real world.

This wasn't the real world either. It was a twisted kind of theater, a "reality-based" drama that had nothing to do with what really went down out there on Twentieth Street. Damon, having fired his lawyer, was now about to get kicked off the show himself. He was going out in flames, too.

"Ladies and gentlemen, I ain't gonna sit up here and tell you what a good guy I am, and that's why you shouldn't execute me, even though I did this horrible crime. Cuz I didn't do this crime. The mitigating factor here is innocence. Someday, we will discover who did this crime, who shot Charlotte King. If you kill me, and that 'someday' comes along, how will any of you live with that? The mitigating factor here is you're not positive I did this. You may have convicted me, but there is a chance you're wrong. What I told you up there, what my witnesses told you up there, that was the truth. It's just a matter of whether you want to believe it or not. So if you have any doubt in your heart that I did this, don't take my life. Don't make a mistake you can't correct. Don't avenge one murder by committing another. I'm flesh, I'm blood, I got a mom who's always loved me and always will; I'm young, I ain't hardly lived yet. So if you ain't one hundred percent sure I'm guilty, don't give me a sentence that is one hundred percent irreversible."

Damon sat back down next to me. The courtroom was totally quiet, except for the squeak of the artist's chalk. The judge broke the silence by clearing his throat into the microphone. He sure knew how to suck the drama out of a moment. He gave the jury their final instructions.

"You must decide whether the aggravating factors outweigh the mitigating factors."

What the hell did it really mean? It was supposed to give guidance, to prevent the arbitrary and inconsistent application of the death penalty that had been the hallmark of capital cases before the 1972 moratorium. But it didn't do much, really. The jury could still assign whatever weight it wanted to anything. It was just a lot of airy fluff, designed to make the death penalty look reasoned and justified, instead of what it was—lightning striking.

As the jurors filed out, perhaps for the last time, I saw nothing but grim faces. I didn't see mercy.

They showed no mercy. Quickly, they showed no mercy. Five hours.

"Jurors, how find you?"

"We find that the aggravating factors outweigh the mitigating factors."

That's all she had to say, Madame Foreperson. The whole procedure was sanitized. She never had to utter the dreaded "death" word. It was just a weighing of factors, not a killing.

The jury was excused. Damon's jaw was clenched. His eyes were red, but his face showed nothing. His mother sobbed quietly in the first row. I took a deep breath and slumped onto the table for a second or two. Then I pulled myself up and turned to Damon, taking his shoulders in my hands, so he had to look right into my eyes.

"Damon, it's not over."

CHAPTER 44

IWALKED HOME in A daze, too shocked to think. I was turning the corner toward my building when suddenly a man was walking next to me. He seemed to have materialized out of nowhere. It was Yates.

"Gold, listen. It's over. You did a good job. You lost. The black kid's gone down, and the case is over. So let it lie."

"What's it to you, Yates? Why you bothering me on the street?"

"Don't jawbone with me. I don't play verbal games. I'm speaking to you for a reason. The reason is, now that the trial's over, and your boy lost, I want you to fuck off. Got it? Nothing personal, but the case is over. Time to move on. I trust you will. I don't want to see you on my radar screen again, understood?"

"Worried about your public offering? What've you got to hide? Thought you were squeaky clean."

"You got a big mouth. That's okay. You're a lawyer. You can't help yourself. You did your job. Great. Now your job is over. I am strongly advising you to go on to the next case."

He was gone.

CHAPTER 45

ONCE I GOT HOME, I poured myself a stiff vodka tonic. I paced back and forth across my living room, replaying my encounter with Yates. The guy was threatening me. Now that the trial was over, he was going to keep an eye on me. He was telling me to let it lie, let it die, or else.

I don't take kindly to that kind of pressure. To me his little veiled threats were just confirmation of his guilt. He didn't scare me. He motivated me.

Like most public defenders, I've lost a lot of trials, and I'd been devastated from time to time, but this was in another category. If I didn't do something to change it, Damon was going to die, not for several years, to be sure, but still, they were going to kill him. It might be a decade before all of Damon's appeals were exhausted. There was a distant horizon, with a sun only slowly setting, but the dark would arrive.

One night, down the road, they'd strap him to a gurney and kill him. Unless I figured something out.

Stephens called. Layden called. Goodman called. My ex-wife called. They all wanted to know how I was doing. Fuck 'em all. I didn't trust myself to speak to anyone. Fuck the judicial system. Fuck the appellate process. Fuck the goddamn rule of goddamn law. It hadn't worked for Damon. The rules made everything appear to be orderly, and just, and measured, but they didn't make things come out right. I no longer wanted any part of the game. I hadn't done anything with my skills except legitimize a process that didn't work. Stephens and I had done a good job for Damon. Good enough that there were now no real issues for him to press on an appeal. He'd received "effective assistance." It was just another nail in his coffin. Nothing more.

That evening, I was almost relieved when Stephens knocked on my door and demanded to know if I was still alive.

"Yes, I'm still alive," I said, opening the door.

"God, you look like shit. Why don't we go out and find something to distract you. Damon's case is going to be appealed for the next decade. Sooner or later, you're going to have to stop beating yourself up, and resume your life."

"Later, Rob, later. Not sooner."

The phone rang.

"Let it go," I yelled. "Let it go."

"Okay, okay, easy now, Arch."

The answering machine clicked on. It was Kathy Dupont.

"Hi, Arch. Just called to say I'm real sorry about the case. I know you're feeling lousy. Hey, *my* case is over. It got dismissed Friday. So now you've got no excuses. Why don't you come see my show? The Executive Lounge. It's kinda hot. Maybe it'll distract you. Hope I see ya, cutie."

"Who the hell is that?" asked Stephens. "Some slutty girlfriend you've been hiding from me?"

"Yeah, right. When's the last time I had any kinda girlfriend?"

"So who is she?"

"Ex-client. A stripper. You met her for thirty seconds in my office. Remember? Big tits. Pouty look. She's from another world. Beauty queen from South Carolina. Comes to big city to make it. Ends up taking off her clothes at fancy strip joints."

"Sounds great. Real career move."

She sounded a little resentful. She came and sat next to me.

"I'm sorry. I thought we'd win this one. You did a great job. You know that, don't you? We got kicked in the ass by that rebuttal case. Damon's lack of control did us in. Don't blame yourself. Okay?"

"You're very sweet," I said.

I took her in my arms and tried to kiss her. It was a stupid thing to do. She pulled away.

"Arch, I like you a lot. You're a great lawyer. You're a good guy. You're handsome as hell. But I don't want to get started. I'm pulling out of here now. Packing up and moving on to the next trial, that one in Buffalo. So what's the point? Maybe someday, if my life changes, and we're in the same place for a long long time. Hey, we'll go on a couple of dates."

"I'd like that," I said. "I'd also like to spend the night with you right now."

"Sorry, Arch."

She gave me a long kiss on the mouth, just to prove how sorry she was. I could feel her petite shape up against my big frame. I liked it. I liked it a lot. That didn't seem to matter.

She left.

I sat and stewed for a while, and then I went out to see Kathy Dupont dance.

CHAPTER 46

THE EXECUTIVE LOUNGE was still trying hard to be upscale and tasteful. The velvet ropes and bouncers in tuxedos, the discreet signs that gave no hint of the activities inside, it was all trying to say something other than "strip joint." The thirty-five dollar cover charge certainly kept out the riffraff.

Inside, the elegant decor, the rich leather banquettes, the tuxedoed staff, the chandeliers, the curtains, the tablecloths, also were all trying to say something other than "strip joint."

It was a strip joint.

Six girls were dancing on a raised stage that ran down the center of the room, curving this way and that. Each girl held on to her own pole, running from the stage to the ceiling. There were enough smoky mirrors strategically placed so that whichever way you looked, you saw some part of the female anatomy undulating to the thumping music.

The girls weren't naked, yet. They were topless, but each still had on a thong bottom. Kathy Dupont was nowhere to be seen. Tables ringed the stage, and men in suits sat at most of them. Some of the men were just grinning stupidly and staring at the dancers. Others seemed to be in conversation and not paying too much attention.

The whole thing made me uncomfortable. I loved women, and I loved sex, but this turned me off. Was it the feeling that these women were being exploited? Was it just the knowledge that I didn't like the kind of men who came to these places, guys who didn't care what was in a girl's head and didn't mind if there was plastic in her tits?

"Will you look at these chicks!" I heard the man next to me saying to his buddy. "I mean, I've never seen bodies like that, have you?"

Most of the men in the club didn't seem to share my reservations. The shine in their eyes said that they found this exciting. If you focused in the right way, these were sexy girls. No doubt about it. I couldn't do it. It was probably for the same reason I couldn't prosecute people, or chase the almighty dollar on Wall Street.

The music died down, and the women climbed off the stage and headed toward the bar, where grinning men with hard-ons were bumping elbows trying to buy their favorite dancer a drink.

No sign of Kathy.

Just then, the music started up again, and six new girls sashayed out onto the stage. Kathy Dupont was first. She was beautiful. Maybe just because I'd seen her in another setting, she seemed real to me, not just a plastic doll up there. I remembered that night, in arraignments, when I'd met her, and Damon, two files I happened to pick up from the top of the basket, a lifetime ago.

As I stared at Kathy, in my peripheral vision, I saw two men come in and wait to be seated. As I focused on them, I realized one of the men was Yates.

Motherfuck.

A waiter was seating them. Yates, as usual, looked like an investment banker in his elegant suit, but I knew better. He and his buddy, a large handsome black man, also elegantly dressed, sat at a table with a "reserved" sign on it not three feet from Kathy Dupont's perfect little writhing body. Yates's companion gave the waiter a tip. I heard the waiter say "Thank you, Mr. Smalls."

Perfect name for the guy. Obviously, he and Yates were regulars.

Yates was clearly transfixed by Kathy. From the moment he walked in the room, his eyes followed her every move. His face was a little red, and his eyes glowed with pleasure. His mouth was slightly open. Every few seconds he licked his lips in a slow circle. The guy was a creep. Meanwhile, Kathy had just noticed me. She smiled and winked. Her back was to Yates. I could see her mouth form her usual greeting.

"Hi, cutie."

The sight of Yates made me sick. His fascination with Kathy Dupont made me sicker. I couldn't take my eyes off his companion either. The black man called Smalls. He bore a striking resemblance to Damon.

I left before they saw me.

CHAPTER 47

THE NEXT DAY in the office, Stephens was packing up her files. I was ranting and raving.

"His homeboy did it. A big black guy who's built like Damon. Must be Yates's bodyguard, or whatever. He probably did Dr. Stern, too, and stole Charlotte's hard drive."

"Arch, believe me, it's over. We lost the goddamn trial."

She was speaking gently, but her words hurt me. She didn't think there was anything left to do but appeal. She was a pretty smart cookie. Was she right?

"Come on, Stephens, stop thinking appeal, and start thinking how we're gonna come up with some new evidence in this case. We gotta do something. We can't just sit around and read the trial transcript."

"That's my thing, bro. That's what I do. I'm not into cops and robbers. I don't like leaving my desk, except to get more coffee."

"Don't you think it was kind of a coincidence that Kathy Dupont got me to come to her show the night Yates walked in? Think something's going on there?"

"I think you got a big imagination. She doesn't even know Yates has any connection to you at all. He's just another swinging dick to her. Life is full of coincidences. What's it got to do with Damon's case?"

She gestured over at the transcript, five thousand pages of it, sitting in ten boxes stacked up next to the door. Somewhere in those pages, according to Stephens, was a way to get Damon a new trial, or at least life without parole. It meant little to me. I believed in my gut that Damon was innocent. How Stephens felt, I wasn't so sure anymore.

"I can't just sit around. I can't let it lie."

Stephens laughed.

"What's so goddamn funny?" I demanded.

I was in no mood for humor.

"You see a black guy same size and build as your client, and next thing you know, you've decided *he's* the guilty guy. You're just as racist as the cops, for Christ sake. If it isn't Damon, well then, it must be the next big black man I see."

"Fuck you, Stephens. You don't know what you're talking about."

"Listen, Gold, you're starting to lose it. Damon went

down. It happens. All the time. We did the best we could. He's got years of appeals left, and he's got some really good issues."

"Your faith in the system is stunning to me."

She was indignant.

"It's not about my faith in the system. I just don't see what else we can do at this point."

"Rob, you keep reading and writing. I'm taking a more proactive approach."

"Good luck, cowboy. Don't get hurt."

Her stuff was all packed. She said good-bye. We kept it low-key, but I knew something big was getting away. I hoped it wasn't gone forever.

CHAPTER 48

I SAT AT MY DESK, wondering what to do next. I took a mental inventory of what I had, and it wasn't much. I called Goodman. Nothing doing. Still no crack in the mystery disk. I thought about Kathy Dupont, and the way Yates was leering at her last night. I thought about Tom Twersky, always calling me for work. I thought about Hyman Rose, telling me to fight like hell for that black boy. All of a sudden I realized what I had. I had my clients. Yates had his ex-FBI, -IRS, -SEC, and God knows what else, with all their access. I had these guys. You play the hand that's dealt you. Plus, I had one other thing. I had the disk, even if I didn't know what the hell it said. It looked like I was going to have to use it, with or without the password. As long as Yates *thought* I knew its contents, did it really matter if I didn't?

I started by calling Kathy Dupont and asking her out to dinner. I felt a little guilty. She liked me, probably because I wasn't trying above all else to get into her pants. I was going to take advantage of her affection, for Damon's sake. Part of me was afraid that she was already Yates's girlfriend. It didn't seem likely, but I'd have to see how she reacted when I told her my plans.

She was happy to hear from me. I told her to meet me at Caliente, a Mexican place in the Village where no one would pay any attention to us.

"Why, all of a sudden, the dinner date?" she wanted to know, when we were seated in our booth. "What's up?"

She pronounced "up" as if it had two syllables.

"I need your help."

She looked crestfallen.

"Aren't you attracted to me?"

"Why does it matter?"

"It's how I relate. I can't help it. It's the only reaction I know how to deal with. Give in, or withhold."

"Well, I am attracted to you. There's no guy under the age of ninety out there who isn't. What's the difference?"

"Well, that's nice to know."

"My pleasure, ma'am."

We sipped on our drinks.

"Kathy, you know who I saw, when I went to your club the other night?"

"A lot of horny men in suits?"

"Yeah, but one in particular. Very handsome guy. Tanned. Named Yates. He runs the outfit where Charlotte King worked."

"Charlotte King?"

"The woman Damon's supposed to have killed."

"Really. No shit."

"Is he a regular?"

"Let's see, handsome guy in a suit, gray hair, tan. Sorry, that's not enough."

"How 'bout this? Always sits next to a big handsome black guy in a suit."

She snapped her fingers.

"Oh, yeah. I know who you mean."

She laughed.

"Small world, isn't it, Arch? I mean, that guy Yates wants to date me. He stuffs my panties with hundred dollar bills every night and asks me out. 'Course I refuse. You know that's not me."

"He wants his private plaything."

"Arch!" she said, with annoyance. I decided then and there to take a chance and trust her. I didn't have much choice. I needed Kathy Dupont. Not spiritually. Not physically. I needed her purely for strategic reasons—to get me to Yates.

"Kathy, there's some very heavy shit going down. Your help will make a big difference."

"Whoa, counselor, since when does the great-looking litigator need my help? I don't like the sound of it."

I told her what I knew and suspected about Yates, about Dr. Stern's murder, about the hard drive. I explained to her that Damon was innocent, that I thought Yates had Charlotte killed, that, in all probability, Smalls did the dirty work. That would explain the description of a large black man in a black coat, which Damon happened to fit.

"Where does l'il ole Kathy D. fit in?" she wanted to know.

"Kathy, this is asking a lot, but it's for a good cause— saving an innocent young man from the death penalty. If it wasn't about that, I wouldn't—"

She cut me off. "Cut to the chase, Arch, for Christ sake."

"Okay. It's like this. You told me, the first night I met you in arraignments, that you didn't turn tricks. Obviously you still don't. But we need you to pretend. We need you to set up a date with Yates, just to get him somewhere we want him. If he knows I'm coming to a meeting, he'll arm up, and bring extra bodies. But if the thinks he's just going somewhere to have a really good time with a stripper, he won't. He'll let his guard down, at least a little. And that's when we'll step in."

"We, who the fuck is we?"

"Me, and a couple other guys. With guns. We'll protect you."

"Arch, I feel sorry for Damon, but not sorry enough to risk my life. This just isn't my problem."

"I'm afraid it is," I said grimly. "Because I'm never going to let you forget that an innocent kid got executed because you wouldn't help catch the real killer."

She couldn't believe how serious I was all of a sudden.

"You don't give up, do you?"

"Wouldn't it be nice if you used some of that unbelievable sexiness to do some good in this world, instead of just lining your bank account?"

"Fuck you."

"What *do* you care about? Besides your money, and your own little problems."

"Fuck you again."

We weren't getting anywhere.

"Look, think about it, okay? Quickly. Because right now, you're all Damon's got."

I left. Our burritos hadn't even arrived, but I'd lost my appetite. As I walked out, she yelled after me.

"Asshole. I thought you wanted to have dinner with me!"

A lot of heads turned. I'd bet there were fifteen guys at the bar who *did* want to have dinner with her. I just wasn't one of them, right now.

CHAPTER 49

HYMAN ROSE LIVED five blocks from the last stop of the F train in Queens, in an ugly little house, one of fifty identical brick and aluminum-sided units built after the war in a hurry by developers who thought general contractors were architects. Each house had a green-and-white awning over an upstairs balcony, one and one half baths, two bedrooms, a bay window in the living room, and a dining room looking over the tiny backyard, big enough for a small above-ground pool, nothing bigger. A solid grasp on the bottom rung of the middle class, circa 1950.

I'd called him first, to see if he was up and about and could handle the intrusion.

"Hyman, how are you?"

"I'm feeling okay. I *am* eighty years old. Let's not forget it."

I heard a hint of acceptance in his voice, even serenity. I was sitting at his kitchen table, first-generation Formica, fluorescent light overhead, greenish-blue hue infecting the room. Everything looked like it was dying.

"What's it all about, sonny? Damon Tucker sending his family after you?"

He let out a cackle.

"Whadaya really think? Kid do it?"

I told him the whole story.

"Yunno, each little part of it don't add up to nothing. Maybe you just need to get yourself on some of that new mental medication they're putting everybody on. Calm yourself down. But when you step back and look at the total picture, well, it don't look good. The clincher is this guy trying to scare you. Thatsa clincher."

He paused for second, scratching his white hair.

"How you gonna save this schwartze, Arch? Whatsa plan?"

"It's in the works, Hyman, but I need this place for a little rendezvous with Yates. Just one night. Okay?"

He looked at me like I was a crazy person, but he didn't say no.

I went out for a walk, on the streets, the anonymous streets of Queens, full of little brick houses with white iron gates and green awnings, a place where normal people led normal lives.

I went into a drugstore to buy a soda and saw the latest high-tech disposable gimmick, marketed to those without credit—a disposable cell phone. Fifty bucks for two hundred minutes, big clunky phone included. No identification needed. All prepaid. Perfect for the new high-tech, low-profile Arch Gold.

As I walked and thought, my dead father's last words to me popped back into my head.

"There's two worlds out there, Arch. The legit world, and the world you come from. Now, you're going legit. But never forget, even out there where you're headed, sometimes you have to break the rules to do the right thing."

Dead twenty years, and he still spoke to me.

I wasn't just going to sit around like some goddamn "officer of the court" while Damon was sentenced to die for something he didn't do, and Yates was threatening to hunt me down like a prize piece of big game if I tried to do anything about it.

Thank you, Noah. So much for legit. Legit didn't seem to be working out too good for Damon Tucker. Legit could get you death row. Legit could get you a nice big lethal injection.

I pulled out my clunky new cell phone and called Tom Twersky.

CHAPTER 50

WHEN I TOLD TWERSKY I needed a gun, he got very concerned.

"Mr. Gold, that ain't for you. That ain't for you. You got other weapons. You're the courtroom guy we bring in *after* the gunfights. You can't join the gunfighters."

I met him in a bar on Fourth Avenue in Brooklyn that nobody ever pays any attention to, a bunch of local drunks. I liked the privacy.

Twersky was already in a back booth, one with high wooden walls. He had a cigarette dangling from his mouth. He smiled, without dropping the cigarette. He was always happy to see me.

He handed me a black backpack. I took it over to my side of the booth. He leaned over and spoke softly.

"That's a .38 pistol. Not an automatic. Much more reliable. Less ammo, though. Only six shots, and not a clip reload. All I could find right now."

He looked at me quizzically.

"You ain't planning to use this, are you?"

"No. I might need it just to keep from getting shot

myself."

"Wrong, Mr. Gold. If you show a gun, you're more likely to get shot than if you don't show a gun. It doesn't matter if the other guy's armed. That's a statistical fact. I read it."

I scratched my head.

"I've never shot a gun."

"I ain't surprised," said Twersky.

We drove in his car to a spot underneath the Verrazano Bridge I'd never imagined. We were standing under the bridge. We could see its entire underbelly, curving almost more than a mile to Staten Island. We had a great view, but nobody could see us, much less hear us, as the cars and trucks roared overhead, and the surf broke against the rocks.

Tom pulled a six-pack of beer cans out of his trunk. We lined them up on the rocks and stepped back about thirty feet.

"Take it out, man, I'm gonna show you what to do."

"You're crazy, Twersky, what if someone comes?"

"Ain't nobody coming, Gold. Let's see the gun."

I pulled it out. It felt heavier than it looked on TV. Twersky showed me the lock and safety and how to shoot using two hands in front of my face.

I shot at the beer cans. The thing popped loudly, like a big firecracker. The gun jumped back a little in my hand, but not as much as I'd expected. I missed.

"It ain't that easy to hit a man from thirty feet. Revolvers, in most case, work only at close range. Ten feet, or less. After that, unless you're Buffalo Bill, it's a crapshoot. 'Course, in my gig it don't matter. I'm just looking for effect with a gun. I ain't trying to hit nothing."

"You *are* a gentleman, Tom. You have the common good at heart."

Twersky had plenty of bullets. I needed 'em. I got a lot of practice reloading the chamber. It took me twenty-five shots to hit all six beer cans from fifteen feet. But I got better. The next six-pack, from his bottomless car trunk, took me only fifteen shots. The third, ten.

Tom wasn't impressed. He was staying on message.

"If you got to shoot somebody, Mr. Gold, close range is the way to go."

I had no plans to shoot anyone. I wanted to talk to Yates, not get into a gunfight with him.

CHAPTER 51

IT'S A DIFFERENT FEELING, walking around with a gun. Handguns are illegal in New York City, except for law enforcement, or if you have a "carry permit," which is almost impossible to get unless you're a private eye, like Yates. When you're packing an illegal gun, rule number one is, don't do anything that is going to give the cops a reason to search you. I can't tell you how many fellas I've represented who jumped the turnstyle and got caught for a farebeat, while carrying a loaded pistol. Those guys had to cop to felonies, and most of them ended up doing a year on Rikers, even if they had no record at all.

So I was crossing at the green, not in between, and paying my subway fare. No littering either.

When I got to my office, there was a voice mail from Kathy Dupont. I called her back.

"Arch, I've been thinking a lot. I'm willing to help."

"That's great!"

"Yeah. Just make sure I don't get hurt."

"Promise."

Was it to save Damon, or so she could live with herself? I didn't know, and I didn't care. When someone does the right thing, I don't ask if it's for the right reason. I'm just grateful.

I told her the plan. Again, I wondered if I was crazy to trust her and decided I didn't have much choice.

CHAPTER 52

FROM A BATHROOM WINDOW in Hyman's house, I saw Yates and Smalls pull up in a black Lincoln Town Car. Yates got out, stretched, and looked around, straightening his necktie. Smalls stayed in the car. So far so good. I felt the gun in my pocket. I didn't want to have to use it. Sure, Yates had killed two people, but on the other hand, those were premeditated, surgical strikes planned ahead. Coming to a tryst with a stripper, backed up by Smalls, would he be armed? I hoped not. Gunfighting was not part of the game plan. I only wanted answers.

Outside, there was a housepainter, all in white, scraping the front windows of Hyman's house. For once in his life, Twersky looked like he was earning an honest dollar, even if it was just a costume for him. His job was to intercept Smalls if he tried to come in.

Testosterone rules, I said to myself as Yates knocked on the door. I'd guessed right about this guy. Norton Gorham. Still looking for Mommy.

Kathy opened the door. She was wearing nothing but a black minidress. Boy, did she look hot.

"Welcome to my humble home, Dave," she said, almost

purring.

She led him to the bedroom.

"Look, Dave, there's a nice big mirror. You like that, don't you?"

He pushed her down on the bed. He grabbed her legs and pulled her pelvis up to his crotch. He ripped off her panties. It was all done in a couple of seconds. Economy of motion. This guy was a real romantic. I had let him get going a little with Kathy, because I was hoping he'd take off some of his clothes and maybe separate himself from his gun. It wasn't working out. I stepped out from the bathroom.

"Leave her alone, Yates. She was just to get you here, so we could talk."

He turned around and glared at me. Kathy got up, pulled down her dress, straightened her hair, and spat, hard, right in his face.

"You fucking pig."

Yates ignored her. He was focused on me.

"Gold. Fucking Gold."

He wiped the spit off his face with his arm.

"It's all over, Yates. The whole thing is over."

"What are you talking about? I came here to fuck this stripper. Is that still a crime? I'm not sure."

"I know the whole story. Charlotte. Dr. Stern. Norton Gorham. The hanky-panky with the books and the client lists. I know everything."

"What in God's name are you talking about?"

His face was turning a deep red, but he wasn't stepping out of role yet. He was, however, getting angry.

I pulled out a black floppy disk. Totally blank, but he didn't know that.

"Chapter and verse. From Charlotte to her shrink, to me, the day before you had him killed. Was it you or Smalls who took care of poor Dr. Stern?"

Yates's face twitched a bit. The veneer was cracking.

"Norton Gorham. Still mad at Mommy." I shook my head.

"What is it you want from me? What is it you want? You want money? I'll give you money, just so you'll leave me alone."

"All I want, Yates, is justice for Damon."

Yates shook his head. "Too bad, Gold. You should know by now, there's no justice. Not for you. Not for Damon."

Suddenly his gun was in his hand, far more quickly than I'd expected. He shot me as I reached for mine. As I heard the firecracker pop of the gun, I felt the burn in my chest. I was sucking air. My lung was shot. I lay on the ground, watching Yates, as my blood pressure dropped. He leaned over me and took the disk out of my hand. I was in a dream. Positive and negative switched back and forth. Time slowed down. Nice special effects. I felt no pain. Doctors call it shock. It doesn't feel too bad.

Yates turned and pointed the gun at Kathy. She screamed. It seemed to echo forever. Then, a shot. Yates flew backward, landing next to me. My dream wasn't over yet.

From the floor where I lay, old Hyman Rose loomed larger than life as he stepped into the room, blowing on his gun. I faded out.

CHAPTER 53

"How are his bloods?"

"Elevated."

"Gases?"

"Depleted."

Apparently these people were talking about me.

I've always liked waking up in strange beds. I like that moment when you become conscious of where you are, and where you aren't, sift through your memories, sort out what your senses are telling you, and rejoin the world from a new location. This time, though, I gradually came to understand that I was in a hospital bed, and there were two tubes going up my nose and down the back of my throat into my gut.

They seemed totally unnecessary to me, so I removed them. I'm exaggerating. I only attempted to remove them. One of these two people who knew about my depleted gases stopped me. Perhaps she had my best interests at heart. Totalitarian tool.

"Mr. Gold. You need those tubes. You're very sick."

"Honey, I don't know who you are, but nothing could possibly justify this garden hose up my nose."

I wish I'd said that. But I couldn't talk. My eyes, and contorted face, must have communicated something.

"Are we going to have to intubate him?"

I didn't like the sound of that. I tried to remember what got me here. Apparently this nurse was not only stronger than me, she was also capable of reading my mind.

"Mr. Gold, do you remember why you're here?"

Truth was, I didn't, not yet.

"You've been shot. In the lung. You almost died. But you're going to be fine. All better. If you let us take care of you."

I guess I didn't have much choice. I turned my head to look down at my arm. It was cuffed to the bed. I was in the Bellevue Hospital Prison Ward.

I faded out again.

CHAPTER 54

I SURFACED FROM MY NARCOTIC HAZE and saw Kevin Layden leaning over the bed. The clock on the wall said 1:30, but I didn't know the day. The tubes down my nose and throat stopped me from talking. The morphine they were dripping into me stopped me from gagging on the tubes or feeling the pain in my ripped-up chest.

I was weak. I could barely move even the parts of me that weren't wrapped or chained.

I was a prisoner, just like Damon. I'd managed to get myself strapped to a gurney years ahead of him, although my life was supposed to be saved, not taken.

"Goddamnit, Gold, when are they going to take those fucking tubes out? We need to talk."

I nodded, and with my one free arm, I made a motion like writing.

"Fine. I've got a pad. But let's start by bringing you up to speed. Look, I don't want to bother you, but you've been in here now for two full days, and shit is happening. You know, you've been charged with weapons, second degree. That's a heavy felony. Minimum three years upstate. Christ, we need to know what's going on."

He stopped to see if I was listening. My eyes were locked on his. He continued.

"What the hell were you doing in that house? With a gun! I mean, that's some crazy shit, Arch. What in God's name were you thinking about?"

He walked to the door, opened it, and bellowed "Nurse" in just the sort of tone that sends all hospital staff running to a different floor. After several minutes, a nurse showed up.

"Ma'am, it's very important that I speak to this patient. I'm his lawyer. Is it possible to take the tubes out for a few minutes?"

Shortly, a young white coat appeared, who introduced himself as the chief resident, and agreed to detube me for our meeting. A few minutes later, I could croak out my thoughts in a hoarse whisper. Was this what Charlotte King sounded like on the sidewalk as she died?

"Nice to see you, Kev."

"You, too, Arch, glad you're alive," said Kevin.

"Coupla questions," I whispered.

"You're not the only one, you fucking lunatic. I'm going to represent you on your criminal case."

He made a visible effort to calm himself down.

"I want to wait 'til you're better to yell at you."

He took my free hand.

"Arch, I wish I could say they're treating you like a hero but they're not. Not yet."

"You know, Damon is innocent."

"Sure, Arch. You'll tell me about it. Relax."

"Is Yates dead?"

Layden looked at me with a frown, realizing for the first time that I hadn't been conscious for the end of the big scene. I didn't know how the story ended, and I needed Layden to fill me in.

"What about Hyman and Kathy and Twersky?" I asked.

"They're all alive, if that's what you mean. Hyman and Twersky are both charged like you, with weapons, second degree. They're thinking about adding murder two for Hyman. He's a few doors down. Cancer's back big time. He's hurting. I don't think he's getting out of here."

Guns are tricky. You may be the white knight in a case, but if you have an illegal gun, the DA won't let it slide. They want you to pay some penalty for a hot gun, even if you're on the side of the angels. Right now, I didn't get the idea that the people in power thought I was on the side of the angels. Angels aren't cuffed to their sickbeds.

"Listen, Layden," I croaked. "Yates had Charlotte King killed. My guess is he killed her because she knew something about his company and was blackmailing him when he wanted to take the company public. He also killed Charlotte's shrink, Dr. Stern, because he figured she told him the story. Then he tried to kill me, when I confronted him about all of it."

I had to pause. My voice was almost gone. I got out one more sentence.

"Doesn't Stoddard understand that Damon is innocent?"

Layden put up his hand to stop me.

"Easy, Archie. Go easy. One thing at a time, kid. Why don't I tell you what I know before you tell me what you know. How's that?"

I'd heard *that* line before. Layden was talking to me like a criminal defendant. Let's face it, that's what I was.

"Here's what I know, Arch. A stripper named Kathy Dupont—ex-client of yours—Yates, and you are all convened in the house of an old bookie dying of cancer named Hyman Rose, whom you also appear to have done some legal work for, on the side. A fellow named Smalls is waiting outside in the the car. Another ex-client of yours, the fearsome Tom Twersky, is standing guard by the door. When the cops come, they find you half dead on the floor, shot in the chest, still holding a gun that has been fired once. Yates is lying dead, sprawled next to you, gunshot to the chest. Smalls is outside the front door, unconscious. Hyman Rose and Twersky are sitting on the couch, guns on a table, out of reach. Those guys are too smart to scare trigger-happy cops. When the police rush in, Rose tells them the story. Says Yates was lured there by Kathy Dupont, so you could confront him over his involvement in Charlotte King's death. Yates pulls first and shoots you, after you start waving a disk around. He takes the disk off you and then turns to shoot the stripper. You'd all be dead, except for our aged hero, Hyman Rose, eighty years old, riddled with cancer, who takes out Yates with a shot to the chest. Smalls tries to come in and gets clobbered by Twersky, wielding a blackjack. Remember any of this?"

I shook my head.

Layden sat in silence. He wanted my best explanation, and he wasn't going to rush me. He leaned his head down to hear my weak whisper. I told him about my trip to Pittsfield, and about seeing Smalls and Yates at the strip club. I told him about the hard drive and taking the disk from Dr. Stern, which we still hadn't cracked. I explained how I'd bluffed Yates about what was on the disk, and then he'd started shooting.

Then I told him the best part of all. The whole final scene had been videotaped. I'd bought the stuff at a place called the Detective Store, a discreet but remarkable little shop in the Village stocked with things you thought were illegal or unaffordable. In our brave new world of affordable high-tech gadgets, you can spy on the cheap. For a few grand, borrowed from Hyman Rose, I'd picked up a couple wireless video cameras the size of beer bottle tops that fit inside a standard smoke detector. For sound, I'd picked up some tiny wireless pen mikes. The cameras and mikes beamed their signals back to a special VCR that I'd set up in Hyman's living room.

"You've got a videotape?"

Clearly, Layden thought it sounded too good to be true.

"It should show the whole thing."

"No shit! Where is it?"

"Either still in Hyman's house, or the cops found it. You're my lawyer. Why don't you find out?"

"Hope that tape is around, Arch, because we're gonna need it. This is the biggest media circus since OJ. Believe me. We've got a famous private investigator, shot dead. We've got his pal, who looks kinda like a hit man, under arrest. We've got a stripper, we've got an old bookie dying of cancer who's one of the shooters, and a career stickup guy who's braining people with a billy club. We've got our own death penalty defense counsel shot, and almost dying. That's one hell of a crime scene."

It all seemed to have reinvigorated Layden. His mood had definitely changed. I guess the excitement of getting me out of trouble, and nailing Charlotte King's real killer, was enough to make him forget about his own problems for a while.

"And what about this floppy disk?" Layden wanted to know.

I told him to retrieve it from Goodman and turn it over to the DA's office, even if we didn't know what was on it. It was time to come clean, now that Yates was out of the picture. Maybe Stoddard could call in Bill Gates and get the frigging thing open. I was sure it would be one more illuminating piece of evidence against Yates.

"What's Stoddard saying?" I asked.

"Nothing. Nada. Everything's 'under investigation.' The papers have all noted that Yates employed Charlotte King and that you defended Damon. They've also dug up that you were Kathy Dupont's lawyer on her last assault case. They all say there's 'speculation' that Yates was involved in Charlotte King's death. But basically, they've all got more questions than answers."

"What about Smalls?"

"He's not talking. Yet."

Layden sat back and closed his eyes. The room was quiet except for the low buzz of the medical equipment keeping me alive.

CHAPTER 55

HYMAN ROSE IS pointing his gun at Yates.

"Any reason why I shouldn't shoot you again, ya lousy douche bag psycho fuck?"

"No. Please. Don't kill me. Please don't kill me. We can work it out."

Yates is begging for his life. Hyman wants more.

"Tell me the truth, scumbag. The truth. Then maybe I won't finish you off. Did you or Smalls kill Charlotte King? Which one of you did Dr. Stern? Tell me, or you're gonna die."

Yates is weary. He's losing a lot of blood. He doesn't answer.

"What did she know, Yates?"

"She knew too much, that little bitch. We were gonna go public. We were gonna make millions. None of this had to happen. She didn't have to fuck around. She didn't have to get greedy."

He's speaking softly now. He's white as a sheet. He's on

his way out.

Hyman isn't moved. "You're a piece of shit," he says, as Yates stops breathing. He puckers up his wrinkled old mouth and blows on his gun.

"Whoever said an old bookie couldn't shoot straight? Kept this thing oiled for thirty years waiting to use it on a fuck like this. Kathy, call the cops."

Layden flicked the remote in his hand, and the video stopped. We were watching it in my hospital room. Stoddard was our special visitor. She was paying close attention, believe me.

Layden found the video right where I'd left it, in the VCR hidden in the cabinet in Hyman Rose's living room where it had been recorded. The Crime Scene boys were looking for blood, prints, DNA, whatever. They never thought about hidden cameras or videos. They were focused on the bedroom, where all the carnage took place. They didn't even notice the unlabeled video, until Layden gave 'em the heads-up.

So we all got a good look at Yates's last moments on earth, in living color.

By the next day, Stoddard's investigators were all over Yates's books and records, looking for a motive— something wrong with the company that Yates had to keep quiet. Eventually, they found what they were looking for. Turned out, Yates represented both sides in many Wall Street deals. He made his clients sign confidentiality agreements, insisting that if his presence in a deal was known, his effectiveness was compromised. In fact, many of his investigations were a sham. He didn't really investigate anything. He just looked over the information he'd gotten from both sides and decided how much of it to give out to the other side. Each side thought he was working for them exclusively. This wasn't just unethical, it was criminal.

Of course, his client/matter list was embedded in his computer with a sophisticated password, which he alone knew. It was his deepest darkest secret. Except fucking Charlotte King broke the password. She was that clever. He started out sleeping with her, and he ended up paying her a fortune to keep quiet. How relationships do evolve! Some end, too, quite abruptly. Apparently when he decided to go public, and cash out, Yates concluded Charlotte King was too risky to keep around, and he had her killed. He knew she was in therapy and decided he'd have to kill the shrink, too. The shrink wouldn't talk while she was alive, but once she was dead, he might go to the cops with what he knew.

One surprise. The disk I'd taken from Dr. Stern's office turned out to be blank. Sure, it had that "Yates" file on it, and nothing else, but when the DA's office finally cracked it, it was just one sentence. "I don't even know where to start." I was puzzled, but it didn't seem to matter. There was still a strong case against Yates. In fact, the final exquisite piece of evidence was provided by Detective Bill Blakeman, the pleasant cop who'd given me Dr. Stern's wife's phone number in Boston, months ago. Turned out, shortly after Dr. Stern was murdered, Crime Scene had found an unknown fingerprint on Dr. Stern's toilet seat. Detective Blakeman pulled it out, after he heard about Smalls. It matched up to Smalls's right index finger.

It still hurt to laugh, but I couldn't help myself when this piece of news came through. It's a common mistake hit men and burglars make. Criminals forget about fingerprints when they're urinating. Pissing is one of the few innocent acts in their sordid lives. They usually can't open their flies or pull out their dicks with gloves on. Since they're not worried about getting prints on their own organs, they take off the gloves. It works out most of the time, but Smalls must've had manners. After he took off his gloves, and pulled out his dick, without thinking he raised the toilet seat.

Good manners get you nowhere. If you don't mind killing somebody, you shouldn't mind pissing on their toilet seat.

CHAPTER 56

I WAS SITTING up in my hospital bed a few days later when there was a knock on the door.

"Come in," I said, in a voice that was almost back to full strength. The steady stream of visitors, official and personal, had died down. The press had backed off a little. I was slowly healing. I could breathe now without tubes, and I could eat real food. No cuffs chained me to the bed either.

Damon came in. He stood at the foot of my bed, looming over me, smiling.

"You're the man, Mr. Gold."

He took my hand and squeezed it. He was grinning from ear to ear.

"You saved my life. I'll never forget it."

Stephens came all the way from Buffalo to visit me one day. She took my hand and held it to her heart.

"We almost lost you, Arch." There were tears of relief in her eyes. It was nice to know she cared, even if she was in some faraway jurisdiction.

CHAPTER 57

LAYDEN WORKED OUT a deal for me. It was tougher than you'd imagine. The folks running the law machinery don't like cowboys, even when they deliver up the bad guys. You are *not* supposed to take matters into your own hands. Only the police are allowed to play with real guns.

I told Layden that any deal for me had to include Twersky and Rose. I couldn't watch these guys do time for saving my life. Layden took care of it. He understood the politics of the situation and pressed Stoddard hard.

Above all, Stoddard wanted to get elected. She didn't want to go down in history as the first black woman DA in New York who, by the way, couldn't actually get *elected*. Since the press had turned Twersky and Rose into mini folk heroes, Stoddard knew she'd look too mean if she made either one of them do time for their good deeds. Since she already looked bad getting a conviction against an innocent kid, she wasn't going to look doubly bad by trying too hard to nail the guys who'd set everything right. So Twersky was put on felony probation—a real gift, considering his record—and no charges were filed against Rose, who had only a few months to live, anyway.

Smalls never did talk, except to say yes when asked if he wanted twenty-five to life. After trial, he'd get life without parole, or death. He decided not to risk it.

As for me, buying a hot gun and carrying it around loaded was forgiven. Stealing property from Dr. Stern's office was forgiven. Breaking into Charlotte King's apartment was forgiven. Just a couple small things, in return. I had to plead guilty to a misdemeanor, criminal possession of a weapon, fourth degree, not that big a deal, really, and I had to give up my law license. Sort of. I would be permitted to reapply to the bar in one year, if I stayed out of trouble. I had no plans, other than to stay out of trouble.

I kept working at the PD's office, as a "paralegal" since I couldn't actually represent clients or appear in court until I had my license back. I'm the most overqualified paralegal on earth. I review trial records of recent cases, looking for possible posttrial motions that must be made to the trial judge prior to a direct appeal to a higher court. It's a calm, studious existence. I read thousands of pages of transcripts—witnesses testifying, judges ruling, lawyers objecting, defendants complaining—I read about what I used to do. I'm happy for the change.

It's been a few months now. On the surface, my life is almost back to some semblance of normality. I've healed, although I have some nasty-looking surgical scars, and my left lung hurts when it's going to rain. Layden tells me I've aged.

My thoughts are not always pleasant. My concentration is bad. It's a daily act of will for me to forget the violence I've just lived through, to put it away somewhere in the back of my mind where it won't haunt me every day.

The media's backed off a bit. For a while, they were following me everywhere. Everyone wanted to interview me. I'm not used to the hero thing. If you ask me, I'm strictly antihero material. I just want to be left alone.

So I sit at my desk, reading through case files. Today, I was reviewing the thick record in a case where the trial judge had thoroughly screwed up a *Batson* challenge by defense counsel during jury selection. *Batson* is a United

States Supreme Court case that says the prosecutor may not use preemptory challenges to knock off potential jurors in a racially biased way. I was looking through the case file, trying to determine the racial composition of the prospective jurors. I was trying to find defense counsel's jury selection chart. Most lawyers make it on a legal pad turned lengthwise. They create sixteen boxes, eight over eight, filling up the page. Each box represents one of the sixteen seats in the jury box. To begin picking a jury, the clerk spins the wooden "wheel," which contains the juror cards of all fifty jurors who are in the courtroom, in the "audience." Sixteen names at random are selected from the wheel and called up to sit in the jury box, where they answer questions from the lawyers and judge. As each juror's background is revealed, counsel writes down the information in the corresponding box—name, occupation, age, neighborhood, ethnicity, and so on. It's an easy and accurate way to keep track of each juror's characteristics, so that later, when all the jurors have been led out of the courtroom and you're no longer looking at them, you can quickly decide who to knock off and who to keep. I find that each box triggers the memory of that particular juror.

I flipped through a few more papers and, suddenly, right in front of me, on a legal pad, was the familiar chart, sixteen boxes, eight over eight.

C. Clark Merril U.W.S.	F. Amber teacher L.E.S.	G. Davis CPA U.E.S.	K. Layden NYC PD	C. King Exec. Yates Ass. U.E.S.	J. Reic Post- man Sly Town	K. Holt Dis- abilty harlem	A. Rollins Prff. NYU E. Vilage
W/m	W/F	W/m	w/m	W/F	B/m	b/m	w/m
T. Jones law- ywer SEC U.E.S.	A. Rivera secu- rity E. Village	S. Wong acct Deloit Asian/	D. Klien writer NY Mag U.E.S.	J. Ortiz super L.E.S.	A. Daniels florist U.W side	Thom- as secre- tary MTA Harlem	J. West teacher Harlem
W/F	His/m	m	W/F	His/m	w/m	b/f	b/f

There it was, in some attorney's handwriting, staring me right in the face. Layden sat next to Charlotte King during jury duty, in September 1998, just two months before she was killed. What the fuck? My mind took off, racing with all the possibilities. Was it definitely them? No doubt. I could confirm it later, but there was no mixing up Layden, head of NYCPD, and Charlotte King, of Yates Associates. This little seating chart left no doubt that they'd been together for at least an hour. That's how long it usually took to go through a panel of sixteen. Could he forget about her two months later? How was that possible? Was there something to hide? I picked up Layden's phone, to give him a call. I thought better of it. It could wait. I wanted to know more. I had a couple stops to make before talking to the attorney-in-charge.

CHAPTER 58

STODDARD WATCHED the Yates video with me again. It was only eight minutes long, although it seemed like an eternity at the time.

"Thanks, Bernice, I just needed to see it again."

It was true, that familiarity allows forgetting. As long as the tape remained mysterious to me, I would speculate about it. Once it became familiar, it lost its mystery, and I could put it, and maybe even the event itself, up in my mental attic, out of the way of daily living.

But that wasn't why I was looking at it. I wanted to see if Yates really did confess. The fact is, he didn't. When Hyman, God bless his soul, says, "Tell me the truth!" Yates responds with "She knew too much, that little bitch." Then he says, "She didn't have to fuck around. She didn't have to get greedy." Not exactly a crystal-clear admission. And it had a new meaning now. Charlotte King *had* been fucking around—with Kevin Layden. Of course, Smalls's fingerprint on Dr. Stern's toilet seat certainly nailed Yates for that murder, but it wasn't direct evidence of his role in Charlotte's killing.

I didn't share my murky thoughts with DA Stoddard. She was still worrying about me.

"What you've been through, anything that helps you get it behind you is okay with me."

"Bernice, I really appreciate it." I meant it, too.

CHAPTER 59

LISA LAYDEN'S TOWN HOUSE was on a beautiful street, steps fromLCentral Park West, a setting unchanged in 120 years, except for the cars. I was sitting with her in the living room, a dark space with massive wood panels, fifteen-foot ceilings, and ornate moldings, sculpted by long-dead artisans. She was the same perky, preppy-looking woman I remembered from numerous office Christmas parties over the years and more than several dinners in this dark Victorian setting they called home.

She grew up in a big fancy house in the suburbs that was so nice, with so much land, it felt like the country, and then she went to a prep school that was so nice, and with so much land, it felt like a college, and then she went to a college that was so nice, and had so much land, that it felt anticlimactic. So she found a guy who was different, but smart, and handsome, and tall. She fell in love with him, even though his politics seemed to indicate he might not make piles of money, as had her forebears.

Luckily, when you yourself have piles of money, you can marry down, dough-wise, as long as you marry up morally and intellectually. That she did. Everything was golden, until Charlotte King.

"Have you figured it all out?"

Lisa was looking at me quite defiantly. Behind that well-bred measured presence was a will of steel. I don't think Layden realized that, when he so recklessly let himself get drawn into Charlotte King's sick world. Right now, Lisa wasn't sure whose side I was on, and where my ultimate loyalties lay. I couldn't blame her.

I pulled out the original jury seating chart. It seemed like a good way to begin. Physical evidence.

She didn't need to be convinced.

"Look, I threw him out. You know why?"

She looked down and took a deep breath. She wasn't the type to cry on me.

"Charlotte King sent me a videotape. Back in November. A very well-made tape. After all, she was in the spy business."

She let out a bitter laugh. "That girl knew what she was doing."

I wasn't sure exactly what she meant. She clarified it.

"She made my husband feel very good. In slow motion."

So, Layden *did* know Charlottte King. In every sense of the word. That wonderful family man had given in to temptation. I thought back to that December morning in the office, after I'd picked up Damon in arraignments— Layden pretending he didn't know from Charlotte King— Layden telling me Lisa had just kicked him out.

I refocused on the moment, though my head was reeling.

"I'm sorry, Lisa. I'm sorry you had to look at that."

"I'm not. It was happening in either case. This way, I have no illusions."

She choked up a little but stayed controlled.

"Arch, what do you want?"

"I want information. I want to know who killed Charlotte King. Was it Smalls, working for Yates, or was it your husband? Or was it you? What did Kevin tell you, Lisa? I need to know."

She shook her head.

"I can't answer your questions. I'm not going to defend myself, and I'm not going to get him in trouble. Not more than he's already in."

Looking at this woman who was tough as steel, I knew she didn't kill Charlotte King. She was raised to believe in punishment, not revenge. She'd sooner throw her husband out than kill his mistress. Suddenly I understood the timing. Lisa didn't kick him out because of his affair. Back in early December, she'd known about that for a while. She'd watched that video more than once. No, Lisa kicked him out because she was afraid he'd *killed* Charlotte King, and *that* really scared her.

"So what is it? Kevin went out and shot Charlotte to prove to you that you were still the one? That's what you're afraid of, aren't you? That you drove him to it. You feel guilty. That's why you won't turn him in. Even though he's confessed to you, hasn't he?"

She stared me right in the eyes, still defiant, like a torture victim with information who wouldn't talk.

"Aren't you afraid of him?" I asked.

"No."

"Why not?"

"Because he doesn't hate me. He hated her. He hated her because she ruined his life. She cost him the thing he loves more than himself—his three children. I didn't do that to him. I just reacted. And I might have taken him back. If . . ." She decided not to finish the sentence. She *was* tough as nails. And she wasn't turning in her husband.

"Arch, don't do anything. Okay? I'll send him away. He'll go. We'll never see him again. Please, Arch. Please. Just let him go."

She walked me to the door, to say good-bye. She leaned up and kissed me. For the first time, she had tears in her eyes.

"Some girl's going to get lucky with you."

Luck hadn't smiled on *her*. She and her family had gotten caught in the Charlotte King wrecking machine.

CHAPTER 60

THE NEXT MORNING I got in early. I was sitting at my desk, thinking about the Laydens, and Charlotte King, and Damon Tucker, when Kevin Layden came into my office and closed the door. He slid his long frame into the plastic chair across from my desk.

"Arch, I'm leaving. I've resigned."

I didn't react. I wasn't surprised.

He was running, as his wife has ordered him to do. He had no better choice, no choice at all, really. Now, I was his final hurdle, although I don't think he understood it yet.

"Where are you going?"

"I'm moving to the country. To think. Write a book. Get away from my misery."

"And the kids."

He was putting on a brave face. "Lisa's making it so difficult for me, I—"

"She doesn't want her kids hanging out with a murderer, is that it?"

"What the hell are you talking about?"

He leaned over in the chair and put his head in his hands. After a few moments he looked up, his mouth unnaturally wide open, twisting in a spasm of agony.

"I'm not a bad man."

"The Kevin I've known for ten years, who diligently

defended anyone who came through arraignments, that
Kevin, he wasn't a bad man. What happened to that man?
Well, I think it all began the day you sat next to Charlotte
King in the jury box of Judge Amron's courtroom."

Kevin face got a little redder, and his jaw tightened.

"One of the cases I was looking over, the one with the
Batson issue. It had a jury selection chart. The standard-
looking thing. Sixteen boxes, eight over eight, one box for
each seat. You sat next to Charlotte King, in seats four and
five, middle of the back row. I'm sure you were together
for at least an hour. No memory of that?"

Layden was looking and listening, barely breathing.

I continued, "That got me thinking. Was it really possible
that you didn't remember her, two months later? Then I
went back and looked at the video of Yates before Hyman
nailed him. In fact, he never actually admitted to killing
Charlotte King."

Layden was staring at me, waiting. "Go on, Arch."

"That's because he didn't kill her. But after she was
killed, he had to kill Dr. Stern. While Charlotte was alive,
Yates had things under control. He knew she was in
therapy, but he also knew that the money was keeping her
happy, paying for the goddamn therapist, in fact, at two
hundred and fifty bucks per hour. That shrink wasn't going
to violate his sacred doctor/patient privilege, unless he
thought *Charlotte* was about to go kill somebody, which
she wasn't. Then, when Charlotte was killed, everything
changed. Then Yates realized that Dr. Stern might go to
the authorities. He had to take him out."

I paused for a second, while he absorbed it all.

"You are a creative thinker, aren't you, Arch?"

"You shot her. You shot her because she destroyed your
life, sending that graphic video to your wife. Lisa, the
cute perky preppy girl with the trust fund, she didn't like

it one bit. She threatened to throw you right out. A week later, Charlotte was killed. Your wife suspected you from the beginning, didn't she? She was afraid she pushed you to it. To prove yourself to her, once again. That's why you told her, Kevin. You got all twisted around and decided that killing Charlotte could bring your family back together."

Layden was shaking his head.

"You can't prove a thing. It's all circumstantial. She said 'black male' before she died. That doesn't include me, does it?"

"You know what I think? She didn't say 'black male.' She said 'blackmail.' That's what she was doing to Yates. That's what she was, a blackmailer. She thought *Yates* killed her. She didn't know it was you, as she lay there on the sidewalk bleeding to death. Does that make you feel better?"

"None of that adds up to a case, and you know it. Lisa will *never* testify. She'll assert her marital privilege."

"What about the videotape?"

"She's destroyed it."

"What if I testify?"

"To what? I haven't admitted anything."

"To the fact that your wife told me you confessed to her."

"Double hearsay. Not admissible."

He was right. No judge would let me get up on the stand and say that Lisa Layden told me that her husband told her . . .

We both knew the rules of evidence.

"All anyone can ever prove is that I had an affair with her, and I covered it up. That's all."

After a short silence, I spoke.

"Why, Kevin? Why did you risk everything for a little fun with Charlotte King?"

He stared at me with those scary eyes of his.

"Arch, you hit your fifties, something happens. You realize—this is it, this is life. No more illusions, no more fantasies. No more possibilities."

His voice started to break. He kept going.

"In some ways, that's okay. My kids. They're better than anything I could have ever imagined. But it's bad, too. My wife . . ."

He looked like a ghost. His voice was far away.

"There wasn't much passion left in my marriage, Arch. I'd accepted it."

His voice became desperate. He wanted me to understand something I would never get.

"You can't imagine what it was like when I met her in Judge Amron's courtroom, in the jury box. She was a seductive, brilliant creature. I got greedy. I got stupid. I got involved with her."

I nodded. He continued.

"She seemed so fascinated by me, from the moment she met me. I was pure, in her eyes, a white knight. We sat in that jury box together for about an hour. Then afterward, when we were both kicked off, we walked out together. We had lunch. That's how it began."

He stopped. He was no longer used to talking about anything that mattered, to anyone, not since his life went in the shitter. Now he was groping, forcing himself to speak.

"She decided I was the man for her. She wanted me to leave my wife and marry her. I was shocked. For not one second had I ever thought of leaving my family. I live for my kids, you know that, Arch."

Tears were streaming down his cheeks and landing on his beard.

"I told her no. That made something change in her. I

didn't realize she was evil, until it was way too late. She decided to destroy my life. She sent my wife that video of us—together."

Suddenly he stood up, and in a violent gesture, swept his hand across the bookcase, sending stuff flying around. A few things smashed.

"Taping this? One more for the Gold archives?" He towered over me for a moment, then he teetered a bit and sat down.

"No, I'm not."

"My wife wanted to throw me out after she watched that video. You know, she had all the money. She bought that lovely 1876 town house we live in. Finding out your husband had an affair, a fling, that's one thing. Watching it on a video, in slow motion, that's another. She couldn't forgive, she couldn't forget. And Charlotte King knew exactly how it would play out, too. She planned it perfectly. She knew exactly how my wife would react, that the video would be all my wife needed to sue me for divorce and get full custody. She knew it would destroy me not to see my kids. She was right."

"What she didn't realize is that you'd decide to take her down with you." I paused, getting angrier. "What did it feel like to discuss Damon's defense with me, on that first morning at work, after you shot her? You sat there and told me I'd have to go ID, told me I'd never find the real shooter."

He looked at me in silence.

"You never expected an arrest, did you? God, you must've been shocked when I turned up in your office talking about Damon Tucker. There was only one way it could get worse—and it did, when Leventhal died, and Stoddard took over. What were you feeling, Mr. Attorney-in-Charge, when you watched Damon get death for your crime?"

No response.

"Did you know she'd been sleeping with Yates, or did you learn that from me?"

"I found that out the hard way. She filled me in on that after I tried to end our relationship. She got so angry—in a way I'd never seen before. Told me that once she got her hooks into a person, they could never get free of her. Told me all about what she had on Yates. She was so sick. She liked playing a chess game with him. She told me that right at the end. That's when I first realized she was going to ruin me."

"You know why she fell for you, Kevin? You're the anti-Yates. Yates was all power, no convictions, no principle. You were nothing but principle, once."

"Now what am I?"

"You're a goddamn killer, trying to get away with it, that's all you are now."

"I'm not a bad man, Arch. All my life, I did the right thing. Until she came along to destroy me."

"You going to kill me next?"

He said nothing.

"You worked awfully hard to get me out of this mess, didn't you, Kevin? And to pin this whole thing on Yates. That videotape of mine, it saved *you*, didn't it. Things really started to look up for a while, didn't they? You were getting away with murder, and Damon was going free. A happy ending, almost."

"If you'd never poked around, we wouldn't need that tape, would we?"

"There's no 'we' anymore. Only one of us was willing to sit back and watch an innocent man face execution."

He looked at me stone-faced.

"What about the disk, Kevin? What about that? You

took it from Goodman, just like I told you to. But you didn't turn it over to the DA, did you? Did you keep it? Or destroy it? I'm sure you just took a blank disk, created a file called Yates, with that one sentence in it, 'I don't even know where to start,' and gave that to the DA's office. You were hoping, maybe, they'd think it was the real thing. You couldn't afford to turn over the real one. None of us know what's on that one, do we? It could've pointed the finger at you. Funny, wasn't it, getting the whole story from me, and then getting to review all the evidence I led you to before deciding whether or not it helped you? I guess you decided the video was okay, because it nailed Yates, but the disk—too risky."

He was listening intently. I had more.

"I thought back to two different things you said when we first found out Stoddard wanted death for Damon. They were little tip-offs, but I didn't see them at the time. First, you said, *Why can't Leventhal wait another couple months to infarct? Who gets executed in this county is supposed to depend on when one old man's heart gives out?* Think about that for a minute. Why would it matter *when* Leventhal died, if *someone*, one of our many clients, was going to face the death penalty? Why would you, as head of the office, care *which one it was?* Only one reason. You knew Damon was innocent. You wanted them to go after one of our typical guilty clients. It killed you, given how you'd spent your whole career, that they were going after an *innocent* defendant. Of course, the fact that you were the killer just made it a little harder. How much harder, I don't know. You seemed to carry on quite well."

"You've got a hell of a memory," he murmured.

"On Christmas Eve, when you spoke about not seeing your kids. You said *not seeing them, being told you can't watch them grow up, being shut out—it's kind of like dying.* It wasn't just kind of like dying, for you. It was also a reason to kill. Too bad it just happened to put Damon on death row, Mr. Public Defender."

"Are you going to try to turn me in?"

"I don't know what I'm going to do."

I've represented so many guilty people. Even a few evil people. I've never passed judgment. I've always just done my job. What was my job now? Layden wasn't a client. He hadn't been caught or charged with a crime. He was my friend, as much or as little as that meant.

An evil woman's been killed. An innocent man's been freed. An evil man, a murderer, has also been killed, after he nearly killed me. Another murderer is doing twenty-five to life. So the good guys have almost won. Except the chief good guy, a man I admired for most of my adult life—well, is he a good guy, or a bad guy? Poor Layden. He got sucked into something he never understood. He gave in to temptation, and his entire life fell apart. He'll never see his kids again, the things he loves more than himself. That love, that loss, fed the hatred that made him a killer.

He got up to go without a word. I didn't stop him.

He was right. It was a weak case. Without more evidence, they might not even be able to charge him.

But there might be more evidence out there. Nobody knew for sure. I fought with all the loyalty, the years of friendship, the sorrow I felt for his misfortune. In the end, the part I couldn't forgive was that Layden was willing to let Damon fry to save his own skin.

I picked up the phone and called Stoddard.

EPILOGUE

STODDARD TURNED UP plenty of evidence against Layden. Cell phone calls. E-mails. Gifts. Witnesses. The day concierge at the Tribeca Grand remembered Charlotte and him regularly shacking up there during the day. Charlotte paid for the rooms on her Yates expense account. So there was an electronic trail. Yates would have been proud.

Maybe Kevin followed it all. Maybe he read the press accounts of the whole thing. More than one commentator noted the irony of jury duty leading to a trail of murder and mayhem.

They found his body in a cabin in Vermont, in the middle of nowhere. He was dead, but his laptop was still humming, running a program trying to crack that locked disk.

He'd slit his wrists and bled to death. I know it was a great relief for him. I can imagine the slow warm euphoria, the release from the hell he'd created for himself on earth. I say a prayer for Kevin Layden every day.

Kathy Dupont went back to whatever small town she'd come from in South Carolina. First, she slept with me, and that was damn nice. I would've looked after her if she'd stuck around, but she didn't trust me long-term. Smart girl.

Twersky was changed, after that gunfight. He quit the stickup business for good. He still calls, looking for work. I buy him lunch whenever he comes around. Last time I checked, he was driving a cab. He saved my life, and I saved him decades in jail. We both owe each other, big time. It's a nice relationship.

Stephens is still fighting the death penalty, all over the country. The movement is picking up a little steam, lately, in part because of Damon's case.

Damon went back full-time to City College. He says he wants to be a criminal defense lawyer. Someday, maybe he'll come work with me.

DA Stoddard was defeated in the general election that year.

The governor set up a commission to look into the mistaken conviction of Damon Tucker. On Christmas 2000, the dawn of the new millennium, he ordered a moratorium on executions in New York State.

I was at Hyman Rose's bedside when he died. I made sure he wasn't in pain. I told him he'd been a good man. We shed some tears together, me and that tough old bookie who saved my life. I got to say good-bye.

Last night, I spoke with my father. I told him the whole story. He was very real, last night, in my dreams, just a little older. He said, "Kid, you did good."

When I woke up, for the first time in many months, I had a smile on my face. I get my law license back in the fall. I'm ready for the next case.